THE TRIDENT SERIES II

BRAVO TEAM

AUSSIE

Book 4

USA TODAY Bestselling Author
Jaime Lewis

This is a work of fiction. Names, characters, businesses, events, and incidents are the products of the author's imagination. Any resemblance to actual persons, living or dead, or actual events is purely coincidental.

The Trident Series - AUSSIE
Copyright © 2025 by Jaime Lewis

All rights reserved. No part of this book may be reproduced or transmitted in any form or by any means without written permission from the author.

ISBN: 978-1-952734-62-5

TABLE OF CONTENTS

Prologue	1
Chapter 1	4
Chapter 2	7
Chapter 3	17
Chapter 4	30
Chapter 5	43
Chapter 6	47
Chapter 7	55
Chapter 8	65
Chapter 9	69
Chapter 10	78
Chapter 11	81
Chapter 12	91
Chapter 13	99
Chapter 14	119
Chapter 15	129
Chapter 16	141
Chapter 17	144
Chapter 18	155
Chapter 19	169
Chapter 20	176
Chapter 21	193
Chapter 22	197
Chapter 23	200
Chapter 24	208
Chapter 25	214

Chapter 26	220
Chapter 27	228
Chapter 28	242
Chapter 29	249
Chapter 30	255
Chapter 31	259
Chapter 32	262
Chapter 33	267
Chapter 34	276
Epilogue	282

PROLOGUE

Ava Porter pedaled through the darkness as the cool and damp Seattle night air prickled her skin. It was just after eleven when she reached the small park behind her house. She hopped off her bike and glanced nervously toward the two-story home in the distance. If Jim and Roxy found out she had a bike, they'd take it from her, just like they took everything else from her. She quickly locked it to the metal bike rack near the swings and pocketed the key.

Her fingers trembled slightly as she tucked her tip money, just under twenty bucks, into her bra. It wasn't much, but it was all she had, and it had to be hidden. If they found it, they'd take that too, claiming it as rent or some other lie. She pulled her jacket tighter around herself as she walked down the narrow trail toward the house. Her heart was already racing in anticipation of what she would find waiting for her.

She reached the driveway and paused for a moment, staring up at the darkened windows.

The house looked like the picture-perfect family home from the outside—neatly trimmed lawn, fresh paint, a porch swing. To anyone passing by, it seemed welcoming, safe even. But Ava knew better. Once you stepped inside, it was like living in a horror movie. Every smile was fake, every kind gesture hiding something sinister.

It was quiet—too quiet. The younger kids they fostered were always asleep by now, but Jim and Roxy were usually awake and lurking. She hesitated, her gut screaming at her to turn around, to run. But where would she go? She forced herself to push open the front door, the familiar creak sending a shiver down her spine.

The house was still, an eerie calm settling over it. Her pulse quickened. There was no sound of the TV, no clinking of beer bottles. There was nothing. Ava swallowed hard, her senses on high alert. Every fiber of her being told her to get out, to run back to her bike, and disappear into the night. But she ignored it, as she always did. She was used to pretending everything was fine.

She made her way to the basement door, trying to move quietly, but the silence made each footstep sound like a shout.

Her footsteps echoed as she descended the narrow, creaking staircase after her shift at the fast-food joint. Something felt off. The air was thick and heavy with an eerie stillness that made her stomach churn. They knew. She didn't know how, but they knew.

The moment her foster father's silhouette appeared at the bottom of the stairs, her heart froze. His dark eyes bore into her, hard and unforgiving. "Get down here," his voice was low and menacing. She hesitated, her legs trembling, but before she could turn to run, he was on her, his grip like iron around her arm.

"You thought you were smart, didn't you?" Her foster mother's shrill voice followed as the woman appeared behind him, her lips curled in a sneer. "The social worker told us everything. You little bitch!"

Panic surged through Ava's veins. The world blurred as she twisted, trying to break free, but it was useless. She knew it. He dragged her down, her feet barely touching the remaining steps. She didn't even get a chance to scream before the first blow landed.

The beating was calculated and practiced, just like every other time. Her foster parents were always careful where they hit. Her body bore the brunt of their fury, bruises blossoming in places no one would see. They never hit her face or any other part of her body where it could be noticeable because they knew better.

Pain shot through her side as his boot connected with her ribs. She bit her lip to stop herself from crying out, but the tears came anyway, hot and angry.

"You think someone's going to believe a little trash thing like you?" Her foster mother's voice hissed in her ear as Ava curled into herself. "If you open your mouth again, you'll regret it."

The words echoed in her mind as she lay on the cold concrete floor, her body throbbing with agony. She couldn't stay there. Not anymore. This had to be the last time.

She vowed then and there, lying broken and bleeding, that she would run away. Far away. She would start over, build a life of her own, away from the suffocating cruelty of this house.

Suddenly, the darkness of the basement faded into nothingness and was replaced by the sound of something shrill.

BEEP...BEEP...BEEP...

CHAPTER ONE

Ava sat up, her chest rising and falling rapidly as the remnants of her past and the nightmare clung to her. The beating, the cold basement floor, the suffocating fear—it all felt so real. She rubbed her eyes, forcing herself to breathe.

"It's just a dream," she whispered to the empty room. "You're not that girl anymore."

She wasn't seventeen, cowering in the shadows of her past. No, she was thirty-two, stronger, wiser, and no longer under anyone's control.

She swung her legs over the side of the bed, her bare feet meeting the cool hardwood floor. Her heart still raced, but she focused on grounding herself, on reminding herself that she'd made it out of that hell hole that the Porters had called home. She had her own life now, her own purpose.

She glanced at her phone on the nightstand. It was six-thirty. She had a full morning ahead of her. She had to stop by the office to make a few phone calls and pick up some documents before heading to the courthouse.

A court hearing for one of the kids she oversaw loomed ahead of her, a day that could change the trajectory of a young life. That's why she chose social services, to make sure no kid would ever have to feel like she did—unseen, unheard, betrayed by the very system that was supposed to protect them.

Ava stood and stretched her arms above her head before moving toward the bathroom. As she walked down the tiny hall separating her bedroom from the master bathroom, her eyes caught the framed picture of Evelyn, her adopted mom, smiling back at her. She paused, her fingers brushing the edge of the frame as memories surfaced.

It had been fifteen years since she ran. She could still remember the night vividly as she slipped out of that hellhole of a house with only a backpack and a little over two thousand dollars she had scraped together from months of working at that fast-food joint. She'd waited until her foster parents had passed out, slipping out into the night like a shadow, her heart pounding with both fear and the thrill of freedom. She was determined to get as far away from Seattle as she could.

Seattle had been her starting point, but it was the bus ride from Wyoming where her life truly changed. She met Evelyn on that bus, an older woman with kind eyes and a calming presence. They had talked for hours, and something in the warmth of Evelyn's voice made Ava trust her in a way she hadn't trusted anyone in years.

By the time the bus rolled into Virginia Beach, Ava knew that the beach town would be her new home. Evelyn had offered her a place to stay and a fresh start, but without her, Ava wasn't sure where she would've ended up. Maybe on the streets, maybe worse. But Evelyn had given her more than shelter. She gave her hope. A future. A real family.

Ava's lips curved into a small smile, her heart swelling with gratitude.

She shook herself from the memories, reminding herself that today wasn't about the past. It was about the kids who needed someone to fight for them. Someone like Evelyn. Someone like her.

Stepping into the bathroom, she turned on the shower, letting the steam fill the small space. The hot water would be her reset, washing away the lingering weight of the nightmare and preparing her for the day ahead.

As she stepped into the shower and under the hot water, she reminded herself once again that she was no longer that scared girl in the basement. She was Ava Morgan, a strong, determined woman and a voice for those who hadn't found their own yet.

CHAPTER TWO

Ava sat in one of the stiff leather chairs in Judge Holten's chambers. Her fingers twisted the thin silver bracelet she wore around her wrist. She tried to appear calm for Christian's sake, but her stomach churned with unease.

The walls in the office were lined with shelves of law books and framed degrees, but there was something cozy about the place, with a few potted plants and photos of her grandkids breaking up the formal austerity.

Beside her, Christian, a fifteen-year-old boy, stared at his hands, fidgeting with the frayed cuff of his sweater. Ava could see the nerves in his tight posture, though he tried to mask it with indifference. His dark brown eyes would periodically shift toward the door the judge had disappeared through just minutes ago. He reminded her so much of herself at that age—quiet, observant, trying not to get too attached to anything or anyone. It was a survival tactic. It broke Ava's heart.

Ava hated this part, the waiting, the uncertainty. It was a cruel limbo for a boy who had already been through too much. Christian didn't need to say it out loud. She knew he was bracing himself for more disappointment. His track record with foster parents was abysmal. Time and again, he'd been let down by people who had no business fostering in the first place. She'd seen the damage it had done to him, how each rejection chipped away at his ability to trust. And now, here they were, waiting to hear if his latest set of foster parents were going to give up on him, too.

She shifted in her chair, glancing at Christian. "You holding up okay?" she asked softly.

He shrugged but didn't look at her. "It's not like this is the first time," he muttered. She could hear the sadness in his voice.

"I know," Ava replied, her voice stead. "But it doesn't make it right."

When he didn't say anything, Ava decided not to push. They sat in silence.

The door to the judge's office remained closed, and the low hum of voices behind it was barely audible. Ava's stomach continued to churn. She didn't have a good feeling about this. The last time she'd seen Christian's foster parents, they'd been all smiles and reassurances, but she did catch the edge of disdain in their tone when they talked about him. They had made small, subtle comments about him—he was a bit difficult and a little defiant.

It had made her furious. Christian was a bright, resourceful kid who'd been let down by every adult who was supposed to protect him. He didn't need perfect parents. He just needed someone who'd stuck around long enough to earn his trust. He needed someone like Evelyn.

"Do you think they're gonna keep me?" Christian asked, his voice barely above a whisper.

He was trying to sound indifferent, but Ava could hear the tiny thread of hope buried underneath. "I don't know, Christian," she answered honestly. "But whatever happens, we'll figure it out together. You're not alone in this."

Before either one could say another word, the door opened, and Judge Holten stepped in carrying a file in her hands. Her expression was carefully guarded, but Ava had spent enough time in her courtroom and outside the courtroom to recognize the slight crease in her forehead that meant bad news.

Judge Holten, a woman in her mid-fifties with sharp eyes softened only by her familiarity with Ava, sat behind her desk.

Being that Christian's foster parents hadn't joined them, told Ava everything that needed to be said.

Even though she didn't show it outright, Ava could tell that Judge Holten appeared clearly irritated by the situation as well.

Ava sat up straighter, bracing herself for the news.

Christian's shoulders tensed, and he shot Ava a quick glance before fixing his eyes on the judge. She'd never seen him look so young and vulnerable as he did at that moment.

Judge Holten looked at Christian and then at Ava. "I just spoke with the Hodges," she began, her voice calm but serious. "And I think we need to have a frank discussion about what happens next."

Ava noticed how Christian's shoulders slumped in defeat, and she reached over and gave his hand a quick squeeze. He didn't pull away, and that gave her the smallest glimmer of hope. Whatever came next, she would fight for him. He deserved that much and so much more.

"Christian, can you tell me a little about how things have been at the Hodges' house?"

Christian shifted uncomfortably in his chair. "It's been okay, I guess," he mumbled. Ava shot him an encouraging look, and he continued, "They just don't really get me. I like different stuff than the other kids. I'm not like them. I keep to myself, but they say I'm causing problems."

The judge nodded, her gaze softening as she listened. "What kind of problems?"

"I honestly don't know. I try not to bother them. They want me to be more like the other kids in the house. But I'm not. I'm me, and I have different interests."

Ava clenched her jaw. She knew this story too well. Christian's foster parents didn't understand him, and instead of working through it, they labeled him a problem. The fact that they couldn't even be bothered to sit in on this conversation proved how little they cared.

Judge Holten leaned back in her chair, her expression hardening slightly. "I won't lie. I'm a little disappointed in this situation. However, that is not directed at you, Christian. Looking over your file, it appears you are a very smart young man. You have all A's and B's in school and taking Honors classes. That is amazing for someone in your situation. I don't see that often, and that alone tells me that you are not the problem." She paused for a moment and took a deep breath. "The issue we have is finding a better solution for you, Christian." She glanced at Ava, and Ava gave her a tight nod in agreement.

"After speaking with the Hodges, they are petitioning to return Christian to the state." She turned her attention to Christian. "Christian, I don't believe the problem is with you," the judge said kindly, and Christian's face lifted ever so slightly.

"I agree," Ava chimed in, her voice firm. "Christian is a good kid. He's respectful and smart, and he is just trying to figure out who he is. He's a normal teenager. Though maybe a little more mature than most at his age." She looked over and winked at Christian, which earned her a small smile in return.

Judge Holten sighed. "It seems the best course of action is to return Christian to the state's care effective immediately."

Ava had known this was coming, but hearing it still felt like a punch to the gut. Christian didn't flinch, but she saw the way his shoulders hunched just a little more.

The judge turned her attention to Ava. "Ava, are there any suitable placements available for Christian?"

Ava hesitated, already knowing the answer. "Unfortunately, there are no vacancies for teens at the moment. Group homes are at capacity, and with Thanksgiving and Christmas coming up, it'll be hard to place him anywhere before the new year."

Judge Holten frowned, clearly displeased. "So, what do you suggest?"

Ava's heart raced. She hadn't fully thought it through, but the answer was clear. She glanced at Christian, his downcast face breaking her heart. This wasn't just some kid she was responsible for. This was a boy who reminded her too much of herself—lost, alone, misunderstood. And she had the power to help him the way Evelyn had helped her.

Taking a deep breath, Ava looked back at the judge. "As you know, I'm approved to foster, but I've never taken a placement before, as I didn't want to risk getting too attached." She paused, feeling the weight of her own words. "But Christian is different. He deserves someone who understands him, especially through the holidays. With the court's permission, I'd like to foster him until the New Year, at least."

Christian's head snapped up, his wide eyes locking onto Ava. He was shocked, and she didn't miss the way his lips twitched upward, the hint of a smile crossing his face.

Judge Holten looked equally surprised, her eyebrows raised as she considered Ava's proposal. "You want to foster Christian?"

Ava nodded without hesitation. "Yes, absolutely. Someone once took a chance on me, and it changed my life. I want to do the same for him."

The judge was quiet for a moment, flipping through Christian's file. She was no longer just a judge. At the moment, she was Ava's friend, and Ava knew the weight of what she was asking. After a long pause, Judge Holten looked up, her gaze serious. "Are you sure this is what you want to do?"

Ava didn't blink. "Yes."

A smile tugged at the corners of Judge Holten's mouth. "Very well. I approve your request, and Christian will remain in your care throughout the holidays. We will schedule another meeting for the first week of the new year. I'll have a few documents for you to sign now, and then I'll have the rest sent over to your office this afternoon."

Christian let out a breath, the tension draining from his body. He turned to Ava, his eyes shining with a mix of excitement and nerves. "Really, Ava?"

She smiled. "Really."

Before she could take her next breath, Christian pounced on her, giving her the biggest hug.

"Thank you, Ava. I promise I won't let you down." His voice was full of emotion.

Hugging him back, she smiled softly as her heart swelled. "I know you won't."

About an hour later, and after signing a few documents and handling some legalities, Christian looked at her with a mix of curiosity and hope. "So, what's next?"

Ava stood, gathering her things. "I don't know about you, but I'm starving. How about we go and get some lunch."

For the first time since they'd entered the chambers, Christian grinned. And for the first time in a long time, Ava felt like she was exactly where she needed to be.

The cozy pizzeria smelled of freshly baked dough and garlic. Ava and Christian sat in a booth near the window, a large meat lovers pizza between them.

Christian had been quiet since they left the courthouse, and Ava assumed he was still processing everything that had happened. After all, she was still sort of shocked herself. She definitely didn't have "agreeing to foster a teenager" on her bingo card for the day.

She took a bite of her slice, watching him as he slowly ate his pizza, glancing out the window every few seconds.

"So, Christian," Ava began, trying to ease the tension she could feel from him. "Let's talk about your room. What are you thinking? Any particular way you want to set it up?"

Christian looked at her, clearly surprised. "My room?"

She smiled. "Yeah, your room. You'll have your own bedroom at my place. I figured we could pick out some stuff you'd like. You know, make it feel like yours."

Christian blinked, then sat back in his seat, staring at her in disbelief. "I thought I'd just sleep on the couch or something. I mean, I don't need a whole room."

Ava smiled softly, shaking her head. "Christian, of course, you'll have your own room. I want you to feel at home. You deserve that."

He seemed stunned, his eyes darting around as if he was still processing what she'd said. "I've never really had my own space like that," he mumbled. "At all the foster homes I've lived at, they just kinda put me wherever."

Ava's chest tightened. She knew how that felt, being shuffled from place to place, never really feeling like you belonged anywhere. "Well, that changes now. My home is your home for as long as you want it. I want you to be comfortable. So, what do you want in your room?"

Christian was quiet for a moment, then hesitated before speaking. "Maybe...I don't know, a desk? Somewhere to do schoolwork and stuff."

"We can do that," Ava nodded. "Anything else? You can go all out, you know."

He shrugged, his nerves showing in the way he fidgeted with his napkin. "I don't know. I've never really thought about it."

Ava leaned forward, her tone gentle. "Take your time. We'll figure it out together."

Christian shifted again, clearly uneasy with the attention on him, but then his gaze met hers. "Can I ask you something?"

"Of course."

"Why'd you take me in? I mean, you didn't have to. You could've just let me go back to the state and let them deal with me."

Ava set her slice down and wiped her hands, her expression softening. She had known this question was coming eventually. "Because I've been where you are," she began, her voice quiet but steady. "I grew up in foster care too. I bounced around a lot, just like you. When I was seventeen, I ran away from my foster parents. They were not good people. They were abusive, both physically and verbally. And the system I was in didn't really care. So, I saved up some money, and I took off."

Christian's eyes widened as his attention was fully on her now. Ava continued, her voice calm, but the weight of those memories was still heavy in her heart. "I didn't know where I was going. I just knew I couldn't stay. Then, I met Evelyn on a bus heading toward Virginia Beach. Long story short, she took me in, no questions asked. She gave me a home when no one else would. She believed in me when I didn't believe in myself. I wouldn't be where I am today if it wasn't for her."

Christian was quiet, digesting her words. After a few seconds, he asked, "So you think I'm like you?"

Ava smiled. "I think you're a lot like me. You're tough, but you don't need to do it all on your own. And more importantly, I don't want anyone telling you what you have to do when it comes to your interests. Your foster parents tried to make you someone you're not, and that's not okay. You deserve to be yourself, Christian. Always."

Christian's expression softened, but he didn't say anything. Instead, he reached into his backpack and pulled out a folded brochure, handing it to Ava. She took it, unfolding the paper. It was a brochure for a college and career fair being held that weekend in the city. But she noticed that on the brochure was the U.S. Navy's emblem with some pictures that Christian had circled.

Ava looked at him curiously. "College fair, huh? Does the military, particularly the Navy, interest you?"

Christian nodded, his face lighting up with a rare enthusiasm. "Yeah, I want to be a Navy SEAL. I've been reading up on it. There are a lot of requirements, like physical fitness, leadership skills, and teamwork. It's tough, but I've been preparing." He leaned forward, his voice gaining more confidence as he spoke. "You have to be really dedicated, but I've been running and working out every day. I know I still have a long way to go, but I want to be ready. And I want to go to this event and learn more. Plus, I heard that one of the SEAL teams are going to be there and will be doing a demonstration."

Ava was genuinely impressed by Christian's ambition, his research, and his drive. It all reminded her of herself when she was his age, determined to find her way despite everything. "Wow, Christian," she said, her tone full of admiration. "I had no idea you were so into this. I'm really impressed."

Christian blushed a little, not used to the praise. "Thanks. I just think it's something I could be good at."

Ava smiled. "I think you'd be great at it. And I'd love to take you to this."

His eyes lit up. "Really? That'd be awesome."

"Absolutely. We'll make it happen."

They continued eating, and the conversation flowed more easily now. Christian seemed more relaxed, more open. As they finished lunch, Christian looked at her with a curious smile. "So, what's next?"

Ava chuckled, wiping her hands with a napkin. "Next? We're going grocery shopping."

Christian's eyes widened with excitement. "Really? That's awesome!"

Ava laughed, a little surprised by his reaction. "You're excited about grocery shopping?"

He nodded quickly. "Yeah! My last foster family never asked me what I wanted to eat. They just bought whatever they liked, and I had to eat it."

Ava's heart ached at that. The idea of Christian never having a say in something as simple as what food he liked felt so wrong. She was determined to make sure he knew that her home, *his* home, would be different.

"Well, you'll definitely get a say this time," she said warmly. "We're going to make sure you have the best home life and the best holiday season that you've ever had."

Christian smiled, and for the first time, it seemed like he believed her.

CHAPTER THREE

The crisp November air had a refreshing bite as Ava and Christian walked through the courtyard of Virginia Beach's City Hall, weaving between booths at the career and college day.

The leaves crunched beneath their feet, a mosaic of autumn oranges and reds. Christian led the way, his backpack slung over one shoulder, moving with a sense of purpose that made Ava's heart swell. She was here to support him, letting him take charge of the day.

He stopped at a few local college tables, asking thoughtful questions about their programs and even visiting a trade school booth with an interest in auto mechanics.

Ava smiled, pride filling her as she watched him do his homework at every booth they passed. His questions were sharp, and his demeanor was calm and mature. He was a fifteen-year-old, far beyond his years. Ava knew his background had forced him to grow up faster, but seeing him like this, confident and in control, filled her with admiration.

After about an hour and a half, they finally approached the military booths, where the Navy's display dominated the scene. Their booth was by far the grandest, with large banners, displays of various Navy equipment and uniforms, and even a few models of ships and aircraft. Given the proximity to Norfolk and the SEAL base in town, it wasn't a surprise the Navy would go all out.

Christian's eyes lit up as he approached the recruiters, two of them standing behind the booth in their crisp uniforms. He immediately struck up a conversation, his enthusiasm evident as he asked questions about different career paths and opportunities in the Navy.

Ava hung back, letting him take the lead, and once again, she was impressed with how well he handled himself. Christian wasn't just asking about general things. His focus was centered around the SEALs.

"This is my mom," Christian said suddenly, introducing her with a proud smile as he turned back toward Ava.

Ava felt a jolt of surprise at his words. *Mom?* Her heart skipped a beat, but she smiled warmly and stepped forward, shaking hands with the recruiters. She didn't correct him.

One of the recruiters, a tall man with close-cropped hair, smiled at Christian. "So, you're interested in becoming a SEAL, huh?"

Christian nodded eagerly. "Yes, sir. I've been studying the process. I know it's hard even to get selected for BUD/S, and I've been reading about the training and what it takes to get through it. It's tough, but I'm getting ready. I've been practicing the PST, and I joined the swim team at my high school."

The other recruiter, a woman with a sharp, professional demeanor, raised her eyebrows, impressed. "You've done your homework. That's a good start. It's one of the hardest things to do in the military, but it sounds like you've got the right mindset."

Christian beamed as the recruiters continued to talk to him, asking more questions about his interest in the military and his schooling. Ava listened, pride swelling in her chest. He was handling the conversation like a pro.

"Well, you came at the perfect time," the male recruiter said, smiling down at Christian. "We've got a SEAL team doing a demonstration in about ten minutes. You should definitely check it out."

Christian's eyes went wide with excitement, and the recruiters handed him a bunch of Navy swag. He got a T-shirt, a keychain, stickers, and a water bottle. He thanked them excitedly, clutching the items to his chest, and then turned to Ava.

"Do you mind if we stay a little longer to see the demonstration?" he asked, practically bouncing on his heels.

"Of course," Ava said, laughing softly. "Today is all about you." She took a few brochures from the recruiters and nodded her thanks before following Christian toward the open field where the demonstration was set to take place.

Christian led them to an area off to the side, away from the main crowd gathering at the front of the field. Ava glanced around, curious. "Why over here?" she asked, a little puzzled that he wasn't trying to get closer for a better view.

Christian pointed to the side, where a group of men that she assumed were the SEALs were gearing up for the demonstration. "This way, I can see everything—front and behind the scenes."

She smiled, understanding now. "Smart," she said, giving him a playful nudge.

The demonstration started soon after, with the team piling into vehicles that Ava could only describe as futuristic dune buggies. Christian leaned over and explained what they were called. The excitement was clear in his voice. "Those are special vehicles for all kinds of terrain. They can handle pretty much anything."

Ava nodded, impressed. She couldn't help but admire how much Christian already knew. As the SEALs raced through the field, displaying their tactical maneuvers, an announcer called out to the crowd. "We need a volunteer to help out the team. Anyone feeling brave?"

Before Ava could even blink, Christian's hand shot up.

The announcer scanned the crowd, and then his eyes landed on Christian, standing off to the side. "You, over there!" he called out, pointing to Christian. "Come on up!"

Ava's heart raced with a mix of excitement and nerves as one of the SEALs jogged over, escorting Christian to where the rest of the team stood. She watched, her emotions bubbling over with pride as Christian beamed, chatting with the SEALs like he belonged there.

As she watched from the side, a figure appeared next to her. She glanced over and felt her breath catch. A tall man, broad-shouldered and in the same tactical clothing as the others, minus all the gear, stood beside her. He had a strong jawline, piercing hazel eyes, and a surprisingly friendly and slightly shy smile. Ava felt her pulse quicken as he met her gaze.

"He seems happy," the man said, nodding toward Christian. "And he really seems to understand what we're doing out there."

Ava smiled, her heart fluttering slightly at the sound of his voice. It had a subtle accent. It was Australian, she realized after a moment. "Yeah, it's his goal to become a SEAL. We were just over at the recruiter booth talking to them about it."

The man grinned, his smile making her heart skip again. "I know. The recruiter told us to pick him if he volunteered."

Ava blinked, surprised. "Really? Why?"

"He was impressed by your son's attitude and how prepared he is," the man said.

Ava felt warmth spread through her. "He's not technically my son," she admitted, glancing down before meeting the man's eyes again. "I'm his foster mom. Well, sort of. It's actually a long story. I'm his social worker, and he's staying with me through the holidays." She had no idea why she had told the man that.

The man's expression softened, and he seemed genuinely interested. "He's a lucky kid to have someone supporting him. And I'm sorry the recruiter mentioned you were his mom."

Ava chuckled softly. "Oh, please don't apologize. I don't mind."

"I'm Aussie, by the way," the man introduced himself, holding out his hand. There was that soft accent again.

Ava took his hand, feeling the warmth of his grip. "Ava," she replied, trying not to let her thoughts run wild about how good-looking he was. His accent, his kind eyes, *oh, be still my heart.* It was all too much.

Aussie's eyes flicked to Christian again. "He's got the drive, that's for sure. What's his story? If you don't mind me asking."

Ava hesitated, but for some reason, she felt comfortable enough to share some of his background. "Christian had a rough start. His mother was a drug addict and a prostitute. She overdosed when he was just three. He's been in the system ever since. We have no idea who the father is. There is no name listed on the birth certificate."

Aussie's expression was full of understanding and no judgment. "Sounds like he's lucky to have you."

Ava smiled, her heart warming at his words. "I feel lucky to have him, too."

Aussie was intrigued by the woman standing beside him.

Ava, as he now knew her name, had caught his eye when Lucas, one of the Navy recruiters he had been talking to, had been talking about the boy who was with her.

When Lucas had first pointed the boy out, it wasn't the kid that had caught his attention. It had been the woman standing next to him with hair as dark as a raven's wing. When the sunlight hit it just right, a blueish hue danced within the long strands that fell down her back in waves. She had been impossible to miss.

When Aussie first approached her, he had been a nervous wreck, which was ridiculous because he was a SEAL who was trained for the toughest missions. Talking to a stranger shouldn't have felt like stepping into uncharted territory.

But the longer he stood there listening to Ava talk about the boy she was caring for, the more he began to loosen up.

From what he's heard, Aussie's respect for Christian grew, but it was Ava's quiet strength that struck him. She didn't seem like someone who sought the spotlight, yet here she was, advocating for a kid who clearly mattered to her.

As the demonstration continued, Aussie stood beside Ava, a comfortable silence hovering between them. When an opportunity arose, he snuck a few peeks at her.

As a small explosive device detonated, Ava jumped.

"Holy crap!" she exclaimed as she held her hand over her heart. "I wasn't expecting that."

Aussie chuckled. "It's quite the show," he replied, looking down at her. Her dark blue eyes sparkled.

"That was really intense," she said, a small laugh escaping her.

"It can be," Aussie admitted. He nodded his head in the direction where Christian was helping Snow, one of his teammates, carry a fake injured person. He had a serious and determined look on his face.

"He seems to really be enjoying himself."

"He does. I'm just glad he got to experience this," she told him.

Aussie wanted to ask more questions, but he didn't want to come across as being nosey.

Moments later, the crowd was clapping as the demonstration came to an end, and after shaking hands with Aussie's teammates, Christian came running back over.

"Ava! Did you see that? That was so cool!" Christian said. The smile on his face grew by the second.

"I did," she told him.

Suddenly, Christian realized Aussie was standing there, and he gave Ava a look as if asking who he was.

Ava smiled. "Christian, this is Aussie. Aussie, this is Christian."

Aussie held his hand out. "It's nice to meet you, Christian. You looked pretty good out there with my team."

Christian shook his hand, and Aussie was impressed with the kid's grip. It was a strong and confident handshake.

"It's nice to meet you too. You're a SEAL too?" he asked, and Aussie grinned.

"I am."

"That's so cool," Christian said.

"Ava here tells me that you're interested in becoming one yourself," Aussie said, directing his attention to Christian.

The boy nodded enthusiastically. "I am. I spoke with the recruiter about it, and he gave me some tips on things that I should focus on and concentrate on. I'm scheduled to take the ASVAB test in the third week of January."

Aussie raised an eyebrow, impressed. Lucas wasn't lying when he said the kid was prepared. "Being a SEAL is a big goal. It takes a lot of hard work and dedication," Aussie told him.

Christian shrugged, but there was a fire in his eyes. "I'm ready for it. Like I told the recruiter, I know it's tough both mentally and physically, but I'm doing everything that I can to prepare myself for it. Do you have any pointers that you can give me? You know things that I might be missing or not doing to prepare?"

Aussie smiled, loving the kid's dedication and willingness to reach his dream.

"Well, you're on the right track already. Going through BUD/s is more mental than it is physical. I've seen some of the strongest men quit because they mentally could not withstand the grueling training that recruits are put through. You see, BUD/s is designed to push recruits beyond their physical limits."

"Was it hard for you?" Christian asked.

Aussie laughed. "Yeah. It was one of the hardest things I think I ever did."

"Was there a time that you wanted to quit? You know, ring the bell?"

"There were numerous times," Aussie admitted, and he wasn't ashamed to say it because if anybody who has gone through BUD/s and said that quitting never crossed their mind, he knew they were lying.

"If you don't mind me asking, what was it that prevented you from ringing out?"

"Pride. I knew I wanted to be a SEAL when I was around your age, and when I got selected into BUD/s, I promised myself that I wasn't going to ring out no matter how badly I wanted to. Anytime I started thinking about quitting, I would think back to a phrase that my mentor, a Master Chief and former SEAL, had told me. And would repeat that phrase over and over in my head until quitting was a thing of the past."

"What was the phrase?"

Aussie grinned. "Don't ring the damn bell. That was the phrase I would repeat."

Christian grinned. "Thanks for sharing that with me. If I get in, I'll have to remember that."

Aussie smiled. "You do that."

"Is there any type of program that could help prepare kids who are Christian's age? I know there is JROTC in high schools, but Christian is focused on core classes," Ava asked.

Aussie felt a surge of respect for both of them—Christian for his resilience and Ava for her dedication to helping him.

Aussie looked at Christian. "If you're serious about this, you should look into the U.S. Naval Sea Cadets."

"Sea Cadets? What is that?" Ava asked, tilting her head.

"It's a youth leadership program for kids interested in the military. The Navy sponsors it," Aussie explained. "One of my buddies has a kid in the program. They get to learn about discipline, teamwork, and leadership. It's a great way to see if military life is really for you before you make the full commitment."

Ava's brow furrowed slightly. "I've never heard of it. How does it work?"

"They have local units across the country. There's one right here in Virginia Beach," Aussie said. "The cadets get together several times a month on the weekends for drills. During the summer months, they host training sessions all around the country. The trainings consist of almost any career offered in the military, including Special Warfare. They get to wear uniforms just like the Navy. They learn about naval history and even get a taste of what it's like to be on a ship. It's not all physical, either. It's about building character."

"That sounds amazing," Ava said as she glanced at Christian.

Aussie nodded. "It is. And it's not just about the military." He looked at Christian. "Even if you decide later that the military isn't for you, the skills that you've learned will carry you through anything you want to do."

Ava smiled again. "Is that something you're interested in?" she asked Christian.

"Yeah. It sounds like a great program."

"If you go out to their website, they have all the information. And they will have the contact information for the Commanding Officer for the local unit here in town."

"Thank you so much for all the great information," Ava told him.

"It's my pleasure." He looked at Christian. "If you ever need some advice or just want to chat, feel free to reach out."

Christian beamed. "Really? That would be awesome!"

Ava looked at Aussie, gratitude in her eyes. "Thank you. That means a lot."

Aussie shrugged modestly. "Happy to help. Besides, it's great to see young people passionate about something."

They spoke for a few more minutes. The conversation flowed easily. Aussie found himself increasingly drawn to Ava, not just because of her beauty but her compassion and strength. She seemed to care for Christian genuinely, and that spoke volumes about her character.

As they wrapped up their discussion, Aussie turned to Ava. "It was great meeting you both. Like I said, if you have a question or if you ever want to talk or anything else, here's my number." He handed her a card with his number written down on it.

Ava took it, smiling. "Thanks, Aussie. And thanks again for everything today. Christian really looks up to guys like you."

Aussie grinned. "The pleasure was mine. Take care, Ava." He looked at Christian. "Keep working hard."

After saying goodbye, Aussie watched as Ava and Christian walked toward the parking lot. He couldn't shake the strange feeling flowing through his body. It felt like a spark of something—interest, curiosity, maybe even an attraction.

Meeting Ava had been unexpected, but he couldn't help but hope he'd see her again.

Ava couldn't shake the thoughts of Aussie as she and Christian walked back to the car. The cool November breeze brushed against her skin, but her mind was still lingering on the warmth of his smile, the kindness in his eyes, and that cute Australian accent that had caught her completely off guard.

There was something rugged about him. Maybe it was his tactical uniform and his confident stance, but also a surprising friendliness that softened his edges. *And okay,* she thought with a grin, *the man was undeniably sexy. Those hazel eyes were captivating and sucked her right in.*

She couldn't help but admire how attentive he had been to Christian, not just brushing him off like some people did with teenagers. No, Aussie had listened. He'd shown genuine interest in Christian's story, in his dreams. And that made her heart swell even more—a SEAL, of all people, caring enough to notice someone like Christian. That kind of awareness was rare, and she hadn't expected it.

As they reached the car, Christian was practically bouncing with excitement, still pumped from the SEAL demonstration and his conversation with Aussie.

He couldn't stop talking about how cool it had been to help out. "Did you see how they worked together, Ava? They're like a well-oiled machine! And when they picked me to participate with them, man, that was awesome!"

Ava smiled as she unlocked the car, listening to him go on, his energy infectious. But just as they were about to get in, Christian turned to her, a mischievous grin on his face.

"And what about Aussie, huh?" he teased, wiggling his eyebrows.

Ava's eyes widened, a laugh escaping her. "What? Christian, come on. It's not like that."

"Oh, it's totally like that," he said, sliding into the passenger seat, still grinning. "I saw the way he was looking at you. He's definitely interested."

Ava shook her head, trying to laugh it off as she started the car. "He was just being nice. He was more interested in you than me, trust me."

"Yeah, because I'm awesome," Christian said with a wink, "but he still gave *you* his number. You should use it."

Ava's fingers tightened on the steering wheel for a second. She had almost forgotten about the number Aussie had casually slipped her before they parted ways. "Christian, stop it," she said with a chuckle, though a part of her couldn't deny the idea was tempting.

She glanced at him out of the corner of her eye, but Christian wasn't letting up. "I'm serious, Ava. You should totally call or text him. I think he's into you. And he's way better than that other guy you were seeing. What was his name? Oh, yeah. Jarod."

Jarod.

The name sent a flicker of tension through her. She'd been dating Jarod on and off for the last year. He was a county judge and was ten years older than her. He was good-looking and had a solid career. He had everything you'd think a woman would want. But there was something about him that always made her hold back.

Maybe it was the fact that being around Jarod felt more like an obligation than anything else. He checked all the right boxes, but there was no spark, no real excitement when she thought about seeing him. They were supposed to have dinner next week, and the idea of it didn't exactly fill her with anticipation. If she was honest with herself, she wasn't even looking forward to it.

"You don't like Jarod?" Ava asked, raising an eyebrow.

Christian shrugged, looking out the window for a second before speaking. "I don't know. There's just something about him that seemed off the few times that I met him. He's nice enough, I guess. But I get bad vibes when he's around."

Ava glanced over at Christian, surprised by how serious he sounded. She knew Christian had good instincts. He'd been through enough in life to read people well. And the fact that he didn't like Jarod struck her as something she couldn't ignore.

But before she could dive too deep into those thoughts, her mind drifted back to Aussie. His easy smile, the way he'd seemed a little shy when he introduced himself, that hint of an accent that somehow made him even more charming. And unlike Jarod, Aussie's presence had excited her and made her heart race in a way she hadn't felt in a long time.

She found herself smiling as she pulled the car onto the road. *Aussie.*

Christian noticed the grin and nudged her playfully. "You're thinking about him, aren't you?"

Ava laughed, shaking her head but not denying it. "Maybe," she admitted, a warmth spreading through her chest. "Maybe I am."

Christian grinned, looking victorious. "Told you."

Ava tried to push thoughts of Jarod out of her mind, and it wasn't that hard. She didn't want to think about her lackluster relationship with the judge right now. Not when the thought of a certain Navy SEAL with an accent could make her smile like this.

As they drove home, Christian rambled on about what they should make for dinner, excited to cook something together. But Ava's mind kept drifting back to Aussie—his smile, his rugged charm, and the phone number burning a hole in her pocket. Maybe, just maybe, it was time to take a chance on something new.

For now, though, she would focus on making dinner with Christian and enjoy the present moment. But she couldn't help but wonder what might happen if she dialed that number.

CHAPTER FOUR

Ava sat across from Jarod at a candlelit table, the hum of chatter and clinking silverware filling the air of the upscale restaurant. The atmosphere was cozy, the lighting warm, but her thoughts were elsewhere, or she should say they were on someone else.

Jarod was speaking, but the memory of Aussie drowned out his voice. That rugged, charming Navy SEAL with the soft Australian accent kept creeping into her mind. It had been a few days, and she couldn't stop thinking about the way he'd smiled at her and how attentive he was to Christian. It felt fresh, different from this stagnant, predictable routine with Jarod.

"Ava," Jarod's annoyed voice cut through her thoughts, sharper than before. She blinked and refocused, realizing she'd missed the last part of whatever he had said. His dark, manicured brows were furrowed, and the muscles in his jaw were clenched. He hated it when she wasn't paying attention to him.

"Sorry, what did you say?" she asked, trying to mask the distraction with a polite smile.

Jarod gave her an irritated look, his lips tight. "I said I heard that you took in that boy." There was a hint of accusation in his tone, something that instantly set her on edge. "Everyone around the courthouse has been talking about it."

Ava forced herself to relax, shrugging it off. "So what? And the *boy* has a name. It's Christian, and he needed a place to stay. It's really not a big deal."

Jarod's eyes narrowed as he leaned in, lowering his voice, though the sharpness didn't diminish. "It was a stupid move, Ava. Getting involved with a kid like that."

Her heart sank, a ripple of anger flaring in her chest, but she kept her face calm. "What do you mean, a kid like that?"

"You know exactly what I mean," he said, a sneer creeping into his voice. "Kids like him have no stable family and no real upbringing. They always end up in trouble. Or in jail. They are failures. I see it every day in my courtroom."

Ava's blood boiled, her grip tightening on the edge of the table. *This man*—how had she ever thought they could have a future together? She took a slow breath, steadying herself before replying. "You realize that I used to be one of those kids, right?"

Jarod's face paled slightly as if realizing he had made a huge mistake. He instantly tried to backtrack, his voice softer now, more appeasing. "Ava, that's not what I meant. You know that I wasn't referring to you and your past."

She raised her eyebrow at him. "Really? Because those *kids* you talked about were me fifteen years ago. Some of us don't have a choice, and we are just shoved wherever there is a room."

"Ava—" Jarod started to say, but Ava was done. She didn't want to hear some lame apology. She had now seen his true colors. And what a shame, considering he was a judge who ruled on juvenile cases.

"No," Ava interrupted, her voice low but firm. She'd had enough. She wasn't going to sit there and listen to someone belittle everything she believed in, everything she stood for. "I know exactly what you meant. And if that's how you really feel about kids like Christian—kids like me—then I think we're done here."

Jarod reached across the table toward her hand, trying to salvage the moment, but Ava had already made up her mind. "Come on, Ava, let's not make a scene. I didn't mean it that way."

"It's not about making a scene," Ava said, pushing her chair back and standing. "It's about realizing that I don't want to be with someone who looks down on the very people I'm trying to help. Or someone that I used to be. Let's just stick to being colleagues at the courthouse."

"Ava, wait," Jarod started, but she was already moving past him, grabbing her bag and heading for the door.

She paused just before exiting and gave him a sarcastic smile. "By the way, your people skills? They could use some work."

The door shut behind her with a satisfying click, but as soon as the cool night air hit her, Ava realized she'd left her coat in Jarod's car. Not that she was about to go back inside and ask him for it. She wrapped her arms around herself, pulling her bag closer for warmth, and sighed. *Perfect.* Now, she needed to call an Uber.

She pulled out her phone and started walking down the sidewalk when she heard a familiar voice that was smooth and rich with that slight Australian accent that made her stomach flip.

"Ava!"

As she turned, her breath caught, and she saw Aussie standing just a few feet away, looking concerned. He was dressed in black slacks, a crisp white shirt, and a matching black sports coat, looking like he'd just stepped out of a magazine. The sight of him sent a shiver down her spine, though the chilly air might've also caused that.

She smiled. "Hi," she managed, though her voice wavered slightly with surprise. "What are you doing here?"

"I was having dinner inside," he said, stepping closer, his eyes searching her face. "I saw you storm out, and I was concerned."

Her heart swelled at the fact that he'd noticed that he cared enough to check on her, even though they had only met days ago. *What kind of man does that?* She barely knew him, and yet here he was, looking at her like she mattered.

"Oh, I'm fine," she said, brushing it off, though she couldn't deny the warmth that spread through her chest at his concern.

Aussie glanced at her bare arms, and without a word, he shrugged off his jacket and wrapped it around her shoulders. The warmth enveloped her instantly, and the gesture nearly made her melt.

"Better?" he asked, his voice soft.

Ava looked up at him, her heart racing for reasons she didn't entirely understand. "Much better," she said her voice barely above a whisper.

He smiled, and the sight of it made her forget all about Jarod. "Want to take a walk?"

Ava nibbled her lip nervously. "Don't you have someone waiting for you in the restaurant?" *Oh, God. Had he been on a date?*

He smiled. "It is just my sister and brother-in-law. We were almost finished anyway."

Hearing he was just with family made her feel a little better.

She looked up at him and nodded. "A walk sounds nice."

As they started walking, Ava felt a strange sense of calm wash over her. The night, which had begun with frustration, now felt full of possibilities.

Sometimes, the universe had a way of clearing the path for something new. And as she walked beside Aussie, she couldn't help but think that maybe, just maybe, something good was about to begin.

Aussie had been sitting at a round table in the corner of the elegant restaurant, savoring the rare opportunity to spend time with his sister, Wren, and her husband, Ben. With the chaos of being a Navy SEAL, Aussie never knew when the next mission would pull him away. It could be tomorrow, next week, or months from now. Their deployments weren't the same as typical military rotations; missions dictated them—some lasting days, others stretching into months or even over a year. Still, he loved the life, loved serving his country, and every time he was home, he made the most of it.

Wren and Ben were passing through Virginia Beach, and this dinner was a welcome chance to catch up. It was also a reminder of just how important his family was to him. Aussie came from a big family. He had three older sisters, all married, with kids of their own. Angie and Rachel had already given him two nieces and nephews each, and they all lived close to each other back in Indiana. The whole family was tight-knit, but Aussie had always been the odd one out, the one who chose to join the Navy and make a life elsewhere. Even so, they supported him in every decision, never holding his career choice against him.

"So, we have a little surprise for you," Wren said, glancing at Ben with a smile. Aussie's fork hovered in the air as he looked between them.

Ben grinned, leaning back in his chair. "We're expecting."

Aussie's face lit up, his chest filling with excitement. "What? That's awesome!" He stood, hugging Wren, then gave Ben a firm pat on the back. "I'm gonna be an uncle again!"

Wren laughed, her eyes sparkling with joy. "We wanted to tell you in person, and since we were passing through, the timing was perfect."

"Best news of the day," Aussie said, grinning ear to ear.

Wren gave him a teasing smile. "It's kinda funny how we all thought that you'd be the first one to settle down."

Aussie laughed, shaking his head. "Nah, you know me. Married to the job." Though after watching Joker, Bear, Duke and now Playboy settle down, it made him wonder if a stable relationship would work for him.

They shared a few more laughs, and the conversation shifted back to family updates, Navy stories, and plans for future visits, which included Christmas. Aussie was completely immersed in the moment until he noticed Wren's eyes shifting past his shoulder, her expression shifting into something more curious, almost bothered.

"What's wrong?" Aussie asked.

She tilted her head toward the far corner of the restaurant. "Dinner doesn't seem to be going well for that couple over there."

Aussie chuckled. His sister had a notorious habit of being nosey, always wanting to know what everyone around her was doing. "Wren, you're terrible. Let people have their awkward dates in peace."

Wren smirked, her eyes still on the couple. "I'm just saying, the woman, who is beautiful, by the way, looks like she's about to lose her shit on the guy."

Aussie rolled his eyes, shaking his head. *Classic Wren*, always inventing backstories for people she didn't know. "Honestly, you'd make a great detective. Or better yet, a gossip columnist."

He was about to make another joke when Wren's eyes widened. "Oh wow. She's definitely had enough."

Aussie turned just in time to see a woman standing up, her expression furious as she pointed at the man across from her. His heart skipped a beat when he recognized her. Her raven-colored hair matched the black skirt she was wearing.

Ava.

He hadn't been able to stop thinking about her since they met last weekend. And now, there she was, clearly upset, grabbing her purse and storming out of the restaurant. His gut twisted with concern.

"I know her," Aussie muttered, standing up. He barely registered Wren's shocked expression before she started grilling him.

"Oh really?" Wren said, her voice dripping with curiosity. "She's pretty. And I mean *really* pretty. What's the story there?"

Aussie waved her off, chuckling as he grabbed his jacket. "Not now, Wren. I'll explain later. Be right back."

Ignoring her barrage of questions, he quickly excused himself and slipped out of the restaurant. He spotted Ava a few feet ahead, her shoulders hunched against the chill as she looked down at her phone. Without thinking, he called out to her.

"Ava!"

She turned, and her eyes widened in surprise. "Hi! What are you doing here?"

He took a few steps toward her. Concern was etched into his features. "I was having dinner inside. I saw you storm out, and I was concerned. Is Everything alright?"

Ava forced a smile, but it didn't quite reach her eyes. "I'm fine," she said, trying to wave off his concern.

But Aussie was a SEAL. He'd been trained to read people, and Ava's body language was practically shouting that something was wrong. She was tense, her hands gripping her purse a little too tightly, and she was shivering—whether from the cold or from the situation, he wasn't sure. Either way, he wasn't about to let her brush it off.

Without a word, he slipped off his sports coat and draped it over her shoulders. She protested weakly, but he didn't listen. "Better?" he asked.

Ava glanced up at him, and he couldn't help but notice how pretty she looked under the streetlights. Her black hair shimmered, drawing out the blue hue mixed throughout her silky locks, and her unique dark blue eyes that looked nearly black held a spark even when she was upset. The slim black pencil skirt and blue blouse she wore hugged her figure perfectly, and the high heels only added to how striking she looked.

"Much better," she replied, giving him a shy, sheepish smile.

He caught himself staring and quickly shifted his thoughts.

"Wanna take a walk?" he asked, hoping to distract her from whatever had happened inside.

When she started to nibble on her bottom lip, he knew she was torn on what to do.

"Don't you have someone waiting for you in the restaurant?" she asked, seeming a bit nervous.

A thought then crossed his mind. He wondered if she thought he was on a date. Was she jealous? Because he felt a little jealous knowing that she was having dinner with another man.

He smiled. "It is just my sister and brother-in-law. We were almost finished anyway."

She was silent as a few seconds passed. But to his relief, she nodded. "A walk sounds nice."

As they started to walk, he shot a quick text to Wren, telling her that he was sorry to cut dinner short, but he had something he needed to take care of. He was not going to get into the details about Ava with his sister. At least not yet.

Wren's response came almost instantly: *Pursuing the pretty woman already? I see how it is. Good luck, loverboy!*

Aussie chuckled, shaking his head.

Ava glanced at him. "Sorry for pulling you away from your dinner."

"It's fine. You didn't interrupt anything important," Aussie assured her. "Besides, I'd rather be here."

Ava smiled, and he felt a little spark of victory. Then, deciding to ease into a conversation, he asked, "How's Christian doing?"

Ava's face lit up, and she started telling him all about how Christian was adjusting to life at her house. She told him that Christian still couldn't stop talking about meeting all of the SEALs at the fair.

"Oh, and we looked up that organization you told us about—the Sea Cadets. Christian is very interested in joining, and I already reached out to the local unit. I called at the right time because they are having an informational meeting this week."

"That's great. As I said, everything I've seen and heard about the program is wonderful."

"Well, Christian is very excited."

"Glad to hear that."

The longer they walked, the more Aussie wanted to bring up the guy from the restaurant. He wanted to know who he was to Ava.

"So, who was the guy that pissed you off?"

He noticed her expression darkened. "That was Jarod," she said with a sigh. "We've known each other for a few years. We dated on and off, but something was always missing."

Aussie's chest tightened at the mention of her dating someone else, but when she said *was*, he couldn't help but feel a surge of relief. "So, it's over between you two?"

She nodded, her jaw tightening. "Oh, it's definitely over after tonight. He showed me who the person he truly is. He said some awful things about Christian."

Hearing that pissed Aussie off. He could feel his blood boiling as Ava recounted everything that Jarod had said. How could anyone talk about any kid like that?

"I just can't believe that I never saw it before now."

"In my line of work, I've met many people who are like chameleons. They have different sides to them. Either way, he doesn't deserve you," Aussie muttered.

Ava smiled at that, and they continued walking, talking about everything from Christian to Navy life. They didn't really get into anything personal about one another. But it was still a pleasant conversation, and Aussie found himself wanting to know more about her.

Before he even realized it, a good hour had passed, and they were both surprised by how much time had flown by.

"I guess I should call an Uber," Ava said, pulling out her phone.

"No need for that," Aussie said quickly. "I can take you home."

Ava hesitated, but then she smiled. "Are you sure?"

He grinned. "Positive. Plus, it'll make me feel better knowing you made it home safely."

"Okay."

They walked to his red Ford F-150, which was parked in the lot across the street from the restaurant.

He opened the door for her and helped her up into the seat.

It wasn't a long drive, and Aussie found himself wishing her house were farther away. He wasn't ready to say goodnight. When they pulled up to her place, he got out and walked around to open her door, helping her down from the truck.

For a moment, they stood there. Their bodies were close to each other, and the tension between them was palpable. Aussie wanted to kiss her, *really* wanted to, but he held back. It didn't feel right—not after the night she'd had. Still, as he looked into her dark blue eyes, he could tell she was thinking the same thing.

Instead, he leaned down and kissed her cheek, feeling her surprise as he did. When he pulled back, she was smiling.

"Thanks for saving me tonight," she said softly. "I really enjoyed the company."

Aussie grinned, feeling lighter than he had in days. "Anytime."

Before they parted ways, he mustered the courage to ask, "I know I gave you my number, but would it be alright if I called you sometime?"

Ava blushed, and the sight made his heart skip. "I'd like that."

They said goodnight, and as Aussie drove back to his apartment, he couldn't stop smiling. *There's something special about her,* he thought. And as he parked and made his way inside, he found himself already looking forward to seeing her again.

Aussie pushed the door open and stepped into the apartment that he shared with his teammate Snow. He tossed his keys onto the small table by the entrance.

He walked further into the living room and found Snow sprawled on the couch in front of the television. A plastic tray was balanced precariously on his knee. He was digging into a clump of cheesy noodles with a plastic fork, his eyes half on the screen. "How was dinner?" he asked, not bothering to look away from the news. "And how's your sister doing?"

Aussie shrugged out of his jacket and hung it on the back of the chair. "Dinner was great. Wren and Ben are doing great. Actually, better than great. And guess what?"

Snow raised an eyebrow, finally glancing over. "What?"

"They're having a baby. Their first." Aussie grinned, the pride in his voice unmistakable.

"No kidding? Congrats to them," Snow said, setting the tray on the coffee table. "That's big news."

Aussie flopped into the armchair opposite the couch, his mind drifting back to dinner. "Yeah, they're over the moon about it. Wren's glowing already. It was good catching up with them. However, I had to cut dinner short."

"Why is that?"

Aussie then told him about Ava being at the restaurant and on her date with that dickhead. The more he explained to Snow about what all the douchebag said about Christian, he could see Snow's expression harden.

When he was finished, Snow shook his head.

"At least she seems smart, considering she left the asshole sitting there in the restaurant. Sounds like a jerk," Snow muttered, stabbing at the remains of his dinner. "Doesn't sound like he's good enough for her or Christian."

Aussie chuckled. "You don't even know him."

"Don't have to," Snow said firmly. "But you seem pretty invested in her. You interested or what?"

Aussie rubbed the back of his neck, a small smile playing on his lips. "She's definitely piqued my interest. There's something about her. She's just different."

Snow grinned, leaning back on the couch. "Good for you, man. Sounds like you've got your eye on someone worth it."

Before Aussie could respond, something on the TV caught both of their attention. The newscaster's voice turned somber as she reported another robbery at a local convenience store.

"This just in—police have confirmed a robbery occurred at a convenience store on Pine and 8th Street late this evening. The cashier was shot but is expected to survive. This marks the fifth such incident in the last two weeks, with suspects continuing to evade authorities. Police believe the robberies may be connected to other violent crimes in the area, including three recent homicides."

Snow set his fork down, his brow furrowed. "That's not far from here."

"Too close," Aussie agreed, watching the footage of flashing police lights and crime scene tape.

Snow crossed his arms, his jaw tightening. "Word is the cops think it's a gang setting up shop in town. Could be tied to some kind of organized operation."

Aussie frowned, his thoughts swirling. "That would explain the pattern—robberies, escalating violence. They're trying to make a statement."

"Yeah, well, I hope they're wrong about the gang part," Snow said grimly. "The last thing this city needs are more bodies piling up."

Aussie nodded, his gaze lingering on the television as the segment switched to weather. His mind, however, stayed on the unsettling news. If the police were right, something big—and dangerous—was brewing in their city.

He leaned back in his chair, the weight of the day settling on his shoulders. Between the crime wave and thoughts of Ava, his mind wasn't going to quiet down anytime soon.

CHAPTER FIVE

Ezekiel Moore stood in front of the large bay windows overlooking the large industrial yard below. This location was one of the many warehouses he owned.

Behind him, the sounds of shuffling feet and muffled voices faded into silence as the room, full of young men no older than eighteen, waited for him to speak. His reflection in the window was sharp and commanding. His salt-and-pepper hair was slicked back, and his gray suit was tailored to perfection, making him look more like a CEO than the dangerous crime leader he was.

The furniture warehouse beneath them was thriving, at least on the surface. Customers came in and bought their overpriced sofas and dining sets, never suspecting that just above their heads was where the real business was happening. Drugs, guns, and broken souls passed through Ezekiel's hands. He controlled it all with a smile and the threat of unimaginable pain.

"Look around," Ezekiel said, his voice smooth but edged with authority. "You see how few of you are left? I'm not blind, boys. I know our numbers are dwindling. We've lost people to jail, to other towns, even to the grave. That isn't good for business. And I don't like bad business."

He turned from the window, his cold, dark eyes scanning the group of teenagers before him. They shifted uncomfortably in their seats, but none dared meet his gaze except two. Barrett and Chase. His top recruits. They both sat with a confidence that came from knowing they had Ezekiel's respect.

Barrett, with his boyish face and lanky frame, could easily pass for a high school student. He had sharp blue eyes that missed nothing and a quiet, calculating nature that made him especially dangerous. Chase, a bit broader and darker-skinned, had a grin that put people at ease, but beneath it lay the heart of a killer. He'd done Ezekiel's dirty work more than once, and the older man trusted him implicitly.

"We need more bodies," Ezekiel continued, stepping closer to the center of the room, his leather shoes echoing in the quiet space. More soldiers. More of others like yourselves to be able to continue doing the job we're doing. You all know what's coming. We have some big deals on the horizon and lots of products to move. We have people depending on us. However, to accomplish our goal of being the main supplier in the area, we need more manpower. So, my question to this group is, where are we going to find it?"

He raised an eyebrow, waiting for someone to answer. One of the younger boys shifted nervously in his seat. "The schools?"

"Exactly," Ezekiel said with a grin that didn't reach his eyes. "Schools are crawling with kids looking for a way to escape. Whether it's boredom, stress, or just their shitty little lives at home, they want something. They want to feel a part of something. And we can give it to them. Drugs, power, money. Whatever it takes to make them ours."

He turned his attention to Barrett and Chase. "I'm putting you two in charge of recruitment. I want new blood. I was given a few names for you to look into. One is at the high school where you found Johnny. You know how to reel them in. Make them feel like they belong. And if they resist. Well, you know what to do." His smile widened, this time with genuine menace. "Don't disappoint me, boys. You get this right, and I'll reward you both handsomely."

Barrett and Chase exchanged a look—both of them understanding the weight of the task before them, but neither flinching. They had earned Ezekiel's trust and knew how to deliver. They were loyal, almost to a fault, and both had no problem spilling blood if it meant staying in Ezekiel's good graces. Hell, just a few hours earlier, Chase and one of the younger kids robbed a convenience store a few blocks over. It was a shame that the cashier got hurt, but they should've just listened and not tried to play the hero.

One of the other boys in the back raised his hand hesitantly, drawing Ezekiel's attention. "What happened to the two who got caught last week trying to sell guns at that parking lot near the mall?"

Ezekiel's face darkened, but his voice remained calm. "Those two? They're handling things the way I taught them. They'll keep their mouths shut, and my people will have them out in a few days. The police have no idea what resources I have in my back pocket. So, don't worry about them. Focus on what I'm asking you to do."

He leaned forward, placing his hands on the back of a chair and fixing the entire group with a cold stare. "Let me make myself clear. I expect results. And soon."

The boys nodded quickly, sinking back into their seats as Ezekiel straightened up and began walking toward the door. Just as he reached it, the door swung open, and Diamond sauntered in.

She was everything her name suggested—glittering, valuable, and untouchable except by the man who owned her. Her long, silver hair flowed down her back, and her short, pink, tight dress left very little to the imagination. Her heels clicked against the floor as she walked straight to Ezekiel, ignoring the eyes of the others in the room. She was used to it. They all knew better than to touch or even look at what was his.

"Ezekiel," she purred, her voice low as she reached him, sliding her hand up his chest.

He smirked, his fingers closing around her wrist as he pulled her closer. "Boys," he said without looking back, "the meeting's over. Get to work."

The teens scrambled out of the room, and within seconds, Ezekiel and Diamond were alone. He led her up the narrow, hidden staircase to the third floor—the floor that no one else was allowed to enter without his permission. It was his private space. A place to escape if things ever went south.

Tonight, he needed an outlet to take his frustrations out, and he knew that Diamond would do anything asked of her.

As they reached his bedroom, Ezekiel shoved the door open and pulled Diamond inside. She laughed softly, the sound dripping with anticipation. He didn't bother with pleasantries, pushing her against the wall, his hand gripping her chin tightly as he tilted her face up to meet his gaze.

"You know why you're here," he whispered, his voice low and commanding.

Diamond nodded, her breath catching as he leaned in, his lips brushing against her ear. "Do what I want, and you'll get rewarded."

Her response was a soft, obedient, "Yes, Ezekiel."

And with that, he led her to the bed, closing the door to the world outside, locking it away with all the dark promises he was about to fulfill.

CHAPTER SIX

Ava sighed as she leaned back in her chair, her eyes drifting to the courtroom clock. It was nearing four in the afternoon, and there was no end in sight with the case she was working on.

The grandparents on both sides of this case—the Wilsons and the Johnsons—were at each other's throats, each fighting tooth and nail for temporary custody of the twin girls who had been removed from their home. Their parents were drug addicts, completely unfit to care for the girls, and while Ava wanted to believe the grandparents had the twins' best interests at heart, the courtroom drama felt more like a power struggle than genuine concern.

The judge had made it clear. *No one's leaving until we find a solution,* she'd said.

Ava rubbed her temples, feeling the weight of the day settle in her bones. Her role in the case was nearly done, but that didn't mean she was getting out of there anytime soon. As she stood up, hoping to stretch her legs, she spotted her friend Sarah and co-worker lingering near the vending machines outside the courtroom. With a nod from the judge that they had a brief break, Ava slipped out of the courtroom and joined her.

"Looks like we're in for another hour, maybe two," Ava muttered, her voice weary as she fumbled for change to buy a bottle of water from the machine. She punched in the code, the machine whirring to life as Sarah stepped beside her, eyeing her with curiosity.

Sarah, always a breath of fresh air in a suffocating system, offered a sympathetic smile. "You've been in there all day. How are you holding up?"

"I'm surviving." Ava grabbed the water and took a long drink before looking back at her friend.

"How's Christian adjusting?" Sarah asked, leaning against the vending machine. "I mean, it's been what? A few weeks now?"

Ava paused, a flicker of surprise crossing her face. She hadn't thought about it much, but the truth was, things with Christian were going really well, better than she had expected. She took another sip of water, her thoughts wandering to the fifteen-year-old boy now living in her home.

"It's actually good," Ava said slowly, a smile creeping onto her lips. "I don't know what the other foster families had issues with. He's been respectful; he mostly keeps to himself, but he's opening up. Honestly, I'm enjoying having him around."

Sarah chuckled, nudging her shoulder. "Sounds like you two were meant to be together. Maybe Christian just needed the right person."

Ava grinned, but before she could respond, her phone buzzed in her hand. She glanced at the screen, her heart sinking a little as she read the text from Christian.

Christian: *Don't forget about the Sea Cadet meeting tonight. It starts at six.*

Panic fluttered in her chest as she checked the time. There was no way she'd make it out of court, back home, and then drive Christian to the meeting on time. *Damn it.* Christian had been looking forward to this meeting for weeks, and the last thing she wanted to do was let him down.

Ava bit her lip, her mind racing through potential options. Sarah noticed the change in her expression immediately. "What's wrong?"

"I—" Ava hesitated, her eyes flicking back to her phone. "It's Christian. He's got this Sea Cadet meeting tonight, and I completely forgot it. There's no way I can get out of here in time to take him."

Sarah frowned, thinking. "Can anyone else help? A friend, maybe?"

Ava's first instinct was to say no, but then a name flashed through her mind. *Aussie.* The tall, dark, handsome, and entirely too sexy for her sanity Navy SEAL. He had told her, more than once, that if she or Christian ever needed anything, he'd be there. But would he actually want to do something as mundane as driving a teenager to a meeting?

Her fingers hovered over her phone screen, debating.

Sarah raised an eyebrow. "I'm guessing that you have someone in mind?"

"Maybe." Ava fumbled with her phone. "There's this guy. Aussie. He told me to reach out if I needed help."

Sarah's eyebrows shot up. "A guy? And you're just now telling me about this?"

Ava rolled her eyes, her stomach fluttering as she scrolled to Aussie's number. *I can't believe I'm doing this.* She pressed the dial button, the phone ringing in her ear. Her heart pounded as the rings went on, and just when she thought he wasn't going to answer, the line clicked over.

"Hey, Ava." Aussie's deep, smooth voice slid through the phone, sending tingles through her body.

God, get your mind out of the gutter, Ava.

"Hey, Aussie," she replied, forcing herself to sound normal and not like she was internally swooning over his voice. "I, um… I hate to ask, but I need a favor."

"What's up."

"I'm stuck in court, and Christian has that Sea Cadet meeting tonight. I was wondering if you could possibly…"

Aussie chuckled softly on the other end, the sound warm and teasing. "Let me guess, you need me to pick him up and take him?"

Ava felt her cheeks flush, embarrassed by how easily he'd read the situation. "Yes," she mumbled, biting her lip. "I really hate to ask, but I'm desperate."

"It's not a problem," Aussie said, his tone light. "I've got nothing going on. I'll make sure he gets there."

Relief flooded through her, but she immediately followed it up with, "I owe you for this. I'll pay you back." She cringed the moment the words left her mouth. *That sounded awful.*

Aussie laughed, and she could practically hear the smile in his voice. "Oh, I'll be looking forward to you repaying that favor."

Her cheeks burned as she realized how that could be taken. "I didn't mean—"

"Relax, Ava. I'm just teasing." His voice dropped, still playful but with a hint of something more. "I've got this. Don't worry."

She managed a weak laugh. "Thanks. I really appreciate it."

"Anytime. I'll see you later, Ava." His voice was like a low purr, and before she could embarrass herself further, she quickly hung up the phone.

When she looked up, Sarah was staring at her, wide-eyed.

"That was Aussie?" Sarah asked, her tone incredulous. "The Navy SEAL you met a few weeks ago when you took Christian to that college and career fair?"

Ava sighed, tucking her phone away. "Yeah. That was him."

Sarah's jaw dropped. "How have you kept this from me? Are you guys like dating?"

Ava felt a mix of excitement and nerves fluttering inside her as she thought back to that night at the restaurant. "It's complicated. I was out to dinner with Jarod, and Aussie just happened to be at the same restaurant. He followed me outside afterward to make sure I was okay. Then he ended up driving me home."

Sarah's mouth fell open in surprise. "And you didn't tell me this because…?"

"I wasn't sure what to think," Ava admitted, her thoughts racing. "But he's…he's really something, Sarah. He's…"

"Amazing?" Sarah finished, her eyes twinkling.

Ava could only nod, a little smile pulling at her lips. Before they could dive deeper into the conversation, one of the courtroom clerks poked her head out of the door.

"The judge is ready to continue," she said.

Ava took a deep breath, but as she turned to follow Sarah back into the courtroom, her mind wasn't on the case anymore. It was on Aussie—and how much she was looking forward to seeing him again.

Ava pushed through the heavy courthouse doors, feeling the weight of the long day finally lift off her shoulders. The two sets of grandparents had finally agreed on a temporary custody arrangement for the twin girls—a rare win in a case that could have easily spiraled into chaos.

Ava smiled, relieved to have been part of a positive outcome, but now all she wanted was to put this exhausting day behind her.

She quickened her pace, eager to reach her car in the dark parking lot when she suddenly collided with someone. Her heart sank as she looked up and saw Jarod.

Of all people, why him?

He stood in front of her, his tall frame blocking her path. Ava's stomach twisted as she remembered the disastrous dinner from the other night, the way his words had cut deep. She wasn't ready to forgive him for that. Not now. Maybe not ever.

She tried to move around him, but he stopped her.

"Ava, wait," Jarod said, his tone pleading as he reached out a hand toward her. "Can we talk for a second?"

No, she thought. He was the last person she wanted to deal with right now. Her mind was still buzzing with everything from the case, and the tension between them was something she wasn't in the mood to handle.

"I really don't have time, Jarod," she muttered, brushing past him, her heels clicking on the pavement as she made a beeline for her car.

He followed her, quickening his steps to keep up. "Ava, please," he called after her. "I didn't mean what I said about Christian the other night. I was just frustrated, and I didn't handle it right."

Ava's jaw tightened as she kept walking, her heart pounding in frustration. *Frustrated?* He hadn't been frustrated—he'd been cruel. She knew the truth behind his words. He didn't believe in her ability to foster Christian, and that wasn't something she could just brush off with an apology.

"I really don't want to hear it, Jarod," she said over her shoulder, not bothering to slow down. "As I said before, let's just keep things work-related from now on."

She was almost at her car when, suddenly, she felt a hand clamp down on her arm, roughly spinning her around. A gasp escaped her lips as her body jerked back toward him.

"Jarod—"

The sharpness in her voice must have struck him because his eyes widened in realization. He immediately let go, throwing his hands up in surrender, his face pale with regret.

"I'm sorry. I didn't mean to." His voice cracked with urgency. "I just wanted to talk to you, Ava. I didn't mean to grab you like that. Please, just listen to me for a minute."

Her pulse raced, rattled not just by the suddenness of his action but by the intensity in his eyes. She took a step back, her heart still pounding in her chest. There was something about the way he had grabbed her. Whether it was intentional or not, it felt like a line had been crossed.

This isn't good.

"Jarod, I don't think now is the best time to have this conversation," she said, trying to keep her voice steady. "I'll repeat myself again. We should keep things between us professional from now on. It's better that way."

He shook his head, stepping toward her again, his tone desperate. "You don't mean that. Ava, we've been good together. You know that. I'll admit that I screwed up. Are you really willing to throw away everything we had over one mistake?"

Everything they had? She wasn't even sure what they even had. Sure, they dated, but that was really the extent of it. She never even slept with him.

But Ava wasn't easily convinced that he was being genuinely remorseful. His insistence only made her more uncomfortable, the tension between them thickening with each passing second. She didn't want any part of this.

"I really have to go, Jarod," she said, her voice firm this time as she turned and pulled her car keys from her purse. "Christian's waiting for me, and I need to pick him up."

He hesitated, his mouth opening as if to say something else, but she didn't give him a chance as she quickly unlocked her car and slid into the driver's seat, her fingers trembling as she gripped the steering wheel. She glanced in the rearview mirror as she pulled out of the parking lot, seeing Jarod still standing there, watching her drive away.

As she left the courthouse behind, Ava's thoughts swirled. There was something about the way Jarod had acted tonight. The way he'd been so insistent and so unwilling to take no for an answer. It made her uneasy. Her gut twisted with a warning she couldn't quite ignore.

Jarod's going to be a problem, she thought, her mind flashing back to his pleading voice and his desperate eyes. He didn't want to let go. And that scared her.

But she shook the thought away, her focus shifting to Christian. That's where her attention needed to be right now. Not on Jarod and whatever was going on with him, but on Christian and making sure she didn't let him down.

Focus, Ava, she told herself, pushing away the lingering anxiety from the encounter. Christian needed her to be present, not rattled. She pressed her foot on the gas and headed toward the community center, determined to shake off the unsettling feeling that had followed her since Jarod had grabbed her arm.

And as her thoughts settled back on Christian and the evening ahead, one comforting thought rose to the surface.

At least I get to see Aussie.

CHAPTER SEVEN

Twenty minutes after Ava's unsettling run-in with Jarod, she pulled into the parking lot of the local community center where Christian's Sea Cadet meeting was being held. The first thing that caught her eye was the familiar red truck parked near the front with a Navy sticker plastered on the back window.

Her heart skipped a beat. She knew Aussie was inside, and the idea of seeing him again made her both excited and nervous.

Ava had replayed her conversation with Sarah from earlier in her head at least ten times by now. *Was she really crushing on Aussie?* She had tried to convince herself it was just a passing attraction, but the butterflies in her stomach every time she thought about him said otherwise.

She took a deep breath as she locked her car up and made her way into the building. As soon as she stepped inside, her eyes found him near the back of the room, standing casually by the rear door, leaning against the wall. Aussie was hard to miss. His broad shoulders, confident stance, and the way he seemed so at ease in any environment made him stand out.

When he saw her, his face lit up, and he waved her over with that easy smile she was starting to think about more often than she should.

She walked toward him, her heart doing that little flutter thing it always seemed to do around him. "Hey," she greeted, her voice steady despite the nerves tightening in her chest. "Thanks again for bailing me out and picking up Christian."

Aussie waved her off, his smile never wavering. "No problem at all. I wasn't doing much at home anyway. I'm always happy to help."

She nodded, grateful. His casual demeanor made it seem like it really wasn't a big deal to him, but to her, it meant a lot, more than he probably realized.

"So, how was your day?" he asked, his tone light but his eyes sharp with interest.

Ava's muscles tensed at the question. She should have known better than to think Aussie wouldn't notice something was off. He was trained to read people, after all. "It was fine," she replied, but her voice faltered slightly. His gaze didn't waver, and she knew she couldn't brush it off. She sighed. "Jarod. Well, he followed me to my car after court."

The mention of Jarod's name made Aussie's expression harden, his playful demeanor shifting in an instant. "He followed you?"

"Yeah, but it's fine. He was trying to apologize for that night at dinner, she said, omitting the part where Jarod had grabbed her. Aussie already looked like he wanted to track the guy down.

"I don't like him following you," Aussie said, his voice low.

Ava quickly changed the subject, not wanting to dwell on Jarod any longer. "So, what did I miss? How's Christian doing?" she asked, gesturing toward the group in the room.

Aussie studied her for a moment longer, his jaw tight, but he let it go. "The commanding officer was just going over some things about the drills and what the program entails. Christian's been asking some really good questions. He's really interested in how the program can help with a future military career."

Ava felt a swell of pride for Christian. He'd had such a rough time with foster care, but seeing him excited about something made her happy and excited for him.

As the meeting wrapped up, Christian spotted them and rushed over, his eyes bright with excitement. There was another boy dressed in a Navy Type III uniform walking with him. "Ava!"

Seeing his smile was what she desperately needed after the day she had.

"Hey! So, how was the meeting? I caught the last part of it," she asked him.

"I really like it. I think it will help me with learning what to expect when I go to enlist after I graduate." He gestured to the boy standing with him. "Oh, and this is Cody," he looked up at Aussie, who was standing there watching the interaction. "you know his dad Frost."

Aussie chuckled. "I do. And it's nice to see you again, Cody."

The young boy grinned. "Nice to see you too, Sir." He then turned toward Ava and smiled. "It's nice to meet you too, Ma'am. I told Christian that if he has any questions about the program, he can call me."

Ava smiled. "Thank you, Cody. That was very nice of you to offer that."

"It's no problem. But I need to head back over to help clean up." He turned toward Christian. "I hope to see you at the next drill."

"Me too," Christian replied.

The boy said goodbye to Ava and Aussie and then rejoined the others who were already starting to clean up.

Christian turned back to Ava and started telling her all about what he learned. Ava smiled at his enthusiasm, her heart warming at how much this meant to him.

"Do you think it is okay if I join?"

Ava smiled. "If this is what you want, I don't see why not. With what you've told me, it sounds great."

Aussie grinned beside her, nodding in agreement. "It's a great program. You'll learn a lot, and it'll give you a good foundation if you're serious about the military."

Christian practically beamed at that, though his excitement faltered for a moment as he glanced at Ava.

"There's an enrollment fee, though. And a packet we have to fill out. I don't want to ask for too much. You've already done so much for me."

Ava's chest tightened at his hesitance. She looked him in the eyes. "Christian, the cost isn't a problem. I want to do this for you. We'll get the packet, fill it out together, and find out when the next drill is, okay?"

Christian's face lit up again, and before Ava knew it, he threw his arms around her in a rare hug. It caught her off guard, and for a moment, she was frozen. When she hugged him back, she felt the sting of tears in her eyes. She blinked rapidly, trying to keep her emotions in check.

"Thank you, Ava," he whispered to her, and she could hear the emotion in his voice.

Aussie must have noticed her struggle because after Christian ran back over to grab the enrollment packet, he gently placed his hand on her shoulder. "Are you okay?" he asked softly.

She gave him a grateful smile, trying to blink away the last of her tears. "Yeah. It just makes me happy to see him so excited about something with everything that he's been through."

"He's lucky to have someone like you in his corner. You truly care about him, and it shows."

She blushed.

"I guess I can say that I've been in his shoes before."

Aussie scrunched his eyebrows together, but before he could ask what she meant by that comment, she changed the topic.

"I know I've said this multiple times already, but thank you again for helping me out. And you really didn't have to stay through the meeting."

Aussie's face reddened slightly, something she hadn't seen before. He looked almost embarrassed or shy. It was a look that was incredibly endearing, especially for someone as confident as him. "Well," he said, rubbing the back of his neck, "Part of the reason that I stayed was because I wanted to see you."

Ava's heart skipped again, and her stomach did that familiar flip-flop. *He wanted to see me?* Her mind scrambled, her nerves firing on all cylinders. She didn't know what to say. She wanted to see him too, but saying that out loud felt like it might tip the balance of whatever was happening between them.

Before she could respond, Christian came bounding back over, his excitement pulling her out of her thoughts. "I got the packet! We just need to fill it out, and I can start!"

Ava smiled, happy for him. "Great, we'll work on it tonight."

Christian's stomach rumbled, and he gave her a sheepish look. "Uh, what's for dinner?"

Ava laughed, feeling the exhaustion of the day hit her all at once. "I'm too tired to cook. Where do you want to go?"

Christian's eyes lit up. "There's this new buffet in town. Can we go there?"

Ava chuckled. "Sure, that sounds good." Then, an idea struck her, and she turned to Aussie. "You should come with us. That is if you don't have any plans."

Christian nodded enthusiastically. "Yeah! Come with us, Aussie!"

Aussie looked surprised for a moment, then smiled. "I'd love to."

"Great!" Ava said, smiling.

As they all walked out to their cars, agreeing to meet at the buffet, Ava felt a mix of excitement and nerves again. Christian hopped into her car, buckling up before he turned to her with a mischievous grin.

"So, are you and Aussie, like, dating now?"

Ava nearly choked on her laughter. "What? No! Aussie and I are just friends."

But Christian's grin only widened. "Uh-huh. I saw how he looked at you, Ava. And how you looked at him."

Ava couldn't help but laugh again, though part of her knew Christian wasn't far from the truth. *Maybe there was something there,* she thought.

Ava sat across from Aussie and Christian at the buffet restaurant, a casual warmth settling over the table as they picked at their plates. Christian's excitement from his Sea Cadet orientation still lingered in the air, and Ava couldn't help but smile, watching him devour his meal with youthful enthusiasm.

"So, Aussie," Ava began, trying to learn more about the man who had come into their lives so unexpectedly, "what do you usually do for Thanksgiving?" She twirled a fork in her fingers, her gaze shifting between him and Christian, wanting to include the boy in the conversation.

Aussie, mid-bite, grinned and wiped his mouth with a napkin. "It depends, really. We're usually on rotation with the team. Right now, we are on rotation. So, Bear, our team leader, and his wife Jocelyn are hosting dinner at their place. If we aren't on rotation, I try to make it home to see my family." He paused, eyes flickering between Ava and Christian. "How about you guys?" he asked.

Christian shook his head, looking both curious and a little shy. "My foster families weren't big on holiday get-togethers."

Ava felt a familiar pang in her chest, the one that surfaced during the holidays when memories of spending them alone haunted her.

Ever since Evelyn had passed away, she'd been on her own for Thanksgiving, Christmas, all of it. Hearing about Aussie's team gathering and the camaraderie they shared made her feel a quiet sense of envy—not jealousy, but a longing for that kind of connection. She admired the closeness he had with his team, something she had never truly had, save for Evelyn.

Aussie must've noticed her silence because he leaned in slightly, his expression softening. "What about you, Ava? What are your plans for Thanksgiving?"

Christian perked up at the question, eyes wide with interest. Ava shifted in her seat, feeling the weight of their attention. "Well, normally, I'd spend it alone," she admitted, her voice quiet but steady. "But this year's different." She glanced at Christian with a smile. "This year, Christian and I are going to make dinner and spend it together."

Christian's face lit up, and Ava's heart warmed at the sight. "Really?" he asked, almost disbelieving.

"Of course," Ava said, reaching over to ruffle his hair. "You're not going to spend your first holiday with me eating takeout."

Aussie watched the exchange, a small smile tugging at his lips. He liked how natural Ava was with Christian and how she took care of him without hesitation. It was clear that she had a huge heart. And seeing her with Christian only made him respect her more.

The evening had been enjoyable. He hadn't anticipated feeling this comfortable around Ava and Christian, but there was something about them that put him at ease. He didn't have to try and go the extra length to impress Ava, and he didn't feel the usual pressure of making himself seem like the capable Navy SEAL. With her, it was just easy to be himself.

He studied Ava, her eyes warm as she listened to Christian talk about his Sea Cadet orientation. She was down-to-earth in a way he hadn't expected, not flashy or looking for attention. She was just real, and that was something Aussie admired. She was also fiercely protective of Christian, and he could tell she genuinely cared about the kid. That spoke volumes about who she was at her core.

In the short time he'd known Ava, he already saw so many qualities in her that he'd want in someone to spend the rest of his life with.

He wasn't like some of the other guys in the teams who didn't want to get attached and just slept around. Aussie came from a big family, and he knew he wanted one of his own someday. The challenge, of course, was his job and what it entailed. It made relationships tough. It was the constant unknowns, the time apart, and the reality that a lot of people couldn't handle that kind of lifestyle. Cheating was common, but not for him. If Aussie ever committed to someone, that was it. No messing around. To him, a relationship was sacred.

He glanced at Ava again, sensing something was holding her back, something that made her hesitant to let herself open up fully.

He didn't know the full story about her past, but from the little snippets that she mentioned, it wasn't hard to figure out that she grew up in a system like Christian. For someone like that, letting someone in probably felt risky. But Aussie didn't mind taking it slow. He had time, and getting to know her better was something he genuinely wanted.

As the meal wound down, Aussie leaned back in his chair, feeling a deep sense of contentment. "I've had a great time tonight. Thanks again for inviting me."

Ava smiled softly. "I'm glad you came. It's been nice having you here with us."

Ava paid the bill, though Aussie initially argued with her about it and insisted that he pay. But after she told him that she was paying him back for taking Christian to his meeting, he reluctantly gave up.

As they made their way outside, the cool evening air wrapped around them. Just as they reached their cars, an older woman pushing a cart stood off to the side, selling single roses. Aussie's gaze lingered on the cart for a moment before he approached the woman and bought a yellow rose.

He turned to Ava, holding the rose out to her with a gentle smile. "For you," he said, "as a sign of friendship."

Ava's eyes widened in surprise, her cheeks flushing slightly. She looked at the rose and then back at Aussie, her expression softening. "Thank you," she whispered, her fingers brushing against his as she took the rose.

Christian grinned, watching the exchange with an amused glint in his eyes.

Aussie chuckled and nodded toward them. "I had a great time tonight. If either of you ever need anything, you know where to find me." He turned to Christian, his tone playful but serious. "And if you've got any questions about the Sea Cadets or the Navy, give me a call. You can also tag along to the shooting range with me sometime if you're up for it. As long as it is okay with Ava."

Christian's face lit up again. "Really? That'd be awesome!"

Aussie laughed, giving him a light pat on the shoulder. "Absolutely."

He walked them both to Ava's car, the air between them easy and warm. Christian said goodnight, and he got into the car, leaving Ava standing there looking up at him, her dark eyes drawing him in.

"Thank you again for dinner. I enjoyed spending time with you guys."

She shyly smiled. "I enjoyed it too."

"Maybe we could do it again sometime," he said, leaving the offer out there.

"I'd like that," she replied, and he couldn't stop his lips from tugging upward into a smile.

He leaned down and kissed her cheek. "Goodnight, Ava."

"Goodnight, Aussie," she whispered before sliding into her car.

He smiled, watching as she got herself settled. "Drive safe," he said and winked before shutting her door.

She offered him a warm smile through the window and waved as she pulled out of the parking lot.

As Ava drove away, Aussie stood by his truck. The warmth from the evening lingered, and as he climbed into his own vehicle, a sense of something new and promising stirred within him.

CHAPTER EIGHT

Christian stood outside the school, shifting his backpack from one shoulder to the other as he waited for Ava to pick him up. The afternoon sun hung low in the sky, casting long shadows across the pavement. He glanced at his phone, checking the time, and smiled, thinking about how his life had changed for the good in just a matter of weeks.

The Sea Cadet program was everything he'd hoped for and more. He was officially part of something big, something that would set him on the path to becoming a Navy SEAL, his ultimate dream.

For a kid who had bounced around foster homes most of his life, finally having a goal, a real future, meant the world to him. He felt a sense of pride he hadn't known before, a drive to not just survive but to thrive. Ava had given him that. Her belief in him made him want to do better in school, to be responsible, and to prove that her faith wasn't misplaced. He had even applied for a part-time job at the local grocery store, bagging groceries. It wasn't much, but it was a step in the right direction. He wanted to show her that he was serious about his future.

Just as Christian shifted his weight to lean against the brick wall, he noticed two figures approaching him from the far side of the parking lot. His stomach twisted as he recognized them—Barrett and Chase. They were older by a couple of years. Both boys were bad news. Everyone knew it. Rumor had it they were into drugs and running around on the streets, causing trouble. Christian had done his best to avoid them at school, but now they were walking straight toward him.

"Hey, you're Christian, right?" Barrett called out, his tone deceptively casual as they neared.

"Yeah," Christian replied, straightening up. Every instinct was telling him that this was not going to be a friendly chat. He forced a neutral expression, trying to hide the unease that curled in his gut.

"What are you doing out here alone?" Chase asked.

"Waiting for my ride."

Barrett and Chase exchanged glances before stepping in closer. Christian's pulse quickened. They were too close. The kind of close that made it clear they weren't here for small talk.

"You know, we've been watching you," Barrett said, his voice low, almost threatening. "You're all alone, no family. No one to really watch your back."

Chase nodded, crossing his arms. "Yeah, man. It must be tough. But it doesn't have to be that way. We can make things a whole lot easier for you."

Christian's throat tightened. He knew where this was going, and he didn't want any part of it. His life was finally looking up, and he wasn't about to screw it up by getting involved with these guys. He shifted his feet, his mind racing for a way out. "I'm good," he said, keeping his voice firm. "I don't need any help."

Barrett chuckled darkly and stepped even closer, so close Christian could smell the faint scent of cigarettes on his breath. "It's not about what you want, Christian. You've been targeted, and if you don't choose wisely, our boss is gonna make your life really difficult. You don't wanna make him mad."

Christian clenched his fists, the threat hanging heavy in the air between them. He wasn't scared of these two, but the idea of someone bigger pulling the strings, someone who could make his life a living hell? That rattled him. But he wasn't about to let them know that. "I'm not interested," he repeated, stepping back, his eyes darting to the street, hoping to see Ava's car.

As if on cue, her little black SUV pulled up to the curb. Christian felt a surge of relief but kept his expression steady. He didn't want Barrett or Chase to think he was running to her for protection. Ava's eyes flicked toward the two boys, concern clear in her expression even from a distance. She had the same look she always had when something didn't sit right with her—brows slightly furrowed and her lips pressed together in a thin line.

"I gotta go," Christian said firmly, stepping away from Barrett. "Leave me alone."

Barrett's smile vanished, his eyes narrowing as Christian turned on his heel and walked toward Ava's car. "This ain't over," Barrett called after him, but Christian didn't turn back. He could feel their eyes boring into his back, making his skin prickle.

He opened the car door and slid into the passenger seat, his heart still racing. Ava glanced at him, her voice calm but laced with worry. "Who were those guys?"

Christian hesitated, the truth clawing at the back of his throat. He didn't want to lie to Ava, but he also didn't want to make her worry. He was supposed to be responsible and show her that he could handle things on his own. "Just some guys from school," he said, keeping his tone light. "It's nothing to worry about."

Ava didn't look convinced, her fingers tightening on the steering wheel as she glanced in the rearview mirror, watching the two boys retreat into the parking lot. "Christian..."

He could tell she wasn't buying it completely, but after a moment, she let it go, starting the car and pulling away from the school. As they drove home, Christian stared out the window, his mind replaying the conversation with Barrett and Chase. Their words echoed in his head—*targeted, our boss, make your life difficult.*

Ava had given him a chance, a real chance at a better life, and he wasn't going to screw it up. He couldn't let those guys drag him down, not when everything was finally going right. He wasn't a little kid anymore—he could handle it. He'd figure out a way to get Barrett and Chase off his back without bringing Ava into it.

But as they drove through the quiet streets, Christian couldn't shake the feeling that this wasn't going to be the last time he'd see them. He glanced over at Ava, who was focused on the road, her expression still tense.

I won't let them ruin this for me, he thought firmly. *I won't disappoint her. I'll handle it.*

CHAPTER NINE

Aussie stood at the shooting range with his team, the distant crack of gunfire filling the air as they all took turns at the targets. His hands rested on his rifle, but his mind was far from the steel barrels and steady trigger pulls. Ever since last week's dinner with Ava and Christian, they had been all he could think about. The quiet conversation, the easy laughter, and the genuine connection he felt. It had all left a mark. He'd enjoyed himself more than he had in a long time, and now, a week later, he found himself itching to see them again.

Thanksgiving was coming up fast, and all he could think about was how Ava had admitted she usually spent the holidays alone. The thought of her and Christian sitting at home with just the two of them tugged at something deep inside him. It didn't feel right. They deserved to be surrounded by people who cared about them.

"Hey, Aussie!" Bear's voice cut through his thoughts, and Aussie blinked, snapping back to the present. Bear stood a few feet away, arms crossed, his brow raised in question. "You've been standing there like a statue for five minutes. What's going on with you?"

The rest of the team paused, turning their attention toward him. Aussie shrugged, trying to shake off the cloud of thoughts. "Nothing, just thinking."

"Yeah, we can see that." Bear grinned, handing his weapon to one of the guys. "You never get that quiet unless something's eating at you. Spill it."

Aussie exhaled, rubbing the back of his neck as he tried to find the right words. "It's nothing major. I've been thinking about Thanksgiving, about how Ava and Christian are probably gonna spend it alone."

A murmur went around the group, the guys shifting their weight as they listened. Everyone on the team knew what it was like to have each other's backs, especially during the holidays. No one ever got left behind.

Bear narrowed his eyes. "Why don't you invite them to dinner at our place? I mean, Jocelyn's already prepping for an army. What's two more people?"

Aussie froze, a spark of hope lighting up inside him. He hadn't even considered it until Bear said something, but now that the idea was there, it seemed perfect. "Are you sure Jocelyn wouldn't mind?"

Bear chuckled and pulled out his phone, already typing. "I'll text her right now, but trust me, she won't care. She loves having a full house."

The other guys went back to their targets, but Aussie stood there, waiting while Bear fired off a quick message. A few seconds later, Bear's phone buzzed, and he looked up with a grin. "Told you. Jocelyn says it's no problem. The more, the merrier."

Aussie nodded, feeling the weight on his chest lift slightly. But then Bear shot him a curious look. "Tell me a little more about these two. You've been real tight-lipped."

Aussie scratched his jaw, debating how much to say. He knew the guys would be supportive, but he wasn't sure how to explain his feelings about Ava—mostly because he hadn't quite figured them out himself. "Christian's a good kid. He's the one who volunteered during that college and career day demo we did a couple of weeks back. Remember him?"

Bear's face lit up with recognition. "Yeah, I remember him. Good kid. He seemed really eager to learn. That's Ava's boy?"

"Well, sort of," Aussie said, adjusting his stance. "Ava's his social worker. She's been looking out for him, and from what I've seen, she's doing a damn good job. She's the kind of person who cares, you know?"

Bear crossed his arms again, clearly interested now. "And what about her? Sounds like you've been thinking about her a lot."

Aussie paused, unsure how to put his thoughts into words. "She's different. Not like anyone I've met before. She's a bit closed off, though. I think it's because of her past. She doesn't let people in easily."

Bear nodded slowly, taking it all in. "You serious about her?"

Aussie hesitated, feeling the weight of that question. "I don't know if it's serious yet. I just know there's something there. She's strong and independent, and she's been taking care of Christian like he's her own. I like that about her. I like that a lot. But I'm taking it slow. I don't want to push her too hard."

Bear slapped him on the shoulder with a grin. "Sounds like you've got your head on straight. Just don't rush it. If she's worth it, and it sounds like she is, take your time. I'm looking forward to meeting them both next week."

Aussie smiled, a strange sense of calm settling over him. "Yeah. I hope they come."

Without wasting any more time, he pulled out his phone and typed out a text to Ava.

Aussie: Hey, Ava. You mentioned that you and Christian were going to cook Thanksgiving dinner. However, I wanted to see if the two of you would like to join me at Bear and Jocelyn's place for dinner. My whole team, along with their families, will be there. Let me know.

He hit send and stared at the screen for a moment, hoping she'd say yes. The thought of spending Thanksgiving with Ava and Christian made him feel more excited than he wanted to admit.

Pocketing his phone, Aussie took a deep breath and returned his focus to the range. He picked up his rifle and got into position, his hands steady as he lined up his shot. The target downrange blurred slightly as his mind drifted back to Ava. He hadn't felt this way about anyone in a long time. There was something about her—something real, something worth waiting for.

As he squeezed the trigger and fired off a round, the recoil kicked into his shoulder, but all he could think about was his phone buzzing with Ava's reply.

Ava sat across from Sarah in the break room, her brown-bagged lunch of a simple ham and cheese sandwich in front of her. She unwrapped it methodically, her mind elsewhere.

Sarah, sipping her iced tea, noticed the distant look in Ava's eyes. The hum of office chatter and the faint smell of coffee lingered in the air, but Ava was miles away, stuck in a conversation she knew she needed to have.

"Everything okay with Christian?" Sarah asked, leaning forward slightly, concern evident in her tone.

Ava sighed, glancing down at her sandwich before pushing it aside. "I don't know. Things were going really good, but the last few days, he's been off," she said, her voice laced with worry. "I think he might be getting bullied at school, but every time I ask him about it, he just shrugs it off like it's nothing. But I can tell. Something's bothering him, and it's starting to really get to me."

Sarah frowned, stirring her tea absently. "That's tough. You know, sometimes kids don't open up to their parents, no matter how much they want to. Maybe he needs to talk to someone else. Someone who's, you know, more relatable to him."

Ava tilted her head, curiosity piqued. "What do you mean?"

"Maybe he needs a guy to talk to," Sarah said gently, her eyes locking with Ava's. "A strong male presence."

Ava's heart gave a little thud in her chest as Sarah's next words came out casually, "What about Aussie?"

A sudden flush warmed Ava's cheeks. *Aussie.* His name stirred up something she hadn't wanted to confront, and she shifted uncomfortably in her chair. Aussie was a good guy—he had an easy smile, was great with Christian, and every time they talked, there was this unspoken connection that left her feeling both comforted and unsettled. Could he really be the answer for Christian? And did she want him to be?

"Do you really think Aussie could help?" Ava asked, trying to mask the flood of emotions that surfaced just at the mention of his name.

"Well, he's someone that Christian knows. He's good with Christian. From what you've told me, he's a stand-up guy. Maybe Christian needs someone like that to talk to," Sarah said, leaning back in her chair. "I mean, you're doing an amazing job, Ava. But maybe a guy would help."

Ava's chest tightened. *Was she enough?* She had always prided herself on being everything Christian needed. She wanted to be his support, his rock, his advocate. But now, hearing Sarah say that, it tugged at a deep-rooted insecurity she tried to bury. What if she wasn't enough? What if Christian really did need someone like Aussie in his life? Someone she could never be?

Sensing Ava's inner turmoil, Sarah quickly shifted the conversation. "So, what about you and Aussie, huh?" She grinned mischievously. "Any other encounters I should know about?"

Ava rolled her eyes but couldn't help the smile that tugged at her lips. "No. He's a great guy, but after putting myself out there with Jarod and getting screwed over, who, by the way, is still trying to apologize, I'm just not sure I'm ready to jump into anything. I've got enough on my plate with Christian."

"Girl, Jarod's an idiot. Forget him." Sarah waved her hand dismissively. "And as for Aussie, if he likes Christian, I don't see a problem there. You're just scared to open up your heart because you've been alone for so long."

Ava flinched, Sarah's words striking a nerve. *Was that it? Was she just scared?* She looked down at her sandwich, no longer hungry. Maybe Sarah had a point. Aussie did make her feel something she hadn't felt in years. But did she have it in her to risk getting hurt again?

Just then, Ava's phone buzzed on the table. She picked it up, her pulse quickening as she saw Aussie's name light up the screen. She hesitated for a second before opening the message.

Aussie: *Hey, Ava. You mentioned that you and Christian were going to cook Thanksgiving dinner. However, I wanted to see if the two of you would like to join me at Bear and Jocelyn's place for dinner. My whole team, along with their families, will be there. Let me know.*

Ava's breath caught in her throat. The message was so genuine, so heartfelt. The thought of spending Thanksgiving with Aussie and his team stirred something deep inside her. But more than that, the idea that Aussie didn't want her or Christian to be alone on the holiday touched her in a way she hadn't expected.

"Well, well, well," Sarah smirked, leaning over to peek at Ava's phone. "Looks like someone really likes you."

Ava laughed softly, her face flushing. "He just invited Christian and me to Thanksgiving with his team. He's just being nice."

Sarah gave her a knowing look. "Ava, that's not just being nice. He's into you. Trust me, guys don't go out of their way like that unless they really care. And the fact that he's inviting you to meet his team tells you something. Those guys don't just bring anyone into their little worlds."

Sarah was right. SEALs were secretive even outside of their jobs. They kept a low profile and usually stayed close to those within their community.

Ava's stomach fluttered, her heart racing as she typed out a response.

Ava: Thank you so much for the invite. It was very sweet of you. I'll talk to Christian about it tonight and get back to you.

She hovered over the send button for a moment, already knowing what Christian's answer would be.

As she hit send, her mind drifted back to what Sarah had said. Was she really scared to open up? Had she been holding back because she was afraid of being hurt again?

Maybe, just maybe, it was time to let herself feel something again.

Christian glanced down at his lunch tray, picking at his sandwich as he sat across from Katy in the bustling school cafeteria. She'd been watching him for a few minutes now, her brown eyes filled with concern, and he knew she wasn't going to let it go.

"Okay, seriously, what's going on?" Katy leaned forward, her voice soft but steady so only he could hear. "You've barely said a word these past few days. Did something happen?"

Christian shrugged, trying to dodge her question with a half-hearted smile. "Just stuff," he said, hoping it would be enough to satisfy her.

But Katy wasn't having it. "Christian, come on. You can talk to me. I promise I won't tell anyone." She hesitated, then nudged his arm gently. "I'm just worried, okay?"

Her words hit him harder than he expected. He knew she cared, but he wasn't sure if he should tell her everything. Barrett and Chase weren't the kind of people anyone should mess with, especially not someone like Katy. She was good, and he didn't want her to get mixed up in anything dangerous.

He looked away, swallowing hard. "It's nothing you need to worry about," he murmured, but the tension in his voice was too obvious.

Katy tilted her head, her eyebrows knitting together. "Is it Barrett and Chase?"

Christian stiffened, not expecting her to be so direct. He knew she wasn't clueless; she'd seen them hanging around him a few times. But he hadn't wanted her to know the whole story. Her worried gaze stayed on him, though, and it was like she was slowly peeling away his defenses with each silent second that passed.

"They want me to join some club," he finally admitted, keeping his voice low.

"A club?" Katy's voice was skeptical. "Or something else?"

He let out a defeated sigh, shaking his head. "It's like a secret club," he said, hoping the phrase would sound innocent enough, but Katy's expression only darkened.

"Christian, that doesn't sound like a club." She paused, taking a deep breath. "I've heard about Barrett and Chase. They're not exactly the kind of people who start school clubs."

He gave her a wary look. "You think I don't know that?" He pressed his lips together. "But they're persistent. And they don't take 'no' for an answer."

"Then talk to Ava," she suggested, her voice gentle. "She would help you. You know she would."

"I don't want to get her involved," he said quietly as his hands fidgeted with the corner of his lunch tray. "Ava has enough on her plate. She doesn't need to be bothered with my problems."

Katy's face softened. She leaned closer to him. "Christian, Ava cares about you. If she didn't, she wouldn't have offered to take you in. Please talk to her. If something's going on, I'm sure she'd want to know."

How could he explain to Katy that he didn't want to involve Ava because he didn't want anything bad to come her way?

He looked at Katy. "If Barrett and Chase come back around, I'll tell her."

Katy smiled, the relief evident on her face, and Christian felt a weight lift off his chest. He didn't know where things would go from here, but for once, he felt a glimmer of hope.

"Thanks," he said quietly, meeting her gaze.

She nudged his arm playfully. "Anytime. Now, want to get ice cream after school?"

Christian grinned, his heart skipping a beat. "Yeah. I'd like that."

CHAPTER TEN

The savory aroma of roasted garlic and herbs filled Ava's kitchen as she stood by the stove, stirring a pot of creamy mushroom risotto and checking on the chicken breasts roasting in the oven, seasoned with rosemary and thyme. She glanced over her shoulder, catching a glimpse of Christian as he carefully laid out the plates and silverware on the dining table. Though he didn't say much, she noticed the slight frown of concentration on his face. It was a look he'd worn often since that day she'd seen him with those boys outside of school.

Once he finished setting the table, Christian moved over to his backpack, pulling out a stack of papers and notebooks. He settled in one of the spots at the table. With his head down, he focused on his schoolwork. Watching him, Ava felt a mix of pride and unease. Christian had always been responsible, but lately, there was a quiet tension in him, something that felt different. He hadn't been his usual open self since she'd caught that uneasy look on his face near those boys, and it nagged at her like a splinter under the skin.

Finally, with a satisfied sigh, Ava pulled the chicken from the oven, sliced it into tender pieces, and brought everything over to the table. As she sat down in her spot at the table, Christian looked up and gave her a quick, appreciative grin before digging in.

They ate in comfortable silence, but Ava's mind kept circling back to her concerns. She decided to ease into it, keeping her tone light.

"So, how's school going?" she asked, glancing at him over her fork. "Anything interesting happening?"

Christian shrugged, not meeting her gaze. "It's fine. Math's kinda boring, but we're starting a new project in history. We have to make a model of a famous landmark. I got assigned the Statue of Liberty."

She smiled, encouraging. "That sounds pretty cool. I'd love to see how that turns out. And what about Sea Cadets? Anything interesting coming up?"

He shifted a bit in his seat, his fork slowing as he thought. "Yeah, sorta. There is a community service project the CO is putting together. With the holidays coming up, we are volunteering to wrap presents at one of the community centers. Then, during one of the drills in December, we will be visiting the local Coast Guard Station. I'm really looking forward to that."

Ava nodded, sensing he was holding back. His replies were short, a little hesitant, as though he was choosing his words carefully. She searched his face, hoping he'd volunteer more, but he kept his gaze trained on his plate. It was like there was a wall between them, one he wasn't ready to break down just yet.

Deciding to shift the conversation, she took a breath, casually mentioning, "Oh, and speaking of plan…Aussie invited us to spend Thanksgiving with him and his team."

At this, Christian's eyes lit up, a spark of excitement breaking through his quiet demeanor. He looked up at her, brows raised. "Wait, seriously? Are we going?"

She smiled at his eagerness, glad to see some of his energy returning. "Well, I told him I'd talk to you first before giving an answer. I wanted us to make that decision together."

Christian blinked, clearly taken aback. "You wanted to ask me what I thought first?"

"Of course," she replied, giving him a soft smile. "We're a team, remember? We make decisions together."

He nodded, still looking a bit surprised but pleased. His gaze softened as he thought about it, and then he gave a decisive nod.

"Yeah, I think we should go. Aussie's cool, and well, I think it'd be nice, you know? Different than just us."

"Alright then," she agreed, feeling a small weight lift off her shoulders. "I'll let Aussie know we're in."

They continued eating, and Ava felt herself relaxing for the first time in days. The tension she'd sensed in Christian seemed to melt away, at least a little. Maybe spending time with Aussie and his friends could help Christian open up. Maybe he'd feel comfortable enough to let go of whatever had been weighing him down.

As they finished dinner, Ava couldn't help but feel a flicker of hope. Maybe sometime around Aussie was exactly what she needed too.

CHAPTER ELEVEN

The warm, familiar chaos of Bear and Jocelyn's house was in full swing as Aussie lounged on the oversized couch with a beer in his hand, his legs stretched out toward the coffee table.

His mouth was already watering from the smell of the roasting turkey in the oven. He had been looking forward to Thanksgiving dinner and was thankful they were stateside and able to enjoy the holiday.

He shifted restlessly, unable to stop glancing at the clock on the wall. He had received a text from Ava about fifteen minutes ago saying that she and Christian were on their way.

Even though Christian sort of met his team during the college and career day event, this would be the first time they'd meet everyone officially. And while Aussie was confident in his choice to invite them, he couldn't help but feel a twinge of nerves. He was proud to introduce Ava to his team. Hell, he wanted them to see what he saw in her. But he also wanted it to go perfectly.

"Man, you've been checking that clock like it owes you money," Nails teased, grinning from where he leaned against the arm of the couch.

"Shut up, Nails," Aussie shot back, though he couldn't keep the grin off his face.

Of course, Nails couldn't leave well enough alone. He leaned over and poked Aussie in the ribs. "Seriously, when is Ava getting here? I'm curious to meet her."

Aussie groaned, trying to swat Nails away. "You'll meet her when she gets here. And let me be clear. I want you to stay *far* away from her."

Nails feigned offense, clutching his chest dramatically. "Me? Far away? Why? I'm a charmer. Women love me. Maybe you're just afraid that she'll realize she's with the wrong SEAL when she meets me."

Jay Bird, the quietest on the team, chimed in from his spot in the recliner. "Let's be real. Nails has been in more relationships this year than I've been to the gym, and that's saying something."

The room erupted in laughter as Nails threw his hands up. "Hey, hey! Let's not throw stones."

Snow chuckled, leaning against the wall. "Nails, you couldn't hold onto a woman if your life depended on it. Pretty sure Ava would run screaming the moment you said, 'Hello.'"

"She wouldn't get the chance," Aussie interjected with a grin. "Because I'd drag you out of here by your collar before you could get a single word out."

Nails laughed, clapping Aussie on the shoulder. "In all seriousness, I really can't wait to meet her. She must be special to have you acting like a lovesick puppy."

Aussie shook his head, unable to hide his smile. "Yeah, she is. Which is why you'll be admiring her from a very safe distance."

Duke, who was sitting next to Aussie, raised his beer in a mock salute. "To Nails. An admirer of all women, keeper of none."

The room roared with laughter, and even Nails couldn't help but join in, shaking his head. "You guys are just jealous."

Aussie leaned back in his seat, laughing along with the rest. "Yeah, Nails. Jealous of how much money you spend on flowers and apologies every week."

That sent the team into another round of ribbing, leaving Nails rolling his eyes and Aussie grinning ear to ear.

As they all settled in to watch the football pre-game show, the front door swung open, and Playboy and Gabby strolled in. The room erupted with cheers and groans.

"About time you two showed up!" Jay Bird hollered from the recliner.

"Last ones to arrive—no surprise there," Snow added, grinning.

Gabby rolled her eyes, but there was a sparkle in them as she held up her left hand, the light catching on a dazzling ring that sat on a very important ring finger. "Well, maybe we were a little late because *someone* decided to propose!"

The room froze for half a beat before erupting into chaos. Jocelyn, Hannah, and Clover rushed over, gasping and squealing as they examined the ring.

"Oh my gosh, Gabby, it's beautiful!" Jocelyn exclaimed, her hands clasped in excitement.

Playboy grinned like the cat that ate the canary as the guys clapped him on the back, congratulating him one by one.

"Congratulations, man," Aussie said, shaking Playboy's hand.

In the middle of the commotion, Snow nudged Aussie and motioned toward the window with his chin. "Look who finally made it."

Aussie turned his head, and his heart skipped a beat as Ava's little SUV pulled up along the curb in front of the house. His stomach flipped, a sudden wave of nervous energy surging through him.

This was it.

Pushing himself off the couch, he ran a hand through his hair and strode toward the front door, his pulse quickening. By the time he stepped onto the porch, Ava and Christian were climbing out of the car. The crisp autumn air hit him, but he barely noticed.

Ava looked radiant, her long black hair catching the sun, and Christian, despite his usual guarded expression, seemed comfortable at her side.

Aussie smiled, his nerves melting away as excitement took over. "Hey, you two," he called out, stepping down to meet them on the walkway.

Ava adjusted her sweater as she and Christian made their way up the walkway to Bear and Jocelyn's house. The fall air was crisp, a slight chill biting at her cheeks, but she felt warm enough in her orange and yellow sweater, her favorite pair of jeans, and brown ankle boots. Christian, looking sharp in his jeans and a green button-up shirt, shot her a teasing grin. She knew that look. It was the "I know you're nervous" grin he'd given her before when she had been in Aussie's presence.

"Oh, you think you're so clever, don't you?" she nudged him, smirking.

"Come on, you're practically blushing already, and we haven't even seen Aussie yet," Christian teased, his grin widening. "I bet he's waiting on the porch right now."

Ava rolled her eyes, though she couldn't deny the flutter in her stomach. She was both eager and nervous to see Aussie, but more than that, she was relieved to see Christian acting like himself again.

When they reached the porch, her heart skipped a beat as she saw Aussie stepping off the porch sporting that easy, inviting smile of his. He looked ruggedly handsome, his jeans fitting him just right, and the navy long-sleeve T-shirt he wore accentuated his broad shoulders.

"Hey, you two!" he called out, meeting them at the bottom of the steps.

Ava smiled back. "Hi there. Sorry, we're a few minutes late." She held up a pan that was covered in aluminum foil. "I know you said that I didn't need to bring anything, but I felt weird not bringing anything. So, I decided at the last minute to bake a cake."

He grinned. "I love cake. I can't wait to try it." He then turned his attention to Christian. "How are you doing, man?"

Christian grinned. "Pretty good."

"Good to hear. Come on in, and I'll introduce you guys to everyone."

As they started up the steps, Aussie looked at her. "You look great, by the way," he said, his gaze warm and appreciative. She felt her cheeks heat up. She heard Christian snicker under his breath.

"Thanks," she managed, trying to keep her composure.

Christian leaned in, whispering, "Ava, you're turning red."

Ava swatted his arm, but Aussie caught the exchange, grinning. "What's going on with this one?" he asked, nodding toward Christian.

Ava hesitated, a little embarrassed. *Oh, shit!* How was she going to explain this? She nibbled her lip again, and she tried to think of something to tell him. But she couldn't think of a damn thing. Plus, she was always preaching honesty to people.

She cleared the huge knot that had suddenly lodged in her throat as she mustered up the courage to tell him the truth.

"Errr...Well, Christian seems to think that we," she gestured between her and Aussie, "are, um, maybe interested in each other."

Oh, sweet baby Jesus. She couldn't believe she blurted that out. She could feel the heat burning her cheeks.

Aussie raised an eyebrow, smirking as he glanced down at Christian, who was now thoroughly enjoying Ava's discomfort. "Smart kid. Seems like he's got a good read on things," Aussie replied, his eyes twinkling. "I think he's on the right track."

Christian laughed, sending Ava a look that clearly said, *"See? Told you so."* Ava couldn't help but laugh, too, her earlier nerves slipping away.

Once inside, they were greeted by a lively chaos of voices, laughter, and the delicious smell of Thanksgiving dinner.

Aussie led Ava and Christian through the bustling house, introducing them to everyone. He started with Bear and Jocelyn, a warm and welcoming couple with two young kids, Amira and Max, who were chasing each other around. Then he introduced her to Joker and Clover, explaining that Clover was Bear's sister.

"It's a big, happy family here," Aussie chuckled as they moved through the crowd, "which brings us to Duke and Hannah." Duke and Hannah were beaming, clearly overjoyed with their adorable baby girl, Isadora, who cooed happily in Hannah's arms.

Finally, they met Playboy and Gabby. Gabby smiled warmly as she shook Ava's hand, her warmth and strength evident.

"And here's the rest of the team," Aussie continued, nodding toward Snow, Jay Bird, and Nails. "Just don't let Nails get too close," he added with a smirk. "The man's got a terrible weakness for pretty ladies."

Nails laughed, unabashed. "What can I say? It's a gift."

Ava chuckled, instantly feeling at ease. Everyone welcomed her and Christian with open arms, and Christian quickly gravitated toward the guys, talking excitedly with them about his own dreams of joining the Navy one day. She caught sight of him animatedly explaining something to Jay Bird, his eyes bright and the tension in his posture gone, if only for the evening.

While Christian was occupied, Ava found herself drawn into the kitchen, where Jocelyn, Clover, Hannah, and Gabby were preparing some last-minute dishes. Jocelyn offered her a glass of wine, which she gladly accepted.

"So," Jocelyn began, a knowing smile on her face, "what's the story with you and Aussie?"

Ava laughed, feeling her cheeks warm again. She sighed. "We're just...Well, I really don't know," she said, glancing down at her glass. "But, I won't lie, I am attracted to him."

"That's how it started for Tanner and me," Gabby said, chuckling.

Ava gave her a confused look. "I thought you were engaged to Playboy?" she asked, and Gabby laughed again.

"Oh, I am. And Tanner is Playboy. I just can't find it in myself to call my future husband Playboy. So, I choose to call him by his birth name."

Ava grinned. "I think I would do the same."

"Now, getting back to Aussie. He's a sweet guy. And it's obvious he thinks the world of you and Christian," Clover piped in as she set out a tray of cookies.

The women shared their stories with Ava, drawing her into their tight-knit circle. Jocelyn explained that she and Bear had been high school sweethearts but had drifted apart over the years. "But then, earlier this year, I was working in Chad, and the team was sent to protect me. It was like fate, pulling us back together." She smiled, her voice laced with nostalgia.

Clover, in her relaxed yet confident way, shared that she'd been a Marine helicopter pilot until a serious injury led her to join Rockwell Security, where she worked with Gabby. "Life takes you where you're supposed to go, one way or another," she said.

Then Hannah chimed in, her eyes lighting up as she talked about meeting Duke. "We met in Hawaii while I was visiting Pearl Harbor. I thought it'd be a vacation fling, but we both fell hard. Now here we are, with little Isadora." She beamed, glancing at her baby girl with pride.

Finally, Gabby spoke up, her gaze steady as she talked about how she'd recently started dating Playboy.

"We've known each other a while, but it wasn't until recently that things fell into place." Her voice softened when she explained her injury, sharing that she'd lost part of her leg while working for the Coast Guard's MSRT team. "But as Clover said, I work at Rockwell and life's good."

Ava listened, captivated by each story. She felt honored to be in the presence of such a close, supportive group of women. For the next hour or so, they all laughed and told stories.

When dinner was finally ready, everyone gathered around the table, filling seats with laughter and conversation. Ava took her place between Christian and Aussie. She was grateful to be surrounded by warmth, acceptance, and a sense of belonging that she hadn't felt in a long time.

As everyone started to eat and continued with their conversations, Ava felt a warmth blossom in her chest as she watched Christian, relaxed and animated, laughing with Bear and Jocelyn's kids even though they were a few years younger.

She glanced at Aussie next to her, and she felt a flutter of hope. Maybe she'd found a place for her and Christian here. And as her gaze met Aussie's, he winked, and she knew that this Thanksgiving would be one to remember.

Just as she was reaching for a dish, Nails, who was sitting across from her, leaned back in his chair with a mischievous glint in his eye and directed a comment at Gabby. "Hey, Gabby, did you hear the news about Vice Admiral Alley?"

Gabby's nose wrinkled in distaste at the name, and Ava's curiosity piqued instantly. She turned to Gabby. "Who's Vice Admiral Alley?"

Gabby rolled her eyes, leaning in conspiratorially. "He's the guy who tried to get me kicked out of the Coast Guard after I was injured.

He's one of those egotistical men who think women don't belong in high-profile positions."

Ava frowned. "What happened?"

"Oh, his little plan backfired, big time," Gabby said with a smirk. "The Homeland Secretary stepped in and made it clear it wasn't his call to make. He called him out in front of everyone during my Medical Review Board hearing. He also ordered an investigation into Alley's action. And I hear that they uncovered a little scheme Alley and his cronies who were in other positions within the Coast Guard were involved in getting people they had a beef with transferred to lower-level jobs or, like in my case, forced them into retiring. Rumor has it that he'll be retiring at the end of the year. Well, either he retires, or he's getting the boot. Oh! And they demoted him one rank."

The whole table broke into laughter, each of Aussie's teammates jumping in with their sarcastic remarks.

Bear leaned back, shaking his head. "Serves the shithead right. Good riddance."

With a laugh, Gabby raised her glass. "Here's to Alley taking an early retirement. The first real thing he's contributed to the Coast Guard."

Everyone cheered, raising their glasses in agreement.

While the conversation flowed, Ava noticed Aussie leaning in closer from where he sat beside her. His voice was low, just for her to hear. "I'm really glad you and Christian came tonight, Ava."

The warmth in his tone gave her butterflies, and her pulse quickened. She looked at him, her face softening with a smile. "Thank you for inviting us. I'm glad we came, too."

Their eyes met, and Ava felt herself get lost in his gaze, her surroundings fading into the background. She knew that if they hadn't been at the dinner table, surrounded by Aussie's family and friends, she would've closed the distance between them right then. She could almost feel the pull as they gazed at each other.

But before she could do anything about it, she noticed Gabby and Clover across the table. They were watching her and sharing amused glances. Blushing, Ava cleared her throat and stood up. "I'll start clearing the dishes," she said, giving herself a reason to escape for a moment.

Aussie was up before she could take a step, grabbing a few dishes and following her to the kitchen. As they set the plates by the sink, Ava felt Aussie's hand snake around her waist. He gently pulled her close, his touch firm yet tender, and she felt her breath catch.

She looked up at him, her heart pounding as his gaze softened, and he spoke in a low voice. "I can't wait any longer."

Then he leaned down, his lips brushing hers, and Ava's mind went blissfully blank. Caught off guard, she froze for a second, but deep down, she knew this was exactly what she wanted. She kissed him back, warmth and electricity flooding her senses.

But just as quickly as the moment started, it was over. She heard voices in the hallway as others started bringing in their dishes. Aussie released her, stepping back smoothly before anyone noticed, but not before he shot her a grin, his gorgeous hazel eyes glinting with mischief. He winked and leaned in close one last time, whispering, "This isn't the last kiss. Not by a long shot."

Ava bit her lip to hold back a smile, her face flushed as she returned to the table. And as she settled back into her seat, she realized with certainty that she couldn't wait for that next kiss.

CHAPTER TWELVE

The following day, Aussie took Christian to the shooting range. Aussie stood beside Christian, nodding as he examined the teen's posture as he got into position, aiming the rifle downrange.

They'd been there for a while, and Christian was a fast learner, picking up on Aussie's instructions with the determination of someone who wanted to do well. But Aussie knew the kid had a ways to go before he was truly comfortable with the weapon.

"Alright," Aussie said, moving closer and resting his hand lightly on Christian's shoulder. "Remember, keep your feet shoulder-width apart. You want a solid stance, or that recoil's gonna mess with your aim." He gave a short, approving nod as Christian followed his direction. "Good. Now, keep that grip firm, but don't choke it. Nice and steady, yeah?"

Christian nodded, adjusting his grip and aiming down the sights with concentration. He fired a few rounds, and Aussie could see he was improving, the shots landing closer to the center.

"Much better," Aussie said, a hint of pride in his tone. "You've got good instincts. Just a little more practice, and you'll be grouping shots like a pro."

Christian smiled, clearly pleased with the compliment, but his expression shifted as he lowered the weapon and glanced over at Aussie. "Do you like Ava?" he asked, trying to keep his tone casual.

The question caught Aussie a bit off guard, but took it in stride, smiling slightly. "Of course, I like her. Who wouldn't? he replied."

Christian looked thoughtful. "No. I mean, really like her."

Aussie felt his chest tighten a bit, wondering where Christian was going with the line of questioning.

Yeah," he admitted, his voice low and sincere. "I do. Ava has got something rare about her. She's strong, smart, and she's got this heart that doesn't quit." He paused, feeling his words. "I'd like to get to know her more. I think she's someone that anyone would be lucky to have in their life, you know?"

Christian looked down, the toe of his shoe scuffing against the ground as he absorbed Aussie's words. "I do know," he murmured, and there was a soft vulnerability in his tone that didn't go unnoticed.

Aussie noticed Christian's gaze drift toward the target as he hesitated before speaking again. "I know she's good to you," Aussie said quietly. "You care about her, don't you?"

Christian shrugged, his face betraying emotions he was trying to suppress. "Yeah. I guess more than anyone else I've known." He hesitated, then continued, "She's the first grown-up who actually believes in me. Listens to me, you know? Not just to tell me what I'm doing wrong but to really hear me."

Aussie's heart ached as he listened. He'd suspected Christian's life hadn't been easy, but hearing him talk about Ava like that made it clear just how much she meant to him. He kept his tone gentle as he spoke. "Sounds like she's made a big difference for you."

"Yeah," Christian said, his voice barely above a whisper. "But she's just keeping me for the holidays, Aussie. After that, I'll be put back in the system. I don't even know where I'll end up. I care for Ava so much. She's like my real parent. But I'm scared to get attached, knowing that in a few weeks, it will all be gone."

Aussie watched him, seeing the fear and uncertainty in his eyes, and he felt a pang of protectiveness for the kid. "That's tough. And it makes sense to feel that way. But don't sell yourself short. Ava wouldn't have taken you in if she didn't care about you, and she's the kind of person who sticks with people she cares about."

Christian took a deep breath, glancing over at Aussie. "I just… I just wish I could stay with her. It's like, for the first time, I feel like someone's giving me a shot. Like she sees something in me that no one else bothered to look for."

Aussie's heart felt heavier with each word Christian said, understanding how deeply he was affected by the fear of losing the one steady, caring presence he'd known. He reached over, resting a reassuring hand on Christian's shoulder. "Ava sees a lot in you, Christian. And from where I'm standing, you're someone worth sticking around for."

Christian looked at him, searching his face for something that reassured him, something that made him feel less alone.

Aussie's phone buzzed, and he pulled it from his pocket to see a message from Ava.

Ava: Hey, what time are you bringing Christian home? There's no rush. I just need to run a few errands and wanted to make sure I'd be back when you got here.

He smiled, typing back.

Aussie: We'll be about two more hours.

Putting his phone away, he turned back to Christian with a warm smile. "No hurry to head back just yet. How about we put in a bit more practice, yeah?"

Christian's face lit up, and he nodded, lifting the gun again as Aussie continued guiding him. As they went through the movements, Aussie felt a deep respect for the kid's resilience, and he knew he'd do everything in his power to help Christian find the stability he deserved.

Ava stepped back from the living room, her hands on her hips as she admired her work. She had just finished setting up a beautiful artificial Christmas tree, strung with lots of twinkling lights, and was now just waiting for ornaments.

Piles of other decorations sat nearby—garlands, stockings, and all the festive touches she'd planned for weeks. She'd even found some small, battery-operated snow globes for Christian to place around the house. This was going to be his best Christmas ever, and she was determined to make every moment count.

She thought back to earlier when she'd gone to put Christian's laundry away in his room. She had stumbled upon a crumpled piece of notebook paper lying on his nightstand. Curious, she had picked it up and smoothed it out, only to find the title "What I Want for Christmas" scrawled at the top. Her heart twisted as she read the first item on the list: *a family to love me like Ava does*. She'd sat on his bed, clutching that piece of paper, feeling the weight of what that simple line meant. She would give anything to adopt him, but she knew the courts were hesitant to approve single parents. Not that it hasn't happened. It's just hard.

The list had a few other items, mostly essentials: clothes, some new shoes, and school supplies. A laptop was on the list, too. Just thinking about how much she cared for him, Ava felt a surge of protectiveness. This holiday was going to be perfect for Christian, no matter what.

About an hour later, she was stirring a pot on the stove when she heard the front door open, and her heart skipped a beat as Aussie and Christian walked in.

Dinner was nearly ready. She'd prepared lemon rosemary chicken, buttery mashed potatoes, and roasted asparagus. She glanced up just as Aussie walked over, his eyes lighting up at the sight of her, and to her surprise, he leaned in, kissing her cheek.

Ava's cheeks warmed, but she quickly smiled, noticing Christian watching them with a huge grin. "So, how was the range?" she asked, her voice slightly higher than usual.

Christian launched into a lively explanation, describing everything from how Aussie had taught him to adjust his stance to how he'd hit a bullseye near the end of practice. Ava listened, joy filling her at seeing him so happy. When he finally paused, she glanced over at Aussie, feeling a quiet gratitude.

"Dinner smells amazing," Aussie commented, and before she could second-guess herself, she invited him to stay.

"Are you sure?" he asked, his eyes meeting hers with a warm glint.

"Yes, of course. I'd love for you to stay," she said, and Christian's eyes lit up with excitement.

As they all sat down to eat, Ava could hardly contain her excitement for what she had planned next. As they finished the meal, she got up and motioned toward the living room. "Christian, I have a little surprise for you," she said.

Christian looked over, his mouth falling open when he saw the tree and all the decorations. "You got a tree?" he asked, his voice filled with disbelief.

Ava chuckled. "I did."

"Can we decorate it tonight?" he asked, moving toward all the shopping bags filled with ornaments.

"Of course, we're going to decorate it tonight."

He grinned from ear to ear and then turned to Aussie. "Will you stay and help?"

Ava's heart raced as Aussie looked from Christian to her. She gave him an encouraging smile, silently hoping he'd say yes.

"Absolutely," Aussie replied, his face breaking into a smile. "I'd love to."

Aussie couldn't remember the last time he'd felt so relaxed and at home. Sitting down for dinner with Ava and Christian, a warm meal on the table, and laughter filling the air made Aussie feel like he'd walked into a moment he hadn't known he'd been missing.

Watching Christian's animated grin as he talked about the shooting range and Ava's gentle smile as she listened, Aussie found himself thinking about the future, about the possibility of something more permanent with them. He couldn't imagine his life without Christian or Ava. Somehow, those two had woven themselves into his heart. He knew it wasn't exactly wise to get attached, but he was already too far gone.

"Will you stay and help us decorate?" Christian asked, his face bright with hope as he glanced from Aussie to Ava.

Aussie's heart did a little flip. "Absolutely. I'd love to," he said, unable to stop the grin that spread across his face. "I don't get to decorate much anymore."

For the next two hours, they transformed Ava's house into a holiday wonderland. The tree sparkled with strings of multi-colored lights, and Aussie found himself placing ornaments on the tree with Christian, letting him take the lead in deciding where everything should go.

Ava joined in, laughing as she hung garlands over doorways. Every so often, Aussie and Ava would catch each other's eye across the room, a shared look that said more than words could. His heart felt lighter with every stolen glance, every moment they shared.

Christian, meanwhile, was having the time of his life. Aussie watched him carefully position every ornament, making sure each one was just right. He'd never seen the kid so happy.

Ava had given him the freedom to take charge of the decorations, and Christian took that responsibility to heart, beaming with every choice he made. Watching him filled Aussie's heart with both joy and a pang of sadness. He wanted Christian to have the stability of a real home and family. And he knew the perfect person who could provide that for him—Ava.

Eventually, the decorations were finished, and the room glowed with the lights from the tree. The house looked warm and welcoming, a perfect holiday scene. As they stood back, admiring their work, Christian's phone buzzed. He glanced down, his eyes lighting up.

"It's Katy," he murmured, then disappeared into his room, phone pressed to his ear.

Aussie smirked, remembering the little tidbits Christian had mentioned about Katy. "Think she might be his girlfriend?" he said aloud, glancing at Ava.

Ava chuckled softly. "He says they're just friends, but who knows with teenagers?" She turned her warm gaze on him. "Thank you for staying tonight. It meant a lot to him. And to me."

Aussie's chest tightened as he followed her to the door, then out to his truck, feeling the chill of the evening air. She looked up at him, her eyes reflecting the twinkling lights from the house. "Thank you for inviting me," he said, his voice sincere. "I had a lot of fun. And I enjoyed spending time with Christian earlier at the range. He's a great kid, Ava. You've done so much for him already."

Ava's face softened a hint of sadness in her expression. "I'm just trying to take it day by day, to make this the best holiday he's had. I know he's worried about what happens after Christmas."

Aussie's heart clenched at the thought. "He told me that earlier," he admitted. "He's afraid of losing this…of losing you. I can tell how much you care about him, too. It's not just him who's worried, is it?"

Ava looked away for a moment, gathering herself. "I'd love to adopt him and be his mom for good. But I know how the courts can be. It's hard for single parents to get approval." She paused, her voice catching. "But I want him to feel loved, even if it's only for now."

He reached for her hand, giving it a reassuring squeeze. "If there's anything I can do, Ava, anything at all, I'm here. I want to see both of you happy. You and Christian mean a lot to me."

Ava's eyes met his, filled with gratitude and something more. He took a step forward and pulled her into a warm hug, feeling the way she relaxed in his arms. After a moment, he gently pulled back, his hands lingering on her shoulders. "I really care about you, Ava. I don't want to rush anything, but how do you feel about us?"

Her cheeks flushed slightly, but she didn't look away. "I like you, Aussie," she admitted softly. "And I'd like to see where things could go between us."

A warm smile spread across his face, and he slowly leaned in, brushing his lips over hers. It was a gentle, unhurried kiss, tender and full of promise as if they had all the time in the world. When they finally pulled apart, Aussie took a deep breath, a soft smile lingering on his lips.

"I'll talk to you soon," he said, giving her hand a gentle squeeze before climbing into his truck.

As he drove away, he glanced in the rearview mirror, watching her standing there until she was just a figure silhouetted by the light from her porch. He felt a surge of hope that maybe Ava could be the one to make him settle down.

CHAPTER THIRTEEN

Aussie pulled off his gloves and tossed them onto the gear rack with a sense of finality. His body was sore, and his mind was ready to unwind after another brutal day of training and drills.

While the others on the team decided to call it a day a few hours ago, he got roped into helping set up a training obstacle in the woods.

He got a whiff of himself and cringed. *Christ, I need a shower,"* he thought to himself as he grabbed a change of clothes and a towel from his bag. Just as he turned for the door to head to the showers, a voice called out from across the room.

"Aussie, a word?" Derek, his CO, stood by the entryway, his eyes sharp and unreadable.

Aussie raised an eyebrow, the hint of curiosity prickling at his thoughts. Derek didn't often pull him aside like this. Still, whatever it was, it wasn't his job to question it, just to handle it. With a silent nod, Aussie fell in step behind Derek, following him through the winding corridors toward the office at the end of the hall.

As they walked, he wondered what Derek could want. They hadn't had any new assignments, at least none that he'd heard of, and he hadn't done anything out of line, as far as he could recall. He pushed the thoughts aside, knowing that he'd know soon enough.

Once inside the office, Derek closed the door with a soft click. He motioned to a chair across from his desk. "Take a seat, Aussie."

Aussie did, sinking back into the chair and watching his CO's face. Derek's mouth pressed into a thin line, and his jaw was tight. He leaned against his desk, crossing his arms as he spoke.

"I just got off the phone with some of the higher-ups. As I'm sure you've seen the recent news about the crime in our town, which also includes three homicides."

Aussie felt his stomach tighten. This was what he and Snow had been talking about the other night. He nodded in acknowledgment.

Derek's expression darkened. "Because of the severity of the crimes, the FBI is now involved. After going over some evidence, the FBI believes that these crimes are the work of a local gang looking to make their mark in the criminal world. The worst part is that they think they're using kids to do their dirty work."

The disgust in Derek's voice was palpable, and Aussie felt his own repulsion stir. Kids? Forcing them into lives that could ruin them, or worse? His mind instantly flicked to Christian, grateful that the kid hadn't been pulled into something like that. He'd had his fair share of tough breaks, but thank god the kid had a good head on his shoulders and hadn't crossed that line.

But then Aussie's mind circled back. Why was Derek telling him all this?

As if reading his mind, Derek continued, "The FBI and PD are stretched thin and they are seeking some assistance."

Aussie's pulse quickened, and his jaw clenched as Derek continued. "They've got leads that some community leaders might be linked to this gang activity."

A new surge of anger rushed through Aussie. He could barely wrap his mind around it. Those who were supposed to lead and protect were allegedly the ones exploiting these kids. The thought made his blood boil.

Derek took a measured breath, his voice cooling. "Every year, the city hosts a big holiday fundraiser. The FBI has an agent who'll attend to cozy up to some of the people they're tracking. But she'll need a date, a cover to blend in."

Aussie's entire body tensed. He realized what Derek was asking of him, and immediately, Ava's face came to mind. He shifted in his chair, glancing away. The thought of posing as someone else's date for a night didn't sit well with him, not when Ava was in the picture—even if things between them hadn't quite found solid ground yet.

But Derek seemed to sense his hesitation. "It's just pretend, Aussie. She only needs a cover, and you won't have to stick by her side all night. If it could help us get these gang members off the streets, it's worth it. And before you ask, Snow and Jay Bird already had plans."

Aussie nodded slowly, his fists unclenching. Derek knew about his interest in Ava. Silence hung in the air. Aussie could feel the weight of it pressing down on his conscience. He knew the stakes, knew the kids who'd be caught in the crossfire if they didn't step up.

"All right," he said finally, his voice even. "I'll do it."

Derek's shoulders seemed to relax. "Thank you, Aussie. As soon as I get all the details, I'll forward them to you."

As Aussie left the office, a knot of guilt settled in his chest. He knew this was just like one of the team's missions. However, the thought of posing as someone's date, even though it was just a cover, felt like a betrayal. Even if he knew Ava might understand, it didn't sit right. Not in the least.

Just as he was about to head back toward the showers, he felt his phone buzz in his pocket. *Now what?* He thought to himself as he pulled it out and looked at it. It was a nine-one-one message from Nails.

Nails: *Dude, I need your help ASAP.*

Aussie: *Where are you?*

Nails: *Bear's house. I offered to babysit, but I'm in way over my head.*

Aussie pinched the bridge of his nose.

Aussie: *Can't you call one of the others to help?*

Nails: *Nobody else will answer me. Please???? I'm desperate, man.*

Ugh! He just wanted to get a shower, go home, and chill for the night. And, of course, call Ava and talk to her. However, knowing that there were kids involved, Aussie couldn't say no.

Aussie: *Fine. Give me twenty.*

Nails: *Fifteen*

Aussie: *Is someone dying?*

Nails: *I might be dead if you don't hurry your ass up*

Aussie shook his head, wondering what in the hell Nails had gotten himself into.

Thirty minutes later, Aussie parked his truck in front of Bear and Jocelyn's house, already grinning as he imagined the scene inside. However, Aussie knew that if Nails had actually asked for backup, it had to be serious.

He walked up the porch steps and swung open the front door, but an eye-watering stench immediately hit him. The unmistakable smell of shit hung heavy in the air. It was so potent he almost gagged. Aussie held his nose, wanting nothing more than to run back out the door, but instead, he muttered, "What the hell...?"

Moments later, Nails emerged from the hallway, holding baby Isadora at arm's length like she was a ticking time bomb. She was wrapped in a couple of towels, and the expression on Nails' face was somewhere between horror and helplessness.

Nails groaned, looking utterly defeated. "Did you know a human this small could expel this much crap?"

Aussie burst out laughing. The sight of the towering SEAL looking absolutely terrified of a baby was too much. He doubled over, clutching his stomach as Nails shot him an exasperated look.

"This isn't funny, Aussie," Nails grumbled, shifting Isadora as if she might explode again. "I thought babysitting was just keeping them alive. They don't train us for this!"

Aussie wiped tears from his eyes, unable to contain his laughter. "Oh, Nails, I didn't know you had such a sensitive stomach. You really didn't think this through, did you?"

Amira and Max stood nearby, pinching their noses and looking horrified, while Sienna, Irish and Bailey's daughter, chimed in. "It's like a monster took over her diaper!"

Aussie glanced around, and his laughter only got louder as he took in the full scene. Yes, it was gross, but it was fucking hilarious.

Baby Isadora had apparently unleashed chaos. There was poop on her, on the towel, somehow a little on Nails' shirt, and even a few splatters on the wood floor.

Even though Max and Amira looked horrified, they were at least trying to help, holding a container of baby wipes and a roll of paper towels like it was an offering.

"I didn't sign up for this," Nails said, still looking helplessly at Isadora, who was oblivious to the chaos she'd caused. "I'm telling you, Aussie, this one's a weapon of mass destruction."

Aussie shook his head, still chuckling. "Alright, big guy, what exactly do you want me to do? You're the one who called me for help."

"Yeah, you've got nieces and nephews," Nails said defensively. "I figured you knew what to do! She won't stop shitting. Every time she toots, more shit comes out."

Aussie stifled another laugh. "I may have nieces and nephews, but between deployments and trainings, I missed the baby stages. So, this isn't exactly in my wheelhouse either."

Nails muttered something under his breath and glanced back down at the grinning baby in his arms. "Do you think Duke and Hannah have dealt with this before?"

"I don't know. Why didn't you call Duke?" Aussie asked, still trying to keep a straight face.

Nails sighed. "Didn't wanna bother them unless it was serious. And she's obviously fine," he added, looking down at Isadora's cherubic, innocent face. "Well, besides the, uh, explosive situation."

Aussie smirked, noticing just how much of a mess this really was. With Isadora, plus the other three kids, the thought of dinner and cleanup was looking like a losing battle.

"You know, we're gonna need backup for this," Aussie said, scanning the disaster zone again. He thought of Ava and how incredible she was with kids. "I think I've got the perfect person to help."

Nails' face lit up with hope. "You thinking of Ava? She's a social worker—she's gotta be great at this kid stuff, right?"

"Exactly," Aussie agreed, already dialing Ava's number.

Ava's office smelled faintly of lavender and coffee, the remnants of the candle she kept under the warmer, and the endless cups of caffeine fueling her day.

Her desk was cluttered with files, post-it notes, and a bowl that held the remains of her chicken Caesar salad.

Across from her, Sarah was perched on the edge of her chair with her sandwich in hand. Her inquisitive blue eyes were zeroed in on Ava.

"So," Sarah said, dragging out the word with a sly grin, "how was Thanksgiving with the SEALs? Did Aussie finally make a move, or are you still just eyeing each other like awkward teenagers at a school dance?"

Ava rolled her eyes, though a small smile tugged at her lips. "It was nice. His team and their families were all really welcoming." She hesitated for a moment before adding, "And...he kissed me."

Sarah nearly choked on her food. "What? He kissed you? Details, now!"

"It wasn't anything huge," Ava said quickly, though the warmth in her cheeks betrayed her. "It was after dinner. We were in the kitchen, and he just kissed me. It was sweet."

Sarah set her sandwich down, abandoning all pretense of eating. "Okay, so? Are you going on a date with him or what?"

Ava hesitated again, biting her lip. "Well, does him coming to the house for dinner and then staying to help Christian and me decorate the tree count as a date?"

Sarah's eyes widened, and her mouth hung open. "You cooked him dinner?"

Ava laughed. "Well, it was sort of a spur-of-the-moment thing." She explained how Aussie had taken Christian to the shooting range, and when he dropped him off, she had invited him to stay for dinner.

Sarah was smiling. "Okay, that is a step in the right direction. But when are you two planning on going on an official date? Just the two of you?"

Ava played with the corner of a piece of paper. "I don't know."

Before Sarah could respond, the door to Ava's office swung open, and Clint, their boss, walked in carrying an envelope and a stack of files. His tall, lanky frame and ever-serious expression made the room feel smaller.

"Hope I'm not interrupting," Clint said, though he didn't wait for an answer. He set the envelope and files down on her desk. "Ava, are you still attending the city's annual fundraising gala this Friday?"

"Yeah. I was going to stop by to make an appearance," Ava replied, sitting up straighter, "but I wasn't planning on staying long. Why? Is there something you need?"

"Well, considering that you are attending with Jarod, I was hoping that you could give this," he said, tapping the large manila envelope that he had set on her desk.

Ava frowned slightly. *Who in the hell told him I was going with Jarod?* "I'm not going with Jarod. In fact, Jarod and I no longer have a relationship outside of work."

Clint's eyebrows lifted in surprise. "Really? Huh. I was under the impression that you two were pretty close these days," he stated. His tone was casual but curious.

"Well, we're not," Ava said firmly, crossing her arms. She hoped that he would take the hint and drop the subject.

"Alright," Clint said with a shrug. "But could you still give this to Jarod?"

"Why can't you?"

"Because I'm not going."

"But just last week, you mentioned that you were."

"I was planning to. However, something came up, and I can no longer attend."

Ava stared at Clint. He raised his bushy eyebrows.

"So? Can you?" He pressed.

She knew there was no way she could say no, considering she had already told him that she was going.

"I guess," Ava said, picking up the envelope and putting it in her bag so she wouldn't forget it.

Clint smiled. "Thanks, doll. I owe you one."

"I'll collect later," she muttered, trying not to roll her eyes.

When the door clicked shut behind him, Sarah groaned. "I swear, sometimes I have to wonder how that dumbass was hired for his position. He clearly has no idea how to run this place."

Ava sighed, leaning back in her chair. "Or he just doesn't care. Either way, we're stuck with him."

Suddenly, Sarah sat up straighter, and her expression turned mischievous as a sly smile slowly spread across her face.

"Well," she started, "since you are going to the gala, why don't you ask Aussie if he wants to go with you? You know, like a date. Make a full night of it." Sarah said, practically bouncing in her seat as if she just thought of the most amazing idea.

Ava laughed softly, shaking her head. "You think so?"

"Absolutely. You said you wanted to go on a date with him, didn't you? And you'll be all dressed up. Oh! And just think, Jarod will be there, and he'll get to see you with your Navy SEAL."

Ava chuckled. But before she could respond, her phone buzzed on the desk. She picked it up and smiled when she saw Aussie's name on the screen.

"Speak of the devil," Ava said, holding up the phone for Sarah to see.

"See, it's fate," Sarah joked.

Ignoring her friend's laughter, she swiped the screen and answered.

"Hey, Aussie."

"Hey, Ava," he said. His warm, deep voice melted her insides. "I hate to bother you, but I could really use your help over at Bear and Jocelyn's place. Well, actually, Nails and I. Think you could swing by?"

Ava glanced at the time. She needed to pick up Christian at school in about thirty minutes.

"Sure," she said into the phone. "What's going on?"

"I'll explain when you get here," Aussie replied. "Just promise you won't laugh too hard."

Ava chuckled, her curiosity piqued. "No promises. I just need to pick up Christian from school, and then I'll be there."

When she hung up, Sarah leaned forward, her grin widening. "So...the SEAL needs rescuing. Guess it's your chance to save the day *and* ask him to go to the gala."

Ava shook her head, laughing. "We'll see." But as she grabbed her coat and headed out the door, her heart was already racing. She was going to see Aussie and ask him out on a date.

ॐ

On the way to Bear's house, Ava swung by the school and grabbed Christian.

"What do you think happened that they needed to call you to help with?" Christian asked her as she pulled her SUV into Bear and Jocelyn's driveway.

"Your guess is as good as mine. Aussie just said that he would explain when I got there. Oh, and I had to promise that I wouldn't laugh."

Christian chuckled. "Well, now I'm curious."

Ava smiled. "Me too. Come on, let's head in."

As she and Christian walked up to the house, she admired the Christmas decorations. The warm white lights decorating the house gave the home a soft glow, giving off a cozy vibe. However, that vibe was quickly shattered the moment she opened the door and was instantly hit by a smell that could only be described as diaper disaster meets biohazard. She scrunched her nose up as she exchanged a knowing look with Christian, who was already pinching his nose, clearly regretting his decision to tag along.

"Here goes nothing," she whispered, holding her breath as they stepped inside.

The first thing she saw was Nails, who was shirtless and appeared freshly showered. He looked as if he'd been through a battle of ages. He was toweling off his hair, and from the faint smell of shampoo, it was clear he'd just survived an emergency decontamination. Aussie stood nearby, smirking, clearly enjoying Nails' suffering.

"Oh my God," Ava laughed, taking in the chaos. "What happened here?"

Nails groaned, gesturing at the scene with an air of resignation. "Let's just say that the explosive poop got everywhere, including me."

Ava couldn't stop her laughter, and even Christian let out a snicker beside her. The scene felt surreal. One tiny baby nearly undid two battle-hardened SEALs.

Just then, Aussie leaned down, catching Ava by surprise as he greeted her with a soft kiss. The warmth of his lips sent a jolt of surprise and happiness through her. The kiss lingered a second too long, and when they broke apart, she could feel the eyes on them.

Nails raised an eyebrow, grinning. "Well, look at that."

Christian, not missing a beat, smirked, folding his arms with a teasing glint in his eyes. "Nice job keeping this little development a secret."

Ava's cheeks burned. "Alright, alright," she said, laughing off the attention. "Can we focus on the matter at hand here? First, let's open some of the windows. I don't care if it's December in Virginia. We need fresh air, stat."

With some reluctance, Nails and Aussie started cracking open windows, letting the cold, crisp air rush in. Ava turned her attention to baby Isadora, who was happily gumming on a shaker toy in her playpen. She was wide awake, clean, and grinning as if she hadn't just caused a biohazard incident.

"Where's her diaper bag?" Ava asked, glancing around.

Nails pointed at the white bag with pink polka-dots by the couch, and she rummaged through it. She was happy when she found the thermometer. Gently, she held it to Isadora's forehead, breathing a sigh of relief when the reading came back normal. "She's fine," Ava said, looking up at the guys. "Nails, did you feed her anything?"

"Yeah," he said, scratching his head. "I gave her some baby food that Duke and Hannah left. It was some green mushy stuff. But I only gave what they said to give her."

Ava laughed. "Well, that's probably what did it. Maybe avoid any more of the 'green mushy stuff' until Duke and Hannah are back." She turned to the guys, adding, "She seems fine, but be sure to let Duke and Hannah know."

"I don't think anybody will miss what happened around here," Nails muttered as he opened up another window.

Meanwhile, Christian had rounded up the other kids, entertaining them with some silly antics until the smell got to be too much for them.

"Alright, we're going upstairs to escape the smell!" Amira announced, holding her nose dramatically as she and Sienna ran up the stairs.

Ava couldn't help but laugh as she watched the girls dart upstairs, trailing giggles behind them.

With the smell thankfully dissipating, she turned back to Aussie and Nails. "Alright, you two. Time to tackle the aftermath." She eyed the remnants of the "disaster zone" on the floor and the walls. She swore that she saw some on the curtain by the front window.

Nails groaned. "I knew you'd say that." He looked toward the kitchen. "The kids still need dinner. Jocelyn left stuff for macaroni and cheese, chicken tenders, and green beans. But," he added quickly, holding up a hand, "I vote that we skip the beans. I can't handle any more poop."

Ava laughed, rolling her eyes. "Deal. Mac and cheese and tenders it is."

She walked into the kitchen and found a mop, some floor cleaner, and disinfectant. She handed it all to Aussie and Nails.

"You guys work on cleaning up the mess, and I'll fix dinner. Oh, and make sure you check the front curtains. I think I saw some poop on it."

With little resistance, the guys began their clean-up efforts, and she got to work in the kitchen. Thankfully, the smell faded to a faint memory as dinner took shape. About twenty minutes later, she set the table and called everyone to the kitchen to eat.

She looked up just as Aussie entered, cradling a now-sleeping Isadora in his arms. Her heart skipped a beat as she took in the scene. He looked like a natural, with the baby resting against his chest.

She blinked, shaking herself out of her little reverie as everyone sat down.

As they started eating, Nails took a moment to thank her. "Thanks for coming, Ava. Really. I don't know how we would've survived without you."

But Ava couldn't take her eyes off Aussie, who was eating while Isadora slept peacefully in his other arm. He looked relaxed, happy—even radiant, and it stirred something deep in her that she hadn't felt before. Her mind wandered to images of him holding their baby in his arms, a thought that both thrilled and startled her.

Holy crap, where did that thought come from?

She looked away quickly and focused on the food on her plate.

Everything seemed calm as the kids whispered and giggled as they munched on their tenders.

That was until Amira, her cheeks smeared with ketchup, turned her bright eyes on Nails.

"Uncle Nails!" she piped up, her tone dangerously curious.

Nails sighed. He was already looking wary. "Yes, Amira."

"Who was your lady friend that was with you last week at Bayside?" Amira asked, her head tilted like she was genuinely trying to solve a puzzle.

"What are you talking about?" Nails asked. Ava could tell he was clearly stalling.

"She wasn't the same girl you were with on Halloween. You know the thick witch—"

Nails spoke up quickly, cutting off the rest of Amira's sentence, and Ava wondered what the reason behind that was.

"How do you know they weren't the same person?" Nails retorted.

Amira looked at him like he was stupid. "Because the Halloween one had really big boobs," she declared, using her hands to emphasize the point.

Ava froze mid-bite, Christian choked on his drink, and Aussie had to cover his mouth with his hand to keep from laughing out loud.

Sienna, sensing an opportunity, jumped in with wide-eyed curiosity. "Do you have a lot of lady friends?"

"What?" Nails asked, looking frightened as two little girls were interrogating him.

"Do you like the one with the big boobs? Or the other one from Bayside?" Sienna asked as she leaned forward, her eyes wide with innocent wonder.

Ava covered her face with her hands, shaking her head, while Christian buried his face in his arms, his shoulders shaking with silent laughter. Aussie was trying his best not to jostle Isadora as he tried to keep his laugh to a minimum.

Nails' face turned bright red as he glared at Aussie. "Are you gonna help me out here?"

"Not a chance," Aussie said between gasps of laughter. "This is too good."

"Why are we talking about this?" Nails groaned, pinching the bridge of his nose. "Can we not?"

But Amira wasn't letting up. "You gotta pick, Uncle Nails! Big boobs or Bayside lady?" Then, her little brown eyes widened as if she had an epiphany. "Or, what about Ms. Vanessa? The lady at the mini golf place who smiles every time you ask her to wash your balls. She nice and pretty."

Ava couldn't take it anymore, and she laughed out loud.

Nails groaned, slumping back in his chair. "This is my nightmare."

Aussie was practically crying at this point. "Cheer up, Nails. At least you've got options, right?"

Nails groaned again, muttering something about needing new friends, while the rest of the table dissolved into another round of laughter.

Once the kids were finished with their dinner, Christian took the kids back upstairs to play, and Nails carefully took Isadora from Aussie's arms. He gave her a wary look. "Alright, little one, no more of that toxic warfare stuff, okay?"

With Nails handling the baby and getting settled in the living room, Aussie lingered in the kitchen with Ava, rolling up his sleeves to help clean up. But as she was about to reach for a dish, he stepped in close, caging her gently against the kitchen island. His face was inches from hers, eyes twinkling with amusement and something else.

"Do you know how hard it was to sit through dinner while you kept staring at me?" he murmured, voice low and teasing.

Ava's cheeks flushed. She tried to look away, but he wasn't having it. He leaned in, brushing his lips over hers in a kiss that was tender, lingering, and left her breathless. She didn't hold back, sinking into the kiss, letting the warmth of it chase away every last bit of embarrassment. But just as things were heating up, they were interrupted by a tiny voice.

"Are you playing the tickle monster game?"

Ava looked up, startled, to see Sienna standing in the doorway. She was eyeing them with all the curiosity of a young child.

Ava looked at Aussie, hoping to get some clarification on Sienna's comment, but she noticed that he was trying, though slightly failing, not to burst into laughter.

Aussie cleared his throat and handed Sienna a couple of juice boxes, but he ignored her question. "Here you go, kiddo. You better hurry back upstairs because I just heard Amira calling for you."

Once Sienna was out of earshot, Ava looked at Aussie.

"What in the world is the tickle monster game?"

Aussie chuckled and then proceeded to explain to Ava how the "tickle monster" game came about.

"Apparently, Sienna walked in on her mom and dad getting a little cozy on the couch one night. Irish told her they were playing the tickle monster game."

Ava's laughter bubbled over. "That was quick thinking. I'll give him that."

"Irish has got his hands full with that one," Aussie admitted, and Ava agreed. Sienna was a little firecracker.

They stood there in the kitchen looking into each other's eyes.

Feeling a little brazen, Ava pushed up on her toes and pressed a soft kiss to Aussie's lips.

Before she could pull away, he wrapped his arms around her waist, pulling her against his body.

"I'm glad I got to see you today," he said, smiling against her lips.

She grinned, feeling the same. "I am, too."

"I guess we better finish the dishes," he said.

She nodded, but really, she wanted to stay wrapped up in Aussie's arms.

He released her, and her heart raced as she went back to washing the dishes. After spending this evening with Aussie, she was ready to take that next step. Before she left, she vowed that she would ask Aussie if he would be her date for the gala.

Aussie leaned against the counter, his hands damp from the dishwater. He could still feel the warmth of Ava's lips against his. He caught himself smiling as he watched her put away a few of the dishes. Being around her had become so natural, and yet, each time they were together, he felt that familiar thrill. The feeling only intensified when he remembered how she'd looked at him while he was holding Isadora.

What would a baby with Ava look like? The thought was quick, unexpected, and made him pause, almost as if he'd crossed some invisible line. They'd only recently decided to take things to the next level. He needed to rein it in—but he couldn't shake that image.

He chuckled to himself, still amused by the memory of Sienna catching them in the middle of a kiss, innocently asking if they were "playing the tickle monster game." The girl had practically become a legend in their circle for that one.

But all joking aside, Aussie felt something stir within him. He had a craving for more than stolen kisses in kitchens and lingering glances.

Ava glanced over her shoulder, a soft, almost shy smile playing on her lips. "I should probably head home. Christian still needs to finish his homework."

Aussie stifled a sigh. The thought of her leaving was like losing the warmth in the room. But he knew she was right. Christian had his studies, and Ava took that role in his life seriously. It was something he admired deeply about her.

"Yeah, don't want to mess with school." He took the last dish and put it away.

As they walked through the living room, they found Nails sprawled on the couch. He was sound asleep with baby Isadora asleep on his chest. Her tiny hand was clutching a fistful of his shirt. Ava stifled a giggle, immediately taking out her phone to snap a picture.

"Tell me that's not the cutest thing you've seen all day," she whispered, holding up her phone.

Aussie chuckled and nodded. "It is pretty damn cute."

"I'm going to run upstairs and get Christian," she said.

"I'll go with you," Aussie replied.

They climbed the stairs, and as they approached Max's room, the murmur of voices caught Aussie's ear. He was about to announce their presence when he heard Amira's voice questioning Christian.

"So, is Ava, like, your *real* mom?" Amira asked, her voice curious but innocent.

Aussie glanced at Ava, whose expression was still, her lips pressed together, her eyes reflecting a hint of vulnerability. She looked nervous.

"No," Christian answered after a brief pause. "But she's the closest thing to a mom I've ever had. So, I kind of think of her as my mom."

Ava inhaled sharply, her hand going to her mouth, her eyes glistening. Aussie placed a comforting hand on her shoulder, gently squeezing, silently letting her know he was there.

The other kids were quick to offer their own experiences, as though this were the most natural thing to talk about in the world. Amira piped up first. "Bear and Jocelyn are our real mom and dad now. They adopted us after they saved us."

"I'm adopted too," Sienna said matter-of-factly. "My real mommy didn't want me, so Uncle Irish and Aunt Bailey adopted me. Now they are my mommy and daddy."

Ava glanced up at Aussie, her face full of gratitude, surprise, and maybe a little wonder. He gave her shoulder another gentle squeeze, pride swelling in his chest as he looked at her, feeling her emotional reaction without her having to say a word.

Finally, Aussie rapped lightly on the doorframe, breaking up the conversation. "Alright, time for you guys to wrap up. Ava and Christian are headed out."

As they said their goodbyes, Aussie walked Ava and Christian to the car, taking their time as they stepped into the brisk December air. Christian climbed into the passenger seat and leaned out, wrinkling his nose playfully. "I don't know if I'll ever recover from that poop smell, Aussie. Like, *ever*."

Aussie laughed, giving Christian a gentle swat on the shoulder. "Hey, you survive one, you're ready for anything."

Once Christian was settled in the car, Aussie turned back to Ava, his gaze soft. "Thanks again for coming over. You saved us."

She brushed it off with a wave, though her smile softened. "I was happy to help. I know you're more used to battlefields than babies."

She hesitated, her expression shy, and then, almost like she was steeling herself, she glanced up at him. "Um, are you, by chance, free next Saturday night?"

Just as he was about to answer and tell her that his schedule was clear, the realization dawned on him that next Saturday was the night of the fundraiser gala. The one he'd agreed to attend undercover with the FBI agent.

His stomach twisted, and he felt a twinge of guilt. "I actually have a work thing that evening."

He could see her disappointment flash across her face, but she forced a small smile, trying to play it off. "Oh, okay. Another time, maybe."

Aussie wasn't about to leave her feeling dejected, not if he could help it. He brushed a hand over her cheek, his voice soft. "If it weren't work-related, I'd cancel it in a heartbeat to be with you. That's a promise."

He leaned down, capturing her lips in a tender kiss, pouring every bit of his apology and affection into it. Her arms looped around his neck, and she kissed him back, her soft sigh the only sound in the still night. He lingered, his hand gently caressing her cheek, savoring the warmth of her mouth against his, the way she pressed close, as though she didn't want to let him go either. When they finally pulled apart, her eyes sparkled, and he could see she believed him.

"I understand," she whispered, nodding. She gave him one last kiss on the cheek before climbing into the car.

Aussie stood back, watching as Ava's car pulled away, a pang of regret settling in his chest. He hadn't wanted to say no to her, not for anything, and watching her drive off left him feeling more than a little frustrated. But he vowed that he'd make it up to her.

CHAPTER FOURTEEN

Saturday arrived, and Ava found herself immersed in a winter wonderland. The Annual Snowball was a vision of winter elegance, capturing the magic of the season with breathtaking decor. Soft blues, crisp whites, and shimmering silver filled the hotel ballroom. Snowflakes of various shapes and sizes hung from the ceiling, casting a delicate glow under the crystal chandeliers. Twinkling lights gave the illusion of gentle snowfall, and tables were draped in white linen with centerpieces of silver branches frosted in faux snow, accented with icy blue glass ornaments.

It was a stunning sight, and Ava couldn't help but feel a little swept up in the beauty of it.

But as she sipped her champagne and walked the room, her dark navy blue gown trailing behind her, she couldn't shake the emptiness of being there alone. She was still a little bummed that Aussie couldn't make it, though she understood he had a job to do. Still, she wished he were here with her, even if just for a dance or two.

As her eyes scanned the room, she offered polite smiles and nods to those who greeted her. She'd barely made it halfway across the ballroom when she felt a hand on her shoulder.

"Ava." A familiar voice greeted her, though it lacked the warmth that once brought a bit of comfort to her.

When she turned, she found Jarod standing there. His tuxedo was perfectly tailored. The smile on his face was overkill.

She forced a polite smile as she tried to tamp down her irritation. "Jarod," she greeted, her tone flat and lacking any excitement.

Ignoring her coldness, he slipped easily into a version of himself she knew well—polished, confident, and slightly arrogant.

"Wow, Ava. You look stunning," he told her as his eyes raked over her body.

"Thank you," she replied. She had no intention to return the compliment.

As the soft music played in the background, an awkward silence settled between the two.

Jarod was the first to speak. "Listen, Ava," he started as he stepped closer. "we really need to—"

"This isn't the place or time to get into that," Ava interrupted, her tone firm but calm. "Clint asked me to give you this." She handed him the sealed envelope, her fingers brushing his briefly before she stepped back, reclaiming her space.

Jarod took the envelope but didn't open it. Instead, his eyes narrowed slightly. "You're leaving already?"

"I only came to make an appearance and to give you that since Clint couldn't make it," she said. "I'll let you get back to the gala." She turned to leave, but his hand closed around her arm, not hard, but enough to stop her.

"Ava, wait," he said, his voice carrying a mix of insistence and something she couldn't quite place.

She stiffened, pulling her arm free with a quick motion. Before she could say anything, a group of men approached, their laughter and conversation cutting through the tension. Jarod turned to them, his expression shifting to one of easy camaraderie.

"Gentlemen, good to see you," Jarod greeted, his tone affable. He pressed his hand against the small of her back as if he had every right to put it there. His possessive touch prickled at her, but she forced herself to remain composed. The last thing she wanted to do was make a scene.

Ava's eyes swept over the group. She recognized a few faces. Some were city officials, and others were donors she'd seen at other events. But there was one man who stood out. He was tall and handsome. But the way his dark eyes were fixated on her made her uneasy.

"Ava," Jarod said, gesturing to the man who hadn't taken his eyes off her, "this is Ezekiel Moore. Ezekiel is an entrepreneur and philanthropist. He owns the largest furniture business in the area."

Ezekiel stepped forward, taking Ava's hand in his and bringing it to his lips.

"It's a pleasure to meet you, Ava," he said, looking into her eyes. His gaze was almost predatory, and his voice dripped with a charm that felt invasive.

She forced a polite smile, gently pulling her hand back. "Likewise."

"We hear that you are involved in social work. What is that like?" Ezekiel asked as he took a sip of his champagne.

Ava was caught off guard by Ezekiel's question. How did he know she was a social worker? But the bigger question was, who was talking about her? She glanced at Jarod and gave him an accusing look. He had to have been the one.

She turned back toward Ezekiel. "Social work can be a rewarding career, Mr. Moore. But at the same time, it is very challenging." She kept her answers brief but professional.

The conversation continued for a few more minutes, but Ava's discomfort grew with every passing second. Finally, as a lull settled over the group, she started to excuse herself.

"Are you leaving so soon?" Ezekiel asked, stepping closer to her. "I was hoping that I could buy you a drink, and we could talk more."

How was she going to get out of this? *Think quick, Ava!*

"I'm afraid that I'll have to decline. But thank you," she told Ezekeil, giving him a big smile.

"Raincheck then?" he pressed.

Oh, damn. This guy is not going to take no for an answer. It was time to pull out the big guns.

"Actually," she said with a small laugh, "I'm seeing someone."

"What? Since when?" Jarod questioned, looking completely shocked, which almost made her laugh.

She smirked. "It's new," she replied with a slight shrug.

Jarod pressed his lips together firmly. She knew he was pissed and wanted to press her on the issue.

Not wanting to stick around any longer, she smiled at the group.

"Well, gentlemen, it was very nice meeting with you all," she said as she took a step back, creating more space between them.

Ezekiel tilted his head, his eyes not leaving hers. "Until we meet again, Ava," he said. His tone carried an unsettling undertone.

With a small smile and a nod, she turned on her heel and moved quickly across the ballroom. Her heart was racing. She needed to get out of there before anybody else stopped her.

Just as she reached the door, she was stopped dead in her tracks. Her feet were literally frozen to the floor. Her heart skipped a beat as she saw Aussie step inside. His tall frame was unmistakable even in the crowd. Relief surged through her. How had he known that she was there? But that relief quickly evaporated when she noticed the woman on his arm.

The woman was stunning, her silver gown shimmering under the chandeliers as she leaned in close to Aussie, laughing at something he said. The sight hit Ava like a punch to the gut. Betrayal and confusion swirled in her mind. Hadn't he said he was working tonight? And yet here he was, looking every bit the perfect date for someone else.

She felt like a vice was squeezing her heart. She turned abruptly, desperate to leave, before he noticed her. But it was too late, as their eyes locked with each other.

Ava's stomach twisted into a ball of knots. The shock on Aussie's face when he saw her was unmistakable, and there was something else—guilt, maybe regret. She looked him straight in the eyes, barely keeping her emotions in check. She willed herself not to cry. There is no way in hell that she would give him the privilege of knowing that he broke her.

"Ava...," he said. Her name rolled off his tongue in a whisper but loud enough that she had heard him.

She looked up at him. "So, this was the 'work thing,' huh?" Her voice was quiet. The hurt veiled beneath a calm exterior.

"Ava, wait—" he started, reaching for her, but she pulled back, swallowing the ache that threatened to break her voice.

"No need to explain, Aussie. I get it." She took a breath, her tone turning colder. "Have a good night."

She turned and walked away, her heart pounding as she waited outside for the valet to bring her car. Her mind raced, hurt morphing into resolve. It wasn't the disappointment she couldn't handle. It was the thought of Christian, and how attached he'd already grown to Aussie. How could she explain this to him? This relationship, just like other relationships in her life, was destined to let her down. She'd taken the chance and had hoped this time might be different. Boy, was she wrong.

The valet brought her car around, and she slid into the driver's seat, exhaling shakily. Then, with a final sigh, she pulled out of the parking lot, ready to put distance between herself and what she'd left behind.

Aussie felt the weight of guilt the moment he stepped into the Annual Snowball on the arm of Agent Elyssa Price.

He knew the job demanded certain things, even bending the line of loyalty if it meant catching the right targets. But tonight felt different. Standing beside Elyssa, dressed to the nines and looking every bit, the part of her date felt wrong. It felt like a betrayal.

"That group is our target for the night," Elyssa murmured softly, nodding in the direction of a cluster of men near the back. Aussie recognized most of the faces from the sheet that the FBI had provided so he could familiarize himself with the ones they were supposed to be observing.

"Got it," Aussie replied, barely keeping his focus on their targets as Elyssa guided him further into the room.

Suddenly, he heard a gasp, and when he turned in the other direction, he saw her. *Ava.* She was standing only a few feet away, looking like something out of a dream.

Aussie felt like the air had been punched out of his lungs. She wasn't just beautiful; she was breathtaking and utterly captivating in a way that made his chest tighten and his pulse quicken. He had always thought she was stunning, even in the simplest of outfits, but seeing her like this was something else entirely.

The floor-length gown she wore was a deep navy blue that shimmered softly under the light. The fabric seemed to flow like liquid as she moved. It draped over one shoulder, leaving the other bare, the asymmetry adding a touch of bold sophistication that was uniquely Ava.

Aussie's gaze traveled down to the train that followed her, subtle yet dramatic, trailing behind her like a whisper. The gown wasn't flashy or overdone—it didn't need to be. It was simple but refined, and it suited Ava perfectly.

It wasn't just the gown itself that struck him. It was how she wore it, with effortless grace and an air of quiet confidence that made his heart pound.

Her black hair was swept to one side. The loose waves cascaded over her bare shoulder, and her makeup was soft, highlighting her natural beauty. But it wasn't just her appearance that had him mesmerized—it was the way she carried herself. Even in a room full of people, she stood out, commanding his attention as if there was no one else around.

Aussie swallowed hard, his throat suddenly dry as Ava's eyes met his across the room. *God, she's incredible,* he thought, unable to tear his gaze away.

As soon as Ava's gaze met his, he knew instantly what she must be thinking. He had told her that he had a work thing, but here he was with another woman on his arm.

His stomach dropped, and he swore under his breath, feeling like the world's biggest jerk. However, he never thought he'd run into Ava.

Then it suddenly hit him. The other day, when they were at Bear and Jocelyn's house, she asked him if he had plans for Saturday. He realized at that moment she had planned to ask him to be her date for this event. Now, he felt even worse.

But what killed him was seeing the mixture of hurt and anger that flashed across her face.

Damn it. She didn't deserve this. And he'd be a fool to think she'd believe his explanation after seeing him here.

"Ava…," he started, but she interrupted him.

"So, this was the 'work thing,' huh?"

Aussie could hear the hurt in her voice even though she did her best to look strong.

He had to explain to her and make her see that it wasn't what she thought.

"Ava, wait—" he said and reached for her. But when she flinched and jerked back, not wanting him to touch her, he felt a crack in his heart.

"No need to explain, Aussie. I get it. Have a good night."

He saw her turn away, her posture stiff as she walked toward the exit. Instinctively, he took a step toward her, desperate to somehow pull her aside and explain without giving away details of the assignment. She wouldn't wait, though. The hurt in her expression was too real, too raw, and he could practically feel her closing herself off to him.

Still, he couldn't help but stare, even as she disappeared through the crowd. She was more than just his girlfriend. She was the woman who had started to make him rethink what he wanted, someone he felt fiercely protective over.

Agent Price noticed his distraction and gently nudged him. "Everything okay?"

Aussie pulled his gaze away from the doors where Ava had vanished, his jaw tightening. "No," he admitted, his voice laced with frustration. "I think I just lost the woman I actually care about."

She raised an eyebrow, understanding dawning in her eyes. "I'm sorry."

He nodded, swallowing the bitterness that settled in his chest. He couldn't afford to let emotions derail the assignment, or Derek would have his ass. "Yeah, me too," he said, steeling himself. "Let's just do what we came here to do."

But as he glanced back at the ballroom doors, all he could think about was the fact that by tomorrow, he might have lost her for good.

Ava stepped through her front door, her heart aching in a way that felt both familiar and bitterly fresh. She'd told herself she could trust Aussie and that maybe he was different. But seeing him at the Snowball with another woman had shattered that fragile trust. She felt like a fool, letting herself get swept up in the hope that maybe, just maybe, someone could care about her without some catch.

The betrayal hurt more than she wanted to admit. She'd set herself up for heartbreak again. If she'd been wiser, she would have kept her distance from Aussie and maintained the walls she'd built to protect herself. Instead, she'd let him in, only to watch him walk into that ballroom with someone else, and the sting of it was cutting deeper than she'd expected. It wasn't just the disappointment. It was the humiliation of believing, even for a moment, that someone like him would truly care.

Taking a deep breath, she promised herself that this was just a setback. She'd bounce back like she always did, stronger and smarter. She didn't need Aussie to feel whole. But the real concern that weighed on her heart wasn't just about herself. It was Christian. He looked up to Aussie. He thought of him as a friend, even a role model. How was she supposed to tell Christian that the person he'd started to trust was no longer part of their lives?

For a moment, she considered keeping everything to herself, at least until she was sure of what to say. Maybe sparing Christian the hurt a little longer would be kinder. But even as the thought crossed her mind, she knew it wasn't fair to him. He needed honesty, and she'd never lied to him before. She'd tell him tomorrow. It was Sunday. Maybe they'd spend it together. She'd find a way to make it feel less like a loss and more like just another step forward.

She sighed as she turned toward the living room, where the soft glow of the Christmas tree illuminated the cozy space. There, curled up on the couch, was Christian, fast asleep. His peaceful expression tugged at her heart as memories of the night they'd decorated the tree with Aussie washed over her. It had felt like a family moment, something she'd never imagined herself being part of until that night. She knelt beside Christian, tucking a blanket around him carefully so as not to wake him.

The weight of the evening seemed to follow her as she finally made her way to her bedroom. She peeled herself out of her dress, leaving it in a heap by the closet, and slipped into the shower, hoping the hot water would wash away the hurt and tension. She scrubbed at her skin as if she could scrub away the memory of Aussie's face, his guilty eyes when she'd caught him with that woman. Her shoulders trembled, but she steadied herself. By the time she stepped out and wrapped herself in her pajamas, she was determined to let this be the last time she'd feel that particular ache.

She climbed into bed and pulled the covers up tight around her. Sleep was elusive, her mind swirling with thoughts of what she'd say to Christian, of how she'd make sure he knew he'd be okay without Aussie. But just as she was finally beginning to drift, her phone pinged from the nightstand.

She reached for it, her heart skipping a beat when she saw Aussie's name flash across the screen. She couldn't do this now, not tonight. Not after the night she'd had. Without reading the message, she placed the phone back on the nightstand and turned away, curling deeper into the blankets and shutting her eyes.

Sleep came eventually, but it was restless, and even in her dreams, echoes of betrayal and regret lingered, blurring with the images of a life she'd once dared to hope for.

CHAPTER FIFTEEN

Aussie leaned back in the creaky armchair in the team's rec room, the familiar hum of the heating system doing little to ease his restless mind. He rubbed a hand over his face, his exhaustion more emotional than physical. Sleep had been elusive after last night's disaster, and the pit in his stomach hadn't eased since Ava had walked away, hurt and angry, thinking he'd betrayed her.

He had tried to text her the moment he got home, typing and retyping a message that he hoped would get her to hear him out.

As of a few minutes ago, the text remained unread. A tiny "delivered" icon mocked him every time he checked his phone. He'd debated calling her, but something about the way she had turned her back on him made him hesitate. Ava didn't walk away unless she was deeply hurt, and he hated that he was the one who caused it.

He had met with Derek earlier that morning to go over the details from the night before. Aussie and Agent Price had managed to strike up conversations with several of the individuals on the Bureau's radar. The men had been polite, careful, and annoyingly vague, offering nothing that set off alarm bells.

Still, something about the night didn't sit right. While none of the conversations screamed "criminal activity" to Aussie, hearing Ava's name on more than one occasion had irked him.

"She's something special," one of the men had said, his tone laced with admiration. *"Smart, gorgeous. A real catch."*

Another man, clearly a bit too drunk, had smirked and leaned toward Jarod, adding, *"And you let her go? Dumb move, buddy. I'd never make that mistake."*

Aussie had to stifle a laugh at the way Jarod's face had tightened in barely concealed irritation. It felt good knowing Ava had told these men she was seeing someone, even if it was up in the air, what she thought about that *now*.

But the casual mention of Ava's name among these men left him unsettled. Was it harmless admiration, or was there something more behind it?

When he'd brought it up with Derek, he had been direct about everything, including the fallout with Ava. Derek had listened intently, his expression thoughtful.

"Give her some time," Derek had said after a long pause. *"Then find a moment to sit her down and explain everything. She's smart, Aussie. She'll see the truth once the dust settles."*

"I don't know if she'll want to hear it," Aussie admitted, his voice low.

"She will," Derek said with quiet confidence. *"And if you need help setting it up, you know I've got your back."*

The offer had meant more to Aussie than he could say, but it still didn't make the weight in his chest any lighter.

Now, as he sat there, the silence of the space pressed down on him. The TV was off, and the usual banter from the team was absent. He felt out of place in his own sanctuary.

Suddenly, the door swung open, and he looked up to see Bear, Joker, and Playboy stride in. They'd been planning a day at the range, and from the looks on their faces, they hadn't been expecting to find him sitting there moping.

"Whoa, Aussie," Bear said, eyebrows raised. "You look like hell. Everything okay?"

Aussie gave a weak smile, though he knew it didn't reach his eyes. "I don't even know where to begin," he admitted as he ran his hand through his hair in frustration.

Playboy leaned against a locker, crossing his arms. "We've got time. Spill it."

Aussie took a deep breath and explained everything that happened, including the part where he was pretty sure Ava was going to ask him to attend the gala with her.

When he finished, Bear's face softened with understanding. "Man, that's rough. I can only imagine what she thought."

Aussie nodded. "Oh, she thought exactly what you're imagining."

"I'm assuming that you've tried to reach out to her," Joker added.

"Yeah, but she isn't answering."

The guys exchanged sympathetic looks, each of them clearly understanding the complications of a job that sometimes required secrecy, even with the people closest to them.

Joker shook his head. "That's a tough break, Aussie. You were just doing your job, but sometimes it can feel like you're on the wrong side of things, especially with the people you care about. And we all know how you feel about Ava."

Aussie felt a pang in his chest and nodded. "Yeah. The hardest part was seeing how she looked at me. It was like I'd betrayed her."

Playboy stepped forward, clapping a hand on his shoulder. "Look, if there's one thing I know about Ava, it's that she's smart and very understanding. She'll understand once you explain. Just keep reaching out to her. She'll see the truth if you keep at it."

Joker joined in with a firm nod. "Playboy's right. This is a tough situation, but once she hears what actually went down, she'll understand. She's been around us long enough to know the job can be complicated."

Aussie looked between his friends, grateful for their support. "I appreciate it, guys. I just don't want to lose her over a situation I couldn't control."

Bear gave him a reassuring nod. "You'll figure it out, man. You've got all of us behind you."

"Thanks," Aussie said, meaning it. He felt a little steadier, the weight of their support helping him cope. The pain of Ava's misunderstanding was still raw, but he felt more determined than ever to set things right.

Aussie's thoughts shifted, his heart catching at the idea of spending the holidays with Ava and Christian. Before last night, he'd actually been considering not going home, instead spending it here and inviting Ava and Christian to join him. They'd started feeling like family—a family he was excited to be part of. But now he wasn't so sure he'd have the chance.

It was difficult for Ava to pull herself out of bed. But she was determined to get past her heartache and move on with life.

After showering and getting ready, she told Christian that she and him were going to spend the day together, which he was very excited about.

She wanted a full day with Christian, one filled with laughter and lots of memories, especially after everything that happened the night before. Her heart felt a little heavier than usual, but she was determined to set aside her pain for his sake.

Their first stop was the indoor mini golf course, decked out with neon lights and decorated with over-the-top winter themes. They each took turns at different obstacles, laughing as they made their way through the course. Christian, with his competitive streak, kept challenging her to beat his score. Ava felt herself relax as they made a game out of trying to "trick shot" around the obstacles, both of them laughing every time the ball ricocheted off the barriers.

Next up was an escape room, something Christian had been excited to try. As they entered the room, he dove right into puzzle-solving mode. They found themselves in a "Pirate's Cove" scenario, hunting for clues to escape a fictional shipwreck. Christian was clever, and he'd noticed clues Ava had missed entirely. Their teamwork paid off as they unlocked the final door with just seconds left on the clock. They high-fived each other, and Ava couldn't help but feel a burst of pride for him.

As they walked out, Christian glanced around, a thoughtful look on his face. "There's actually one thing I've always wanted to do around Christmas," he said, his voice quiet.

Ava looked at him curiously. "Oh yeah? What's that?"

He glanced down at his shoes. "I've always wanted to pick an angel off a Christmas Angel tree. You know, where you pick a name and get gifts for a kid who is in need."

Ava felt a rush of warmth and admiration for him. Even with everything uncertain in his life, his heart was big enough to think about making Christmas special for someone else. She wrapped an arm around his shoulders, giving him a gentle squeeze.

"That's an amazing idea, Christian. Let's do it."

He looked up at her, his eyes lighting up. Ava's heart swelled with love for this boy—no, *her* boy. She realized at that moment that her feelings went beyond the care of a foster parent. She loved Christian, truly, like a mother loves a son. But the thought of him leaving after the holidays made her chest tighten. She'd have to talk with her friend, Judge Holten, to see what her options were. She didn't want to lose him.

They finally found an Angel tree at a nearby shopping center, and Christian carefully examined each of the cards. He picked one for an eight-year-old boy named Jackson. Then, his face lit up with excitement as he turned to Ava. "Look, he has a twin sister! Can we find her card too?"

Ava smiled. "Of course! Let's make sure we get both of them."

They sifted through the cards until they found Jackson's twin sister, Julie. Christian's face beamed with happiness, and they made their way to the nearby stores to get everything on the kids' wish lists. They gathered clothes, shoes, a science experiment kit, a skateboard, and some video games for Jackson, while for Julie, they found a pair of sparkly sneakers, a pink scooter, an art set, and a soccer ball. Ava couldn't help but smile as she watched Christian's enthusiasm as they went from aisle to aisle, his focus completely on making the twins' Christmas perfect.

By the end of the day, they were both exhausted but starving. Christian's eyes lit up as he remembered something. "There's this place, Bayside. I've heard some people talk about it, but I've never been."

Ava smiled, curious herself. "I've heard of it too, but I've never gone either. Let's check it out."

When they pulled into the parking lot, she was a bit skeptical. The outside looked rundown, with peeling paint and faded signage. She glanced over at Christian, who looked just as uncertain.

"Well, I mean, people rave about the food," Christian offered, a small grin on his face.

Ava chuckled. "You know what? You're right. Let's give it a shot. If we don't like it, we can always leave."

When they stepped inside, Ava was pleasantly surprised. The decor was a blend of Chesapeake Bay charm and military tribute, with vintage ship wheels, model boats, and old photos of service members on the walls. The restaurant was bustling for a Sunday evening.

Christian spotted a booth in the back with a view of the water, and they quickly claimed it.

As they settled in and the waitress took their drink order, Ava's phone buzzed, and she quickly silenced it. Aussie's name flashed across the screen, her stomach twisting.

Christian gave her a puzzled look. "That's, like, the fourth time you've done that today. What's going on?"

Ava hesitated. She thought she'd been discreet, but clearly, Christian had noticed. She'd been avoiding thoughts of Aussie all day, but now, she couldn't keep it to herself.

Mustering up all the mental strength she had, she took a deep breath.

"Last night, I ran into Aussie," she said slowly, choosing her words. "And he was with someone else."

"What do you mean he was with someone else? Like one of his teammates?"

Her heart broke more, having to explain this. "No. He was there with another woman. He was on a date."

Christian's face fell, confusion and hurt flickering across his expression. "Wait, what? I don't get it. He said he was busy with work."

"That's what he told me." Ava tried to keep her voice steady.

Christian's fists clenched slightly, his jaw tight. "No way, Ava. There's got to be another reason. Aussie's not like that. He wouldn't do that to you."

Her heart softened at his loyalty, but she knew too well how people could deceive. "I understand why you want to think that, but sometimes people aren't who we think they are."

Christian looked at her, pain etched across his face. "So, what are you going to do?"

She took a deep breath. "I'm going to keep doing what I've always done, Christian. I just keep moving forward. It's all I can do."

Christian was quiet, mulling it over. Finally, he looked back at her, a determined glint in his eye. "I think you should hear him out. I know I'm young, but maybe there's an explanation. Then you can decide."

Ava let his words sink in, touched by his wisdom beyond his years. She realized that maybe, just maybe, he was right. "You might have a point," she admitted, a soft smile tugging at her lips. "I'll think about it."

The waitress returned with their drinks, and Christian grinned as he launched into a new topic, eager to chat about Christmas and school. Ava let the tension ease, feeling a new kind of peace settle in. For tonight, she'd let herself just enjoy their time together. And later, when she was ready, she'd decide what to do about Aussie.

Ava wanted to moan as she took a hearty bite of her French dip sandwich, savoring the warmth of the juicy beef with the melted cheese and tangy au jus. Across from her, Christian grinned as he bit into his massive cheeseburger, trying to hold everything together as the layers of tomato, lettuce, and melted cheddar nearly slipped out.

Everything she had heard about this place was spot on. The food was absolutely delicious. Not to mention the staff was very friendly. She also noticed that there were a lot of military personnel coming in to either grab a bite to eat or hang out.

"Christian," Ava began, smiling, "I'm so proud of you for wanting to pick those two kids off the Angel Tree. You didn't even hesitate. Not a lot of people your age think about others like that."

Christian shrugged, cheeks pinking a bit. "I don't know. I guess I know what it feels like to feel forgotten. And those kids probably have it worse than me. I wanted to help."

Ava's chest ached, touched by his sincerity but saddened by the reminder of what he'd been through. "You're a good person,

Christian. Really. And whatever happens in the future, you deserve to know that."

He nodded but kept his gaze on his food. "We never really did holidays in my foster homes," he admitted, his tone light but distant. "They were mostly focused on the younger kids. And, you know, I was okay with it. I got used to it."

Ava's heart squeezed, and she reached across the table, giving his hand a reassuring squeeze. "This year's going to be different," she said firmly. "We're going to do it right. I mean, we already got the tree. Now, we need to think about baking and decorating cookies, and we will need some wrapping paper to wrap all those wonderful gifts that you picked out for Jackson and Julie. I was also thinking that when Christmas gets a little closer and most people have their decorations up, we could drive around and look at all the lights."

Christian brightened, a hopeful smile breaking through as he took another bite of his burger. Just as they were talking about all the Christmas things they could do together, Ava heard a voice behind her.

"Ava! Christian! Funny seeing you two here."

Ava turned to see Clover, Jocelyn, and Gabby approaching their table. All three of them looked thrilled to see her and Christian. Clover had that usual sparkle in her eyes, Jocelyn wore a warm smile, and Gabby's hand was already on her hip, playfully inquisitive.

"Hi!" Ava said, surprised to see them.

"What have you guys been up to today?" Clover asked, eyes darting between Ava and Christian with an excited energy. Ava felt a twinge in her stomach. She was pretty sure that none of them knew about what had happened last night with Aussie.

"Ava and I spent the day together!" Christian said, looking excited. "We went and played mini-golf and did an escape room. Then we went shopping. Ava, let me pick out some gifts for some kids from an Angel Tree. They were twins."

"That sounds wonderful!" Jocelyn said.

"It was," Ava replied, forcing a cheerful tone. "So, what brings you three in here?"

"Oh, we come here all the time. This is like the hang for the guys. Well, for a lot of military and first responders."

"Really?" Ava asked.

"Yep. It's a little hidden treasure here in Virginia Beach. Mostly, only locals know about it. Plus, they have some of the most amazing food."

Ava smiled. "I'll agree with you about the food. This sandwich is delicious."

"You know, Ava, I never got a chance to thank you for helping Aussie and Nails last week with the kids. Or maybe I should say rescuing Nails. According to Aussie, I heard both you and Christian got a good laugh at Nails' expense. Hell, I still find myself laughing when I think about it," Jocelyn said laughingly.

Ava grinned at the memory of that day. It was fun. Well, until the end, when Aussie had lied to her.

"Hey, what's wrong?" Gabby asked.

When Ava looked up, all three women were looking at her with concerned expressions.

"What do you mean?" Ava asked, looking at the three women.

"You looked lost there for a moment. Like you were sad," Clover said, a frown on her face.

Ugh! Ava really didn't want to get into her and Aussie's situation, but she had a feeling that these women weren't going to back down. Hell, they were probably better interrogators than their men.

She shared a quick glance with Christian, seeing a shared uncertainty in his eyes.

Clover tilted her head, catching on to the silent exchange. "Okay, what's going on?" she asked.

Ava swallowed, glancing at the three women, each of them waiting for her answer. She took a deep breath, deciding to come clean. They would find out sooner or later.

"Umm..things with Aussie and I are a bit complicated right now," she admitted, feeling a tad bit embarrassed.

All three ladies exchanged glances, surprised and concerned.

"What happened?" Gabby asked gently, placing a hand on Ava's shoulder.

Ava took a breath and told them about how she had asked Aussie about his plans for last night, and he told her that he had a work thing.

"Anyway, last night I was at the Snowball, and well…I ran into Aussie there."

"You did?" Gabby questioned, her nose was scrunched up.

"Yeah. And he wasn't alone. He was with another woman."

Clover's mouth dropped open. "No. Way. Are you serious?"

Jocelyn's brows knitted together. "Did he say anything to you when you saw him?"

"He tried, but I was too upset, so I left," Ava explained, trying to keep her voice steady. She was quiet for a few seconds, thinking about about that exact moment when she saw the other woman. "She was beautiful," Ava whispered, looking at the women.

Gabby's eyes narrowed, a mix of sympathy and confusion. "I don't get it. Aussie doesn't seem like the type to do something like that."

Clover crossed her arms, visibly upset. "He told you he had a work thing, and then he shows up with another woman? That doesn't sound right."

Before Ava could answer, Christian spoke up, his voice steady and clear. "That's what I told her, too. I think there has to be an explanation. Aussie wouldn't do that. I know he wouldn't."

Gabby nodded, supporting Christian. "Ava, maybe it's worth hearing what he has to say."

Clover, however, still looked like she was about to march out and confront Aussie herself. "I don't like it, though. He owes you an explanation, no question about it."

The three women looked at her with earnest eyes, urging her to at least give Aussie a chance to explain. They promised her that no matter what, she and Christian were still part of their group.

Ava offered a faint smile. "Thank you. Right now, I just want to focus on enjoying the holidays with Christian."

"Well, if you need anything or just want to talk, you have our numbers," Jocelyn said.

Ava nodded, grateful for their support but unsure if she'd truly she would ever call them. It was nice to know they'd be there if she needed them, but they didn't understand that being around them would make her think of Aussie, and thinking about him made her heart hurt. At least, right now, it did. Maybe that would change with time.

CHAPTER SIXTEEN

Jarod leaned back in his plush leather chair. His fingers were steepled as he watched Ezekiel pace across the polished floor of his office. The courthouse buzzed faintly outside the closed doors, a constant reminder of the delicate balance Jarod maintained between his public persona and his shadowed alliances.

Ezekiel stopped near the window, his gaze fixed on the cityscape outside. "The kids," he began, his voice smooth yet laced with authority. "How are we doing there?"

Jarod smirked, a hint of pride seeping into his tone. "Handled. The ones that got picked up? I saw to their cases personally. They were given a slap on the wrist, a few lectures, and then sent back to their foster homes. Most of those parents don't give a shit what they're up to, anyway."

Ezekiel chuckled darkly, turning to face Jarod. "Good. The last thing we need is any of them running their mouths. These kids may be useful, but they're still kids. We don't need them putting the rest of us at risk."

Jarod nodded, leaning forward to rest his elbows on the desk. "They're scared enough of you to stay quiet. Besides, the system doesn't exactly make it easy for anyone to dig too deep. No one's going to care if a couple of foster kids mess up and get sent back to their so-called homes."

Ezekiel studied him for a moment, then shifted topics so abruptly that it caught Jarod off guard.

"The woman that you introduced me to at the gala, Ava Morgan."

The mention of her name made Jarod sit up a little straighter, and his jaw tighten. "What about her? he said flatly.

Ezekiel grinned, a predatory edge to his expression. "She is one gorgeous woman."

The flare of anger that rose in Jarod was immediate, hot, and unbidden. His lips pressed into a thin line, and he fought to keep his composure. "Ava's business isn't relevant to what we're doing."

Ezekiel raised a brow, clearly enjoying the reaction he'd provoked. "Are you sure about that?"

Jarod's hands curled into fists under the desk. "She's not a problem," he said, his voice cold. "She doesn't know anything."

Ezekiel's smirk faded, replaced by a calculating look. "When were you going to tell me that Christian was living with her?"

Jarod froze, his mind scrambling to assess how much Ezekiel already knew. "How do you know that?"

"Doesn't matter," Ezekiel said dismissively. "What does matter is that I assigned Chase and Barrett to recruit the kid."

"So, tell them to back off," Jarod suggested.

Ezekiel shot him a cold glare. "It's not that easy. They've already made contact with him. This complicates things. You know how clean I like my operations, Jarod."

Jarod nodded, though a small, vindictive part of him relished seeing Ezekiel rattled.

Ezekiel's voice turned sharper. "I've got enough on my plate steering the FBI away from me. They've been sniffing around, but so far, they've got nothing. I don't need any hiccups because some snot-nosed kid goes running to Ava and opens his mouth. I would hate for something to happen to Ms. Morgan."

"I get it," Jarod said smoothly, masking his irritation. "Just tell Barrett and Chase to back off."

Ezekiel studied him for a moment longer before nodding. "I plan to. In the meantime, I'd like you to find out if she knows anything."

"How in the hell do I do that when she won't speak to me?"

Ezekiel grinned wickedly. "You're a smart man. Figure it out. And do it quickly."

With that, he turned and strode out of the office, leaving Jarod alone with his thoughts.

The silence in the room felt heavy, the earlier conversation playing on a loop in his mind. Ava. Christian. Ezekiel's veiled threats.

Jarod stood, walking to the window and staring out at the city below. He couldn't stop himself from thinking about her—how she was doing, if she was still angry at him for everything that had happened between them. His thoughts drifted to the night of the gala when she announced that she was seeing someone. Hearing that had not only shocked him, but it enraged him. The idea of her being with someone else made his stomach churn, though he couldn't decide if it was jealousy or something darker.

After a moment of internal debate, he made a decision. Grabbing his coat, he headed for the door.

He'd take a break from the chaos Ezekiel had stirred up and focus on something else. He'd find Ava, take her to lunch, and see if he could figure out where her head and her heart were.

CHAPTER SEVENTEEN

Ava was hunched over her desk. There was a faint crease in her brow as she scanned through reports, updating notes and timelines on her cases. It had been two weeks since the Snowball event, two weeks of dodging calls, texts, and every attempt Aussie made to reach her.

Several times, she almost answered. She missed him—a lot, and the connection they'd started to build. But every time her phone rang with his name flashing on the screen, a wall of bitterness, pride, and something raw kept her from picking up.

The memory of him with that woman still stung, and it brought her back to every betrayal she'd endured growing up. She'd sworn she wouldn't allow herself to be fooled again—not by anyone, especially not by a man she was beginning to care about.

She hated how the situation with Aussie was affecting Christian, too. He was trying to hide it, but she could see his disappointment. He moped around the house, half-heartedly engaging in his usual routines, clearly missing the friendship he'd developed with Aussie. And while Christian never directly asked about him, she could feel his unspoken questions hanging in the air.

Ava swallowed the guilt building in her throat and sighed, focusing harder on her screen to push everything else out of her mind.

She heard the door to her office open, and when she looked up, she was surprised to see Clint standing in the doorway, holding a few files in his hands.

She hadn't seen nor heard a peep from him since that time she saw him before the Snowball when he asked her to give Jarod that envelope.

"You're back. We were all getting ready to send a search party out for you."

Clint smirked. "Funny. I got tied up at my parent's place. But I'm back now."

She raised an eyebrow, giving him a pointed look. "What's that?" she questioned, pointing to the files in his hand.

"We have three new kids," he said matter-of-factly.

Ava blinked. "Three new kids?" she asked, incredulous. "Clint, we barely have space as it is. We don't even have enough placements for the kids we already have." She motioned to her own file cabinet, which was brimming with folders.

Clint's eyes shifted, a flash of something unreadable crossing his face before his usual hard expression returned. "There's nothing I can do. Just go over the files and work on finding placements. They'll be arriving after the first of the year."

Ava's mouth dropped open. Clint could be brash, but this was a new level. She'd never seen him this edgy. He looked almost nervous.

But then, as if flipping a switch, he plastered on a smile. "Speaking of which, how's Christian doing?"

The question caught her off guard. Clint had never shown interest in her personal life before. Ava regarded him suspiciously, still unsure what to make of this strange mood. "He's good," she said slowly. "Keeping busy with school and the holidays."

"Good, good," Clint replied, his demeanor unsettlingly cheerful. "So, where are you going for lunch?"

Ava blinked again, her side-eye probably sharper than she meant it to be. "Just the deli around the corner."

He nodded, smiling a little too brightly as he headed toward the door. "Enjoy. See you when you get back."

She watched him disappear down the hallway, suspicion simmering in her mind. Shaking her head, she grabbed her coat and purse.

The brisk walk to the deli gave her some clarity. She needed to finish shopping for Christian's Christmas presents. She mentally cataloged what she still needed to buy. There was a pair of black *Vans* that he had his eye on, a few military books he saw when they were shopping the other day and a few other items.

By the time she reached the deli, her mind was buzzing with holiday lists. She ordered a turkey sub with a sweet tea and found a small table in the back corner. She was glad for a quiet moment away from everything.

Just as she unwrapped her sandwich and took a deep breath, she looked up to see Jarod standing in front of her, his expression one of mild surprise.

"Ava? Didn't expect to see you here," he said, pulling out the chair across from her before she could respond.

She clenched her jaw, irritation simmering beneath her polite smile. She'd been hoping for a quiet lunch alone, but apparently, that wasn't going to happen.

"So," he started, leaning back with a casual smile, "how have you been?"

"Fine," she replied, picking up her sandwich in the hope that he'd get the hint.

"I haven't seen you since the Snowball," he continued, oblivious to her tone.

"I've been busy with work and Christian," she said, biting into her sub.

"So, what've you been up to?"

She raised her eyebrow. "Like you care?" she replied, wanting to roll her eyes.

"Come on, Ava. I'm trying here." He leaned forward and lowered his voice. "Look, I know I fucked up. I'm sorry. But I do really care about you. I hate the fact that we can't even have a conversation."

Ava sighed, deciding that maybe answering him would get him to leave. "Christian and I have been doing a lot of holiday stuff. Decorating, baking. Just keeping ourselves busy."

She noticed his slight frown at the mention of Christian, but he quickly masked it. She knew he didn't approve of her decision to foster the teenager, and a small part of her enjoyed his discomfort. Still, he seemed to weigh his next question carefully.

"How's he doing?" Jarod asked, his voice neutral but curious. "What kind of activities does he like?"

Ava's gaze narrowed. Jarod rarely showed interest in Christian, so his questions felt off. "He's been doing great," she said cautiously, wondering why he was suddenly so curious.

Jarod smiled but didn't respond, letting silence linger between them. Ava tapped her fingers on her cup, growing increasingly uncomfortable. More than anything, she wanted to wrap her sub up, take it back to the office, and finish it there.

Then, unexpectedly, Jarod cleared his throat. "Listen, Ava, I was thinking…" He leaned forward, his expression almost apologetic. "Maybe we could go out again? I know our last date didn't end well, but I'd like a chance to redeem myself."

Ava blinked, taken aback. Before she could respond, a warm pressure settled on her shoulders, grounding her, and she felt a familiar strength radiate through her.

Turning her head, she found herself looking up into Aussie's intense, hazel eyes. His facial expression was unreadable, but his presence was undeniable. Her heart skipped, and her emotions whirled between relief, shock, and an ache she didn't want to acknowledge.

Aussie pulled his truck into a parking spot across from the deli and shut off the engine. He and Snow had just finished dropping off some gear at Dam Neck before heading back to the SEAL base.

Lunchtime had rolled around, and Aussie couldn't stop thinking about the deli nearby that was famous for its Italian subs, the kind loaded with layers of meat and topped with a house-made dressing. Snow had readily agreed, and they were both hungry enough to stop for a quick bite.

The deli was bustling when they stepped inside. Aussie took in the familiar atmosphere. The walls were lined with old photos and quirky trinkets, and the scent of fresh bread and herbs filled the air.

They walked up to the counter and placed their orders, both of them going for the Italian subs. As they waited, Aussie's gaze naturally drifted around the room, instinctively scanning exits and taking in every face in the place. It was an old habit from years of being a SEAL.

His eyes swept the room, pausing when they fell on a figure sitting near the back, her back to him. He didn't need to see her face to recognize her. *Ava.* He'd know her anywhere. A wave of emotions hit him, surprising in its intensity.

He hadn't seen her since the gala despite his attempts to reach out to her. The image of her at the Snowball, her hurt and confusion at seeing him with Agent Price, flashed in his mind.

Snow nudged him, catching Aussie's look. "Is that Ava?" he asked, his eyes flicking between Aussie and Ava. "And who's that guy with her? Looks like a lunch date."

Aussie's chest tightened. Was she moving on? He tried to push the thought away, but it lingered, sour and unwelcome. He leaned forward, studying the man across from her. That's when it clicked. He recognized the guy. The same guy she'd walked out on during a dinner date a few weeks ago.

He also recalled seeing him at the Snowball. He had been hovering around a few of the individuals the FBI was quickly investigating.

He watched the pair for a minute. It seemed like Ava might be giving him the cold shoulder, though Jarod's expression looked somewhere between annoyed and desperate.

Over the past two weeks, Aussie had missed her more than he could admit, even to himself. He'd tried focusing on work, drowning himself in tasks and training to keep his mind off Ava. But it was impossible. She was everywhere in his thoughts. And not just her, but Christian too. A few days ago, he'd texted the kid, keeping it casual, and while Christian's response had been brief, at least he'd replied.

But now, watching Jarod lean forward, his expression turning darker, Aussie felt a surge of protectiveness. Jarod's face was tight, an edge of frustration in his posture, and Aussie couldn't stand by and watch any longer.

Aussie strode forward, weaving through the tables until he was directly behind Ava. Gently, he placed his hands on her shoulders. He felt her startle, her muscles tensing at the unexpected contact, but as soon as she glanced up and met his gaze, he saw her relax. There was something in her eyes—relief, maybe even gratitude—that eased his own tension. She looked as surprised as he felt, and the flicker of warmth in her eyes made his pulse quicken. He barely registered Jarod's glare. The only person he cared about here was Ava.

"Hey," he said, his voice low. "Everything okay?"

Ava straightened, gathering her composure. "Yes," she replied, but her voice was firmer than before. "Actually, I was just leaving."

Jarod's mouth tightened. "You're really going?" he asked, his tone sharpening with irritation. It was clear he wasn't expecting her to cut the lunch short.

"Yes, Jarod, I am." She didn't even hesitate.

Aussie hid his grin as he watched Jarod's face redden with anger. This guy clearly had no idea when to back off. Ignoring Jarod's glare, Aussie took Ava's coat off the back of her chair, holding it out for her as she slipped her arms into the sleeves. He felt an unexpected sense of satisfaction when she didn't argue or hesitate but accepted his presence as if she appreciated it.

"I'll walk you out," he offered, his voice steady.

Ava gave him a small nod, and her expression softened. "Thanks."

"Go on," Snow called from the counter, waving him off. "I'll grab the food."

With Ava by his side, Aussie led her toward the door. Even as they walked away, he could feel Jarod's eyes boring into his back, but he didn't care. The world could fall apart around them, but right now, his focus was on the woman next to him.

As Ava stepped outside the deli with Aussie, a wave of relief washed over her. She couldn't help but be thankful he'd shown up when he did. Jarod had been grating on her nerves, not taking a hint that their dating stint was over. She'd been seconds away from saying something she'd regret, and Aussie had saved her from it. Now, having him by her side brought back a flurry of emotions she'd been trying to bury. Seeing him again felt a little overwhelming.

Once they stopped on the sidewalk, Ava turned to face him. She caught her breath, hesitating, before softly saying, "Thank you, Aussie. Really."

He chuckled. That familiar, warm sound made her chest ache. "Anytime, Ava. You looked like you needed the rescue," he teased, a grin lifting the corners of his mouth.

They both went quiet, the air between them thick with things unsaid. It was as if both of them were weighing what to say, and both were afraid to be the first to speak. Finally, Aussie cleared his throat, his expression turning serious.

"Do you have a few minutes?" he asked, his voice low. "I'd like to talk."

Ava nodded, even as a pang of nerves stirred in her stomach. "Yeah, of course."

Aussie took a deep breath, glancing away before meeting her gaze with a look so earnest it almost hurt to see. "I've missed you, Ava," he began, his voice rough around the edges. "I've missed you and Christian more than I thought was possible. If I could go back to the night of the Snowball, I would've followed you out right then and told you the truth." He paused for a moment and then continued. "I can't go into detail because it's classified. But I swear to you, Ava, I would never betray you or Christian. I was there that night because of my job—nothing more, nothing less. And these last two weeks..." He shook his head as if searching for the right words. "I've been miserable without you."

Ava felt her throat tighten, her heart dipping as she realized that Christian and Clover were right. She hadn't even given him the chance to explain. All the missed calls, the messages she'd ignored, letting her past fears get the best of her.

He laughed softly. "Even Clover showed up at my place to give me hell about it all."

Ava managed a small smile, feeling foolish for shutting him out so completely. "I'm sorry, Aussie. I should've taken your calls and given you a chance to explain."

But before she could continue, Aussie gently shook his head and pulled her into his arms, wrapping her in a hug so comforting, so steady, that she melted against him. She could feel the tension from the last two weeks slip away, the hurt and confusion fading in the warmth of his embrace. She let herself relax, breathing in his familiar scent, allowing herself a moment of peace she'd been denying for days.

When she finally looked up at him, their eyes met, and a quiet happiness bloomed inside her. Aussie's gaze softened, his hands resting at her waist, and without a second thought, she leaned up and kissed him, letting all the feelings she'd been holding back pour into that single, gentle moment.

Jarod clenched his fists, watching through the deli's front window as Ava walked away with that man. She'd barely glanced back, leaving him in the middle of the deli like he was nothing.

His jaw clenched as he seethed, eyes fixed on the two of them, now standing close on the sidewalk. Of course, he couldn't hear what they were talking about, but Jarod didn't need to know what they were saying to feel the betrayal burn.

Jarod wondered if this was the guy Ava said she was seeing. Judging from the uniform, Jarod knew he was in the military. That surprised him. He never saw Ava as someone who was interested in military men. Though the guy probably used his charm and muscles to make her turn her head. Jarod bristled as his lips curled in disdain. Ava deserved more than that. She deserved someone with power and influence. She needed someone who could actually protect her and who knew how to move in her world.

And yet, here she was, leaning into this stranger. It was infuriating to watch. Every little laugh, every glance they exchanged twisted something deep inside him. But then he saw her turn toward the guy, her hand resting gently on his shoulder as she looked up at him, and a spark of anger jolted through him. They were too close, far too close. He could see the softness in her expression, the warmth she was giving this man that she should have been giving him.

Then, he saw her tip her face toward the man's, and his stomach dropped. She was kissing him. Right there on the street.

A flash of red clouded his vision as he watched them, his fists clenching harder until his nails bit into his palms. He was barely aware of the people passing him, their curious glances as he stood like a statue in the deli, his eyes fixed on Ava and that man.

Ava is mine, he thought fiercely. *She's always been mine.*

The military guy was nothing. He was just a passing phase, someone who'd vanish when he had to ship out for duty again. Meanwhile, Jarod was stable, someone she could actually count on. He had a reputation, respect, and a place in this town that would last. What did this man have that Jarod didn't? Sure, he had the good looks and the swagger, but that was just surface stuff. Eventually, Ava would see through that. She would realize what she was missing with him, and by then, this man would be long gone.

But even so, the sight of them together felt like a slap. He could almost hear her laughing at him, dismissing him as if he were no one. His blood simmered. *No. No one was going to stand in his way. Not this guy. Not anyone.*

When Ava and the man finally broke apart and turned to walk down the sidewalk together, Jarod's eyes tracked them, his mind spinning with a new determination. He'd have to find out more about this military guy. He needed to figure out his weaknesses, how he'd gotten so close to Ava so quickly. This wasn't over. He wasn't about to lose Ava to anyone, least of all a man who wouldn't last.

CHAPTER EIGHTEEN

Christian had a bad feeling when he entered school that morning and saw Barrett and Chase lingering in the hallway. He hadn't spoken to them since the last encounter he had with them. Throughout the day, he managed to avoid running into them between classes because he took a different way to his classes.

Now, as he walked toward his last class of the day, he tensed seeing the pair standing near an exit. Their eyes were searching the crowd of rowdy teenagers as if they were looking for someone. His pulse quickened, but he kept his gaze forward, pretending he hadn't seen them. He should've known they wouldn't let him slip by.

"Christian," Barrett called, voice low but sharp. He gripped Christian's shoulder. Chase smirked beside him, both guys closing in as they nudged him toward the door. Christian swallowed hard, his hands instinctively clenching. He wouldn't fight, not here and not now, but every instinct was screaming at him to run.

"Let's have a little talk outside," Chase said, shoving Christian's shoulder to steer him through the door and out into the narrow, secluded area between the school building and the gym. The sun was already dipping behind the roofline, casting a shadow over the cracked pavement.

They stopped and spun him, pressing his back hard against the rough brick wall. He could feel the tension coiling in his muscles, every instinct telling him to fight back, to push them off, to swing a fist and defend himself. But he knew better. He was outnumbered, and Barrett and Chase, well, it was a safe bet they were armed.

Barrett leaned in close, sneering. "So, you had enough time to think about our offer?"

Christian lifted his chin, trying to keep his voice steady. "Yeah, I have. And it's the same as before. Gang life isn't for me."

Chase let out a sharp laugh, clearly unimpressed. "Not the answer we wanted, Christian."

A sudden punch to his stomach doubled him over. The air left his lungs in a rush. Before he could recover, Chase drove another fist into his side. His ribs screamed in pain, but he forced himself not to cry out.

"Just be glad we're at school," Barrett hissed, his face close enough that Christian could smell the stale scent of cigarettes on his breath. "Otherwise, we wouldn't let you leave here until you agreed to come work with us."

Christian's whole body was tense, but he refused to show weakness. He forced himself to breathe through the pain, not letting them see that he was in pain. He glared at both of them. "You guys done yet?"

Barrett sneered, tilting his head in mock disappointment. "No, not quite. See, since you still don't want to cooperate with us, we're going to have to go about this another way."

Christian felt a cold weight settle in his gut, but he didn't look away. "What? You're gonna kill me?"

"Oh, no," Chase replied, the cruel twist of his smile sending a chill down Christian's spine. "But we know all about that pretty lady that's taking care of you."

Christian's blood ran cold. "What are you talking about?"

Barrett smirked, "What's her name? Oh, yeah. Ava Morgan. Our boss even has his eye on her. He's got plans for her. She'll be begging for mercy by the time he's done with her."

Christian's fists clenched tight as they laughed. He could barely breathe. He felt as if his heart was being crushed inside his chest. Ava had done everything to save him from the life he'd come from. She was innocent. She was his rock, his safe place. And now, these monsters wanted to tear that apart. Every part of him wanted to lash out, to defend her, to do *something*. But he forced himself to stay still, trapped in their twisted web.

Chase pulled his arm back, fist aimed to strike again when the door behind them swung open. A teacher stepped outside, catching all three boys in the act. Christian straightened, wincing, his ribs still aching.

"What's going on here?" the teacher asked, frowning as his gaze landed on Barrett and Chase's hostile postures.

Chase was quick to flash a fake smile. "Nothing, sir. Just a little chat with our friend here."

The teacher's gaze lingered, doubtful. "Get back inside, all of you. Now."

Barrett and Chase threw Christian one last threatening glare before slipping past the teacher and heading inside. Christian tried to school his face, hiding the pain as the teacher turned to him.

"Is everything alright, Christian?"

He hesitated, throat tight. "Yeah. Everything's fine."

But as he watched the teacher's concerned expression fade, Christian knew he was lying. He couldn't keep this to himself. He had to tell Ava. But then what? How could he drag her into this danger? He didn't want to scare her, and the last thing he wanted was to make her a target.

Then he thought of Aussie. He might be the hope needed to keep both him and Ava safe. However, Ava and Aussie weren't speaking. Even though Christian had to believe that he'd step up if he knew how serious this was.

He looked down at the ground and saw that his phone was shattered, thanks to Chase. The problem now was getting a hold of Aussie.

He then remembered Bayside, the restaurant where he and Ava had grabbed lunch the other day, when they ran into Jocelyn, Clover, and Gabby. He remembered Clover saying that the team hung out there. Maybe he could find someone there who'd help him get a message to Aussie.

Pulling his backpack over his shoulder, Christian gritted his teeth, gripping his side. He walked out of the school and headed toward the bus stop. He fumbled through his pocket for the few bucks he'd need for the fare.

About twenty minutes later, Christian stepped off the bus a block from Bayside. He glanced over his shoulder as he walked. His nerves were already on edge, but the uneasy feeling that Barrett and Chase might've followed him kept him hyper-aware of every shadow and sound. He told himself they wouldn't be this bold. They wouldn't try anything in broad daylight. But the threat of what they'd promised haunted him. And Ava was still at work, probably going about her day without any idea of the danger she was in. This had to be the right thing, going to Aussie, but Christian couldn't shake the feeling that maybe he was only dragging more people into this mess.

When he reached Bayside, he stepped inside and looked around. It was a lull between lunch and dinner, with only a few customers scattered around the tables. Music played from the jukebox, and clinking dishes settled some of his nerves. He looked around, recognizing the familiar layout but somehow feeling out of place.

A woman with dark, shoulder-length hair glanced up from behind the bar. She gave him a welcoming smile and walked over, her friendly expression easing his tension a bit.

"Hey there, can I help you with something?" she asked, her tone warm and welcoming.

Christian shifted his backpack, the ache in his ribs flaring up again. He winced involuntarily, and her gaze sharpened as she took in his discomfort.

"You okay?" she asked, concerned.

He swallowed, nodding slowly. "I was hoping to find someone I know. Or maybe someone who knows how to reach him."

Her brow lifted with mild curiosity. "Well, I'm one of the owners here. Maybe I can help. Who are you looking for?"

Christian hesitated, glancing around and lowering his voice as he leaned in slightly. "I'm looking for a guy named Aussie. He's a SEAL."

She blinked, her expression shifting to something between surprise and recognition. He could tell instantly that she knew exactly who he was talking about, though she tried to keep her face neutral.

"How do you know Aussie?" she asked a hint of caution in her voice.

Christian's shoulders relaxed a bit, and he offered a small, uneasy smile. "My foster mom, Ava. She knows Aussie, and I met him and his team at a college fair last month. I actually had his number, but my phone got broken earlier today at school. And it's really important that I talk to him."

The woman studied him for a moment before nodding. "Alright," she said, her voice softer. "Follow me."

She led him to a small two-seater table near the bar and gestured for him to sit. Her kindness helped settle some of his nerves as she smiled and offered, "Can I get you a soda or maybe something to eat?"

Christian's cheeks flushed slightly. "I, uh, I don't really have any money on me."

She waved it off with an easy smile. "A friend of Aussie's is a friend of mine. Don't worry about it."

Surprised, he couldn't help but ask, "So, Aussie's really your friend?"

Her smile widened. "Yes, he is." There was a flicker of something cautious in her gaze, but she continued with the same kindness. Handing him a menu, she added, "Take a look, and I'll go see if I can get in touch with him. Oh, and I'm Arianna, by the way."

Christian glanced down at the menu but wasn't sure he could actually eat. His stomach felt tight with worry. Still, he nodded as she left, returning a moment later with a glass of Coke.

She set it down in front of him, giving him an encouraging smile. "I couldn't get a hold of Aussie directly, but I was able to reach someone who can."

He looked up, relieved. "Should I wait here? Or should I go?"

"Stay put," she said with a reassuring smile. "What would you like to eat?"

Even though hunger was the last thing on his mind, he could use some food in his stomach. "Um, maybe just a munchie basket? The one with fries, onion rings, mozzarella sticks, and chicken tenders?"

"Coming right up," she said, her friendly smile easing some of his worry.

Christian watched her walk away and then took a sip of the Coke, the cold fizz numbing some of the tension in his throat. He waited, tapping his fingers on the edge of the table.

A few minutes later, Arianna returned with his food, setting the basket in front of him with a gentle smile. She gave him a small nod and then moved back to the bar, keeping herself occupied while he picked at the food. It was the first thing he'd eaten since breakfast.

A little while later, the front door opened, and a man stepped in. He was dressed in a Navy working uniform. Christian's breath caught as he watched the man scan the room, his gaze finally landing on Arianna. She shot him a knowing smile and pointed toward Christian's table.

The man walked over, his face calm but focused. Christian felt a surge of both relief and nervousness as the man stopped at his table, offering a firm but kind smile.

"You must be Christian," he said, his voice low and steady. "I'm Commander Derek Connors. I heard you were looking for Aussie."

Christian nodded, his heart pounding. Here was his chance. This was someone who could help him, someone who might be able to protect Ava, too. And as he looked into Commander Connors' steady gaze, he felt, for the first time since his encounter with Barrett and Chase, that maybe he wasn't alone in this after all.

Derek parked his truck outside Bayside, turning off the engine as he mulled over Arianna's unexpected call. It wasn't often she reached out, and even less often to discuss anything urgent. But her voice had held a tone of quiet concern, and he hadn't missed her hesitation as she explained that a young boy named Christian had come in looking for Aussie. The skittish part had thrown him a bit, though he supposed it wasn't surprising given the rumors about what that kid had gone through.

Of course, Derek knew who Christian was. He also knew plenty about Ava, the woman Aussie had been seeing. Thinking back, Derek felt a familiar pang of sympathy for Aussie and everything that had unraveled during the Snowball. He knew that it had affected Aussie significantly, and he'd been patient, waiting for the right time to talk to her and explain why he was there.

As he stepped through Bayside's door, his eyes immediately caught Arianna's across the room. She gave him a subtle nod toward a table near the bar, where a young boy sat alone, sipping a soda. Derek followed her gaze, noting the boy's tense posture and the way his eyes darted up to meet his. Christian looked wary, a little on edge. Derek knew he could sometimes come across as intimidating, and he made a mental note to soften his approach.

When he neared the table, he offered a warm smile and extended his hand.

"You must be Christian. I'm Commander Derek Connors. I heard you were looking for Aussie."

Christian's eyes widened a little as he processed that Derek wasn't just any friend of Aussie's but his CO. Derek fought a smile as Christian quickly stood, introducing himself with a firm handshake. The kid had some good manners, that was for sure.

"It's nice to meet you, Sir," Christian said as he sat back down.

Derek eased into the seat across from him, making small talk to settle Christian's nerves. "Aussie's caught up with a few things right now, so I came in his place. Arianna made it sound like it was urgent."

Christian shifted uncomfortably, looking a little guilty. "I'm sorry for bothering you, sir. I wouldn't have tried to find him if it wasn't really important."

Derek nodded, sensing the boy's anxiety radiating off him in waves. "I get it, Christian. That's what we're here for. Do you want to tell me what happened? Maybe I can help."

Christian glanced away, his hands gripping his soda. For a moment, Derek thought he might clam up, but then Christian blurted out, "It's Ava. I think she's in trouble."

Derek's brows drew together, his attention sharpening. "Ava? What kind of trouble?"

Christian took a shaky breath and launched into an explanation, telling Derek about two boys from his school. Their names were Barrett and Chase. He spoke quickly, explaining how they'd approached him a few weeks back, asking him to join their "club."

He didn't need to say much more so that Derek could know what kind of "club" they were running.

"And today," Christian continued, his voice shaking. "Today, they cornered me again. Pushed me out one of the side doors where no one could see us. They told me I needed to make a decision, said I've had enough time to think it over."

Derek clenched his jaw as Christian recounted the threats, the warnings, and how they hit him. And then, with a shaky breath, Christian dropped the bombshell. "They threatened Ava, sir. They said if I don't join, they'll go after her. They told me their boss had his sights on her." He paused for a minute and took a breath. "They said that she would be begging for mercy by the time he was done with her."

Christian's voice wavered, his whole body tense, and Derek could see the struggle the boy was going through just to keep himself together.

"Christian." Derek's voice was firm but calm, reaching out a steady hand to him. "Listen to me. Nothing is going to happen to Ava or you. I promise you that."

Christian exhaled, looking at Derek with a blend of relief and uncertainty.

Derek leaned back, his mind running through the situation with laser focus. His thoughts went to the current investigation the FBI was conducting on the gang activity. It was possible, Derek realized with a surge of urgency, that Barrett and Chase weren't just idle troublemakers. They could be linked to the very gang the FBI and police were looking into.

He shot off a quick text to Aussie.

Derek: *Got a situation with Christian. Meet me at Bayside ASAP.*

He got a reply back immediately.

Aussie: *On my way. Be there in 15.*

Derek tucked his phone back into his pocket, giving Christian a reassuring smile. "Aussie's on his way," he told him. "And, Christian, don't worry. We'll make sure everything's okay."

Christian nodded, the tension in his face easing just slightly as he clung to the hope that help was finally on the way.

Aussie climbed back into his truck, shutting the door with a sense of relief. After days of silence and miscommunication, he'd finally set things right with Ava. She had let him explain what really happened at the Snowball. That the woman he'd been with was an FBI agent. Ava had listened, asked her questions, and most importantly, she believed him. They'd shared a quiet moment, and she'd even kissed him, a gesture that said they were back on track.

Snow looked over from the passenger seat as they buckled in. "So, that kiss looked like a good sign," he said with a smirk. "I'm guessing you're back in the clear?"

Aussie grinned, feeling a weight lift. "Yeah, man. Finally. She knows the truth now, and I think we're good."

Snow gave him a nod, chuckling as they pulled out of the parking lot. "About time. I thought you were gonna combust."

They were barely a few blocks from the parking lot when Aussie's phone vibrated on the console. He glanced down and saw a text from Derek that made his brow furrow. All it said was that there was a situation with Christian and to go to Bayside.

Aussie's gut tightened. He'd just seen Ava, but she hadn't mentioned anything. Confusion clouded his thoughts. As they came to a red light, he quickly typed back, telling Derek that he was on his way.

Snow caught the tension on his face. "Everything alright?"

"I don't know. Derek's asking me to come to Bayside. Says it's urgent, something to do with Christian."

Snow's brow lifted in surprise. "But we just saw Ava. She seemed fine."

"I know."

On the way, questions flooded Aussie's mind. Of all people, why was Derek calling him? Why Bayside?

When they finally pulled into the parking lot outside Bayside, Aussie didn't waste a second. Snow followed as they entered, and Aussie immediately caught sight of Derek and Christian sitting near the bar. He saw Arianna behind the counter, who gave him a quick nod. He gave her a wave, then turned his attention back to Derek and Christian.

As he approached, Aussie's eyes locked with Christian's. The boy looked tense and troubled, but there was also a glimmer of relief there as if Aussie's presence meant something to him.

Derek motioned for him and Snow to take a seat. Aussie slid into the booth, his eyes shifting between Derek and Christian as he waited for the explanation.

Derek leaned forward, his tone low but urgent. "Christian came here looking for you, Aussie. There's been a situation, one that involves some local kids. They've been harassing Christian, trying to recruit him into a gang. Today, they pushed him around, threatened him, and" Derek's face tightened. "They threatened Ava too. Said they'd go after her if he didn't join them."

Aussie felt a surge of anger, his hands instinctively clenching. Christian and Ava, both caught in some gang's crosshairs? But then something else clicked. Could this be the same gang that had been stirring up trouble in the area?

He exchanged a look with Derek, and he didn't need his CO to spell it out. He could see it in his posture, in the slight nod of his head, that Derek was thinking the same thing.

Turning to Christian, Aussie's voice softened, but there was an intensity behind it. "Christian, first off, you did the right thing coming here. That took guts. Second, nothing is going to happen to you or Ava. I won't let that happen."

Christian swallowed hard, visibly relieved, though the fear in his eyes hadn't entirely dissipated.

Derek leaned back, his expression thoughtful. "Aussie, we need to talk to Ava. If these guys are targeting her, she needs to know. I'll also give Agent Jefferson a call and fill him in on this situation."

Aussie nodded. "Sounds good. I'll give Ava a call right now and let her know that I have Christian and that we're heading to the house." He glanced at Christian, giving him a reassuring look. "You've got me on your side, alright? We'll handle this. Nothing's going to happen to you or Ava."

Christian nodded, a hint of resolve replacing his earlier fear.

With a final nod to Derek, Aussie rose from his seat, gently patting Christian on the shoulder. "Let's get you home," he said, motioning for the boy to follow him.

"I'll follow you," Derek said as they all headed for the door.

Christian's tension seemed to lessen slightly, knowing that Aussie was by his side. As they walked out of Bayside and headed to the truck, Aussie's thoughts remained on Ava and Christian and the threat hanging over them both. But he knew one thing for certain. He wasn't going to let this gang come anywhere near them.

Ava sat in her office, the quiet hum of the building filling the air as she scanned the files of three new kids who had come into the system. Each page tugged at her heart in different ways, and she was carefully considering which foster families might be the right fit. But despite her focus, her mind kept drifting back to Aussie. She couldn't help it. The past few weeks of confusion and hurt had been rough, and now, knowing the truth about his presence at the Snowball, she felt lighter. Happier.

A smile tugged at her lips as she thought about how she couldn't wait to tell Christian. He'd been so worried, seeing her so down. Now she had good news to share.

As if on cue, her friend and coworker Sarah appeared in the doorway, leaning against the frame with a smirk. "Well, look at you, all sunshine and rainbows. Who knew files could make you so happy?"

Ava laughed, shaking her head. "It's not the files." She looked down, feeling a slight blush rising. "I ran into Jarod at the deli, and then, well, Aussie showed up."

Sarah's eyebrows shot up in surprise, her smile widening. "The Aussie?"

"Yeah," Ava said, chuckling. "He showed up at the right time, too. Jarod was being an ass, as usual."

Sarah moved into the office, perching on the edge of the desk. "And? What happened?"

Ava leaned back in her chair, recalling the moment with a warm feeling. "We finally talked about what happened at the Snowball. It turns out he was there on a classified assignment. The woman with him was part of the cover."

Sarah sighed, a look of pure satisfaction on her face. "I knew it. I told you something wasn't adding up. I'm glad you guys found a way to make things right."

Ava's smile softened. "Me too. It's like this huge weight has been lifted. I can't wait to tell Christian. This has affected him just as much as it has me."

Just then, Ava's phone vibrated on the desk, interrupting their conversation. She glanced down to see a text from Aussie.

Aussie: *Christian is with me, and we need to talk to you as soon as possible. Can we meet you at your house?*

Her stomach clenched. Christian? With Aussie? He was supposed to be in school. Why would Aussie have him?

Sarah noticed the shift in Ava's expression immediately. "What's wrong?"

"Aussie just texted me. He's with Christian, and they need to talk to me right away. But Christian should be at school right now." Concern seeped into Ava's voice.

Sarah's expression grew serious. "That sounds strange. Go. Go meet them. I'll cover here for now."

Ava nodded, quickly gathering her things. "I'll let you know what's going on as soon as I can."

"Okay!" Sarah called after her as Ava headed out the door.

Ava hurried to her car, tossing her bag into the passenger seat and buckling herself in. She pulled out of the parking lot, her fingers gripping the steering wheel a little tighter than usual as worry began to settle in her stomach. She trusted Aussie, but the uneasy feeling gnawed at her as she drove, hoping everything was okay.

CHAPTER NINETEEN

Ava paced the family room, her nerves fraying with each step. She couldn't shake the uneasy feeling in her stomach, wondering what could've been so urgent for Christian to leave school and why he was with Aussie of all people. She bit her lip, stealing a glance at the clock. The longer she waited, the more her mind spiraled with worry.

Just then, the front door opened. Ava's head whipped up, her heart stuttering when she saw Aussie step inside, followed by Christian, and then, to her surprise, Snow and an older gentleman dressed in a Navy uniform.

Ava's first instinct was to go straight to Christian. She closed the distance between them and hugged him tightly. "Are you okay? Why aren't you at school?"

Before Christian could answer, Aussie gently placed a hand on her shoulder. "Let's all sit down. We need to talk, Ava."

Nervously, Ava looked at the man she didn't recognize, feeling Aussie's calming presence beside her. As they gathered in the living room, Aussie gestured to the older gentleman. "Ava, this is my commander, Derek Connors. Derek, this is Ava."

"Ma'am," Derek greeted her with a polite nod, and Ava offered a small, tense smile. The formal introduction did little to ease her nerves.

Once everyone was seated, Derek leaned forward, hands clasped together. "First, I want you to know that Christian here is a brave, smart young man," he said, giving Christian a nod of approval. "And I assure you, he wasn't just playing hooky." Derek's playful smirk helped lighten the mood for a moment, and Ava couldn't help but feel a little more at ease.

Derek's expression grew serious as he continued. "A couple of boys approached Christian at school. It wasn't the first time."

Ava's gaze shot to Christian, who looked back at her, his eyes holding a hint of fear and guilt. The pieces clicked in her mind. "Christian," she murmured, "are these the same boys I saw you with a few weeks ago?"

Christian's shoulders slumped, and he nodded, guilt evident on his face. "I'm sorry, Ava. I should've told you the truth. They aren't good people."

A chill ran through her as the reality of the situation started to sink in.

Derek continued, his tone calm but firm. "These boys have been trying to recruit Christian into their club. And I use the word club loosely as we believe the club is actually a local gang that the FBI and local police are investigating."

Derek glanced at Aussie, signaling him to take over. Aussie shifted closer to Ava, his hand still holding hers.

"Ava," Aussie began, his eyes steady, "this gang is the reason I was at the Snowball with the FBI agent. There were some people in attendance that evening who the FBI believe are connected to this criminal organization. We were undercover, gathering intel."

Ava's heart pounded as she listened, absorbing the weight of each word. She was scared, yes, but more than that, she was terrified for Christian.

Derek spoke up again, his voice reassuring. "The next step is for me to reach out to my contacts at the PD and FBI and alert them to this situation." He looked at Ava, sensing her worry. "For now, the best thing you can do is act like you know nothing. Christian should go to school as usual, and both of you should keep to your normal routines. But stay vigilant. Be aware of your surroundings."

Ava bit her lip, nodding. "Is there anything else I should do? How can I be sure Christian will be safe?"

Derek's jaw tightened. "I hate saying it, but until we have more concrete info, keeping up appearances and your daily life is the safest option. But you're not alone in this, Ava. We're here to support you both."

After a few more minutes of discussion, Derek and Snow stood to leave, and Aussie rose with them to walk them to the door. Ava watched as they exchanged a few quiet words, then Aussie returned to her and Christian in the living room.

"We'll make sure you're protected," Aussie assured her, his gaze steady and unwavering.

Ava hesitated, worry evident in her eyes. "How can you be so sure, Aussie? This is serious."

Aussie stepped closer, placing a comforting hand on her shoulder. "Because you're with me now, Ava. I care about you both, and in my world, that means you're part of our community. SEALs look after their own."

A faint blush colored Ava's cheeks, and Aussie chuckled, lightening the mood. "Besides, until Derek hears back from his FBI and PD contacts and we have a plan, I think it'd be best if I stay here with you and Christian. I promise I'll behave, and I'll even take the couch."

Ava's mind raced at the thought of having Aussie under the same roof, even if only temporarily. She knew he was right that having him there could offer a sense of security, but her heart fluttered at the idea. She nodded, though a blush betrayed her excitement. "I'd feel better if you stayed," she admitted softly, her gaze dropping to the floor.

Christian glanced between them, grinning. "I'm, uh, gonna go catch up on the schoolwork I missed," he said with a small smirk before heading to his room.

Once they were alone, Aussie took Ava into his arms, wrapping her in a hug that she hadn't realized she needed so badly. She closed her eyes, letting his strength reassure her.

"Everything's going to be fine," he whispered, his breath warm against her ear. "My team and I have got you and Christian covered."

He pulled back slightly, looking into her eyes, and before either of them could think twice, their lips met in a kiss that held all the emotions of the past few weeks—relief, love, and the warmth of being together again. Ava melted into him, feeling the weight of her worries lift, even if just for a moment.

She'd missed this. She missed being with him. And right now, with danger looming, having Aussie by her side was exactly where she wanted him to be.

A little while later, Ava took a deep breath as she dried the last dish and placed it in the cabinet.

She had showered earlier, after dinner, and Christian had just gone to bed. She was wearing her flannel reindeer pajamas, a red tank top, and fuzzy socks to keep her feet warm.

She had so much on her mind that she couldn't think straight. She still couldn't believe that Christian was pursued by a gang who wanted to recruit him. She was, however, very proud of him for seeking out help.

She also was still coming to grips with the fact that Aussie was staying the night. Or maybe a few nights. She was nervous as hell about it.

Get a grip. He is staying here to protect me and Christian. He's not here for body-protection duties.

But with Aussie staying here overnight, her heart was doing overtime, and she wasn't even sure how to act around him. This situation was way beyond her usual comfort zone.

As she closed the last cabinet, she heard Aussie's deep, smooth voice behind her. "Need some help?"

She turned and immediately regretted it. There was Aussie, fresh from the shower. His damp hair was tousled, and he was standing there all six feet- something of him in nothing but a pair of blue and white pajama pants.

Ava's jaw nearly hit the floor, and her thoughts did a swan dive from innocent to dirty. *Holy shit, he is gorgeous!* She knew she was staring, but she couldn't stop her eyes from wandering over his sculpted chest and defined abs. Her mind veered into territory she was not prepared for. It was a dangerous, tempting, and absolutely unprofessional territory.

Aussie's amused chuckle jolted her back. "Didn't mean to turn you speechless, but I have to say, I'm flattered."

Ava felt heat rush to her cheeks. "I, uh, y-you clean up well," she stammered, instantly regretting how ridiculous that sounded.

"Well, I'd return the compliment," he said with a teasing grin, "but I might sound biased, considering the view." He stepped closer, and Ava felt her pulse quicken. He was close enough now that she could feel the heat radiating from him.

Aussie leaned down, his face a few inches from hers. "Relax, love. It's not like I'm about to swoop in and ravish you."

Ava bit her lip, trying to keep a straight face, but her heart was racing. She wanted to thank him for agreeing to stay here and for making her and Christian's safety a priority. "Thank you for doing this and for making time for us. I know you didn't have to, and—"

"Ava," he interrupted, his voice soft. "I'd do anything for either of you. There's no need to thank me." He brushed a gentle hand over her arm. "But promise me you'll keep your guard up at work. Don't go anywhere alone."

"I will. I'll make sure to stick with Sarah if I have to go anywhere," she assured him.

He gave her a nod, his intense gaze lingering on her for a moment. Then, before she realized what was happening, he leaned down and pressed his lips to hers. The kiss was soft at first, then grew into something deeper, more electrifying, until her knees felt weak beneath her. Her hands found his shoulders, and for a moment, she felt an emotion she barely recognized. Was she falling in love with this man?

When they pulled apart, her mind was swimming. "We should probably, um, get some sleep," she said, looking sheepishly at him.

Aussie gave her a gentle smile and nodded. "Yeah. Let's call it a night."

They walked into the living room, where Aussie's blanket and pillow were already set on the couch. Ava took one look at it, then back at him, and bit her lip. The man was enormous. There was no way that couch would be comfortable.

He leaned down and gave her a quick peck on the lips. "Goodnight, Ava."

"Goodnight."

But as she turned toward her bedroom, the thought nagged at her of him cramped on the couch while he was doing them a huge favor. Before she could talk herself out of it, she turned back around, marching over to the living room just as Aussie was sitting down.

He looked up, surprised. "What's wrong?"

She took a breath. "I can't let you sleep on that couch. You'll be miserable."

His eyebrows raised slightly. "Are you suggesting I sleep on the floor?" He smirked, teasing her.

"No, I mean," Her cheeks warmed again, but she pushed through it. "You could share my bed. It's big enough for both of us. And we're adults," she added quickly.

For a moment, Aussie just stared at her, surprised, and then he smiled, that charming, disarming grin of his. "Are you really sure about that?"

Ava nodded. "Yes. I mean, you've more than earned a good night's sleep."

He gave her a quick hug and a small kiss on the forehead. "I promise I'll be a complete gentleman."

They headed into her bedroom, and as she turned off the light, Ava felt a shiver of nerves settle in. She lay on her side, trying to keep her breathing steady. Then she heard his deep, accented voice in the dark.

"You okay?"

"Yeah," she whispered, then added, "a little nervous, I guess."

"Are you nervous because we are sleeping in the same bed or because of everything going on right now?"

"Both," she answered honestly.

There was a pause, and then she felt him shift closer. "Slide over here. I swear I'm not going to try anything, but I want you to know you're safe."

She hesitated, then scooted closer until she felt his arm wrap around her, pulling her into the warmth of his chest. Her head rested on his shoulder. He leaned down and pressed a soft kiss to her forehead. "Close your eyes, Ava. I've got your six."

For the first time in a long while, she let herself relax, comforted by the steady beat of his heart and the strength in his arms. And as sleep began to tug at her, Ava knew she'd never felt more protected.

CHAPTER TWENTY

The soft glow of the clock on her nightstand read five in the morning. Ava blinked at the numbers, and a quiet sigh escaped her lips. Wrapped snugly in Aussie's arms, his steady breathing tickling the back of her neck, she felt cocooned in a safety net. For the first time in what felt like weeks, the weight of the world didn't press quite so hard.

Ava shifted slightly, careful not to wake him, and studied the clock again. In just thirty minutes, he'd have to get up. She closed her eyes, trying to push aside the creeping thoughts about the threats looming over her and Christian. For now, she focused on the steady warmth of Aussie behind her and the way his arms seemed to protect her even in sleep.

Why couldn't things stay like this forever?

Before she knew it, the alarm on Aussie's phone buzzed softly. She felt him stir, his grip tightening briefly around her waist before he nuzzled the back of her neck, his morning stubble sending a pleasant shiver down her spine.

"Good mornin', love," he murmured, his voice low and rough with sleep, that slight Australian accent sending her heart into a flutter.

Ava smiled. "Morning."

"I wish I could stay like this a little longer," he said as he kissed the curve of her neck before reluctantly pulling away.

Ava rolled onto her back to watch him stretch before he climbed out of bed, his broad shoulders catching the faint light streaming through the blinds.

He turned to look at her and caught her staring. He gave her a cheeky grin. "This is all yours," he said as he grabbed his toiletry bag and headed toward the guest bathroom.

Ava took her time getting ready, trying to shake off her nerves. She wished that she and Christian could just stay home.

After dressing in black slacks and a pale blue blouse, she knocked on Christian's door to wake him up. "Come on, sleepyhead. Time to get moving."

When she walked into the kitchen, she started on breakfast, the soothing ritual of cracking eggs and flipping bacon, which gave her something to focus on. Her thoughts strayed to Aussie, and when he finally walked in, her breath hitched.

He wasn't dressed in the normal working uniform that she saw most Navy personnel wear. Instead, he wore a long-sleeved shirt slightly fitted, with a three-quarter zip that made him look both professional and effortlessly attractive.

Ava quickly turned back to the stove, feeling her cheeks warm. *Stop it, Ava.*

Thankfully, Christian walked in a moment later, yawning and dragging his feet. "What's for breakfast?"

The trio ate together, the atmosphere light despite everything hanging over them. Aussie joked about Christian's messy bedhead, which earned him an exaggerated eye roll. After cleaning up, they all headed to their vehicles.

"I can drop Christian off," Aussie offered as they reached the cars. "The high school's on my way to the base."

Ava smiled gratefully and nodded. "Thanks."

Before she could open her car door, Aussie stepped closer. He leaned down and kissed her softly. "Be safe, and have a good day."

"I will."

His expression turned serious for a moment. "And remember, call me if anything feels off. And if you can't get a hold of me, start going down the list."

During dinner the night before, Aussie had taken her phone and programmed his team's phone numbers and Derek's phone number in it.

She grinned. "I promise."

Ava watched as Aussie and Christian drove off, a small part of her wishing she could hold onto that morning forever.

The drive to Christian's school felt almost peaceful, the rising sun casting a golden hue across the quiet streets. Aussie couldn't stop thinking about waking up next to Ava. She fit so perfectly in his arms, and for the first time in years, he felt like he was exactly where he was supposed to be.

"Here," Aussie said as he handed Christian a small box from his center console.

"What's this?" Christian asked, looking at the box in confusion.

"New phone," Aussie replied. "Meant to give it to you last night, but things got a bit hectic."

Christian opened it, his eyes lighting up. "Seriously? Thank you!"

"No worries," Aussie said with a grin. "My number's already in there, along with the rest of the team. If anything happens, anything at all, you call me. Got it?"

Christian nodded. "Got it."

Satisfied, Aussie pulled into the school's drop-off lane and clapped Christian on the shoulder. "Have a good day."

Christian smiled faintly, clutching the phone. "Thanks, Aussie."

Aussie watched as Christian walked up to a blonde-haired girl sitting on one of the benches outside of the school. She smiled at him before standing up and walking inside the school with him. Aussie assumed that it must be Katy, the girl Christian talks about.

His chest tightened a little. God, he hoped the FBI could handle the situation surrounding Ava and Christian quickly.

When Aussie arrived at the base, he headed straight for the team's building. Derek was waiting just inside the entrance, arms crossed.

"Morning," Derek said, his tone brisk. "Follow me."

Aussie fell in step behind his commander, who led him to his office. Inside, a man in a suit was seated in one of the chairs.

"Aussie, this is FBI Agent Rod Jefferson," Derek introduced. "He's one of the lead agents on the gang case."

Agent Jefferson stood and shook Aussie's hand. "Good to meet you. Thanks for your help so far."

"No problem," Aussie replied.

The three of them sat, and for the next hour, they discussed the threats made toward Ava and Christian. Jefferson was methodical, taking notes as Derek and Aussie filled him in on the confrontation between the boys from Christian's school.

"We'll have surveillance put on those two boys," Jefferson said. "With any luck, they'll lead us to someone higher up."

Aussie nodded, though his jaw clenched. "What about Ava and Christian? What can be done to keep them safe in the meantime?"

Jefferson hesitated, his expression somber. "Truthfully? Not much, given that we don't know who all the players are. The best we can do is keep watch and hope something breaks soon."

Aussie didn't like that answer, and he could tell Derek didn't either.

Jefferson sighed. "Does Ava have family she could visit for the holidays? Somewhere out of town?"

Aussie frowned. "No, she doesn't." But then an idea hit him. "What if I take them with me?"

Jefferson raised an eyebrow. "Take them where?"

"Originally, I was planning to visit my family in Indiana for Christmas," Aussie explained. "But after I met Ava, I decided to stay here instead. But what if I take them to my parent's place? It's far enough away."

Derek exchanged a glance with Jefferson, who nodded slowly.

"That's a solid plan," Jefferson said. "Getting them out of the area could buy us some time to gather more intel."

Derek leaned back in his chair. "You'd need additional leave. Consider it approved."

"Thank you. I just need to make a quick call," Aussie said as he excused himself from the room.

The door to Derek's office clicked shut, muffling the sound of Agent Jefferson's low voice as he discussed logistics with Derek. Aussie leaned against the wall in the hallway, his mind already racing ahead. Even though he had made up his mind about Ava and Christian staying with his family for Christmas, he knew there was one more person who needed to be in the loop. And that was his mom.

He pulled his phone from his pocket and dialed. The line barely rang twice before his mom answered, her voice bright and cheerful.

"Well, look who's calling! Is this my son who forgot his mother existed?"

Aussie rolled his eyes, his lips curving into a smirk. "It's been two weeks, Mom. Not exactly an eternity."

"That's debatable," she replied. "What's going on? And don't you dare tell me you're stuck in some frozen wasteland or on a mission where you can't tell me anything. I'm not in the mood for that today."

"Relax, I'm not on a mission." Aussie glanced at the closed door, lowering his voice. "Actually, I need to talk to you about something important."

The teasing edge in her voice softened. "What's wrong?"

"I've got a couple of people I'd like to bring home for Christmas," Aussie said, his tone even. "A woman I've been seeing and the teenager she is fostering. Her name is Ava, and the boy is Christian."

There was a brief silence on the other end before his mom spoke, her curiosity palpable. "Okay, back up. Ava? This is the one you mentioned last time, isn't it?"

"Yeah, it's the same person."

"And she's fostering a teenager? How old is he?"

"Fifteen," Aussie said. "He's a good kid, Mom. Really good. And Ava's incredible. She's a social worker who works with kids like Christian. She's tough, selfless, and honestly amazing."

"Well," his mom said with a laugh, "it sounds like you're already smitten."

Aussie felt his ears burn. "Mom."

"Oh, don't 'Mom' me. You don't bring just anyone to meet the family, and now you're talking about two people. This sounds serious."

"It is," Aussie admitted, the weight of his words settling over him. "I care about them. Both of them. And things have gotten a little complicated around here."

"What kind of complicated?" she asked, her tone shifting to something sharper.

Aussie hesitated, glancing around to make sure no one was listening. "Ava and Christian are in some trouble. Nothing they caused, but there's a local gang that's become a threat to them. We're trying to keep them safe, and taking them out of town for a bit seemed like the best option. Nobody knows I'm bringing them to you except my CO and an FBI agent. I promise, Mom, there won't be any danger brought your way."

His mom was silent for a moment, then said with quiet confidence, "I trust you, sweetheart. You wouldn't bring trouble to us. But I want to know more about this Ava."

Aussie sighed, knowing she wouldn't let it go. "She's strong, independent, and probably one of the most compassionate people I've ever met. She's been through a lot, but she's still fighting, still trying to make a difference. And Christian, he's had a rough time, but he's smart and kind. They're good people, Mom."

"And you're serious about her?"

Aussie's voice softened. "Yeah, I am. She's different, Mom. In the best way."

His mom chuckled. "Well, I can't wait to meet her. And Christian, too. Bring them home, Aussie. We'll take care of them."

"Thanks, Mom," Aussie said, relief washing over him.

"And don't think you're off the hook. I'll be talking to Ava about everything about you. I need to make sure she knows what she's getting herself into."

Aussie groaned, but he was smiling. "Just don't scare her off, okay?"

"No promises," she replied with a laugh. "Now go do whatever secret Navy thing you're doing, and I'll get the guest rooms ready."

"Love you, Mom," Aussie said.

"Love you too, sweetheart. Drive safe."

Aussie ended the call, sliding his phone back into his pocket as the door to Derek's office opened. Agent Jefferson and Derek stepped out, nodding toward him.

"All good?" Derek asked.

"Yes, Sir," Aussie said. "I just spoke with my mom, and she is good with us staying with them through the holidays."

"When do you think that you'll head out?"

"I'm not sure. I'll have to talk to Ava. However, I'd like to leave as soon as possible."

"I agree. Getting them out of the area sooner than later is a good call," Agent Jefferson stated.

"Just keep me updated," Derek said.

"Will do."

He shook both men's hands before parting ways and walking outside. He got into his truck and pulled out his phone to call Ava.

"Hey," she answered after the second ring, her voice instantly calming him.

"Hey," he said, a small smile tugging at his lips. "Are you free for an early lunch?"

"Of course. Is everything okay?"

"Everything is fine," he replied. "There's just something that I want to talk to you about."

"Okay. I'm free whenever you are."

"Alright. I'm on my way. I'll pick you up."

"Sounds good. See you soon.

As he hung up, Aussie started the truck, his mind already spinning with details. He'd make sure Ava and Christian were protected at all costs.

᠅

Ava sat at her desk going over some files for a few kids who will be aging out of the system come spring time. Those cases were always difficult because, for most of the kids, as soon as they turned 18 and graduated high school, they were on their own. Most of them didn't keep in touch with their foster families. They were just sent out into the world all alone.

Her thoughts drifted to Christian, and when that time came for him. She vowed that no matter what happened with Christian's situation, she would always be there for him. She was one person that he could always count on.

The sound of a knock on her office door made her look up. Sarah stood there leaning against the frame, her eyes wide with excitement.

"There's a ridiculously handsome man in the lobby asking for you," Sarah said with a grin.

Ava didn't need to guess who it was. But she would have some fun with her friend. "Tall, broad shoulders, gorgeous hazel eyes, a killer smile, and wearing a uniform?"

Sarah's grin widened, and she nodded. "Is that him? Is that Aussie?"

Ava laughed. "Yes. That would be Aussie."

Sarah clutched her chest dramatically. "You lucky, bitch! He's like something out of a military romance novel!"

"Sarah, stop," Ava said, though she couldn't help but laugh.

"I'm serious! If I weren't happily married—"

"Stop," Ava said again, holding up a hand.

"You're no fun," Sarah mock pouted, and it made Ava laugh again.

Ava slipped on her coat, smoothed her hair, and grabbed her purse before heading toward the lobby. Sure enough, Aussie stood near the entrance, his presence commanding even in the mundane setting of her workplace.

He spotted her and smiled, that easy, heart-melting grin she loved. "Ready to go?"

"Yeah," Ava said, trying not to blush under Sarah's not-so-subtle gaze from behind the reception desk.

"You weren't kidding," Sarah whispered as Ava passed by.

"I'll see you after lunch," Ava called back, ignoring her friend's teasing laughter.

In the parking lot, Aussie opened the passenger door of his truck for her, a small gesture that never failed to make her smile.

"You didn't have to come all the way here," Ava said as she climbed in.

"I needed an excuse to see you," he said, shutting the door behind her before rounding the truck.

They drove in companionable silence for a few minutes, the radio playing softly in the background. When they pulled into the parking lot of a little diner just outside the base, Ava raised an eyebrow.

"This place any good?" she asked.

"You'll love it," he promised, cutting the engine.

The smell of freshly baked bread and something sweet greeted them as they stepped inside. Aussie led her to a booth near the window, and a waitress brought over menus.

As they sat down, Ava couldn't help but notice the faint tension in Aussie's shoulders.

"Alright, what's going on?" she asked, folding her hands on the table.

He hesitated, his fingers tracing the edge of the menu. "I met with Derek and the FBI agent in charge of the investigation this morning."

Ava's stomach tightened. "What about it?"

"Derek and I gave him the information about the two boys who have been harassing Christian, and we told him about the threats towards you and Christian. The agent thinks it's best if you and Christian lay low for a bit while they work the case."

"Lay low? What does that mean?" Ava asked, her voice barely above a whisper.

"They're hoping these boys will lead them to someone higher up in the organization," Aussie explained. "But until they have something solid, the agent thinks it's safer if you two aren't easy to find."

Ava sat back, processing his words. "So, what do we do? Move into hiding?"

"Not exactly," Aussie said, reaching across the table to take her hand. His touch was warm and grounding. "I have an idea. What if you and Christian come with me to Indiana to my parent's house for Christmas?"

She blinked, caught off guard. "Indiana?"

"It's far enough from here, and my parents' place is out in the country. Quiet, private, and safe. Plus," He gave her a sheepish smile. "I'd love for you to meet my family."

Ava's heart fluttered at the thought of being included in something so personal. "Are you sure? I mean, I don't want to impose on your family's holiday."

"You wouldn't be," he said. "I already spoke with my mom, and she's excited to meet you and Christian. And it's the best option for now. Derek and Agent Jefferson agree."

Ava chewed on her lip as her mind raced. The idea of taking Christian so far from home felt daunting, but the thought of staying and risking his safety was even worse.

Christmas in Indiana. With Aussie. It wasn't the holiday she'd expected, but maybe it would be exactly what they needed.

"Okay," she said finally. "If you think it's the best thing to do, we'll go. Plus, maybe it'll be good for all of us to get away."

Aussie's shoulders relaxed, and he squeezed her hand. "You're doing the right thing. I promise, Ava, I'll keep you both safe."

She smiled. "When would we leave? There are some things I'll need to take of before we head out."

"I understand. I was thinking the day after tomorrow. Would that work?"

"It should. I'll talk to Christian tonight and let him know. He'll probably be a little bummed because he's been so excited about spending Christmas at the house."

Aussie gave her hand another squeeze. "How about I pick Christian up from school, and we tell him together tonight?"

She thought about it for a second and then nodded. "That will work."

After lunch, Aussie dropped Ava off at work. As she walked back into the office, her mind was spinning with everything she needed to get done before they left.

She hadn't even hung her coat when her gaze landed on a figure in the distance that made her stomach churn. It was Jarod, standing just outside her boss's office, engaged in an animated conversation.

Great. Just what I need, she thought.

As if on cue, Jarod glanced over and caught sight of her. A smile tugged at the corners of his lips, but there was no warmth behind it. He looked like a cat who'd just cornered its prey. But before he could say or do anything, she kicked her office door closed, shutting him out.

She couldn't help but giggle, knowing that she probably pissed him off.

She sat down behind her desk and started making a list of things she needed to get done before they left.

Aussie pulled into the school parking lot right as Christian walked out of the main doors, his backpack slung over one shoulder. The kid had a bounce in his step, but as he climbed into the truck, he let out a dramatic sigh.

"Tough day?" Aussie asked, glancing at him as he merged into traffic.

"Not really," Christian said, shrugging. "Just a lot of tests. I think I aced most of them, though."

Aussie grinned. "Most of them, huh? What about the ones you don't think that you aced?"

Christian smirked. "I probably got a B on them."

They both laughed and for a moment, the easygoing banter lightened the weight that had been sitting on Aussie's shoulders all day.

"So," Christian said, "have you talked with Ava at all today? I know she's nervous about everything going on."

Aussie's grip on the steering wheel tightened slightly, but he forced himself to keep his tone light. "I actually had lunch with her. She's okay. But you're right. She is nervous, and she has a lot on her plate."

Christian nodded, his expression thoughtful. "She worries about everyone else more than herself. I just don't like seeing her stressed. I feel responsible for everything that is going on."

Aussie's chest tightened. One of the things he admired most about Christian was his compassion. Despite everything the kid had been through, he was anything but selfish. But he also didn't like that the kid was beating himself up over the situation at hand.

"Hey, this stuff going on is not your fault. You didn't ask for it."

"I know that, but it is because of me that Ava's life is in danger."

Aussie didn't want to tell Christian about them leaving town yet.

"Well, hopefully, the police can get a handle on the situation quickly. Until then, you've both got me, plus my team behind you," Aussie said.

Christian smiled, then his eyes lit up as they passed a small barbecue joint. "Can we grab dinner from there? Their brisket sandwiches are amazing."

"Brisket it is," Aussie agreed, pulling into the parking lot.

After picking up some sandwiches, mac and cheese, and cornbread, they headed back to Ava's house. As Aussie parked in the driveway, he immediately noticed Ava's car already there.

"She's home early," Christian said as they grabbed the food and headed inside.

The moment they stepped through the door, Aussie felt it. Ava was in the kitchen, pulling some snacks out of the pantry, but something about her posture was off. She was stiff, her movements almost mechanical.

"Hey, Ava!" Christian chirped. "We brought dinner!"

She turned and smiled, though it didn't quite reach her eyes. "Perfect. I'm starving."

"Go get ready for dinner," Aussie said, giving Christian a gentle nudge. "Wash up, set the table, you know the drill."

Christian nodded and disappeared down the hall, leaving Aussie alone with Ava. He set the food on the counter and stepped closer to her.

"What's wrong?" he asked quietly, his voice low and steady.

Ava hesitated, then sighed. "I don't know if I'm just being paranoid with everything going on, but when I got home, there was a car that I didn't recognize parked on the side of the road between my driveway and the neighbor's next door. When I got out of the car and turned to look at it, the person took off."

Aussie's heart pounded. He wanted nothing more than to scoop Ava and Christian up and get them far away from all of this. "Can you describe the vehicle? I can at least give that information to Agent Jefferson, and they can check it out."

"Yeah. It was a champagne-colored Lexus sedan. It had Virginia plates, but I only caught the first two letters. It was XB."

"That's a pretty good description," Aussie said, pulling his phone out and texting the information to the agent.

When he was finished, he looked at Ava. She was biting her lip nervously.

"Are you alright?" he asked her.

"Are we able to leave earlier?"

"We can leave whenever you are ready. I had suggested the day after tomorrow because I assumed you had things you would need to take care of." Hell, he would be happy if they left right after dinner. But he knew that was wishful thinking.

"Ava nodded, her expression softening. "How about tomorrow?"

Aussie nodded. "Tomorrow works."

Before they could say more, Christian returned, setting plates on the table. "Everything okay?" he asked, his sharp eyes flicking between them.

"Yeah," Aussie said, forcing a smile. "Come on, let's eat."

They dished out the food, the aroma of smoky brisket filling the kitchen. As they ate, Aussie exchanged a glance with Ava before clearing his throat.

"Christian, Ava, and I have been talking," he began. "With everything going on, we think it's best to spend the holidays with my family in Indiana."

Christian looked between them. His fork was paused mid-air. "But Ava and I were going to have Christmas here."

"I know," Aussie said gently. "I know how much you were looking forward to it. But we're doing this also to keep you both safe while the FBI continues their investigation."

Christian then surprised him by smiling. "Actually, I don't care where we are for Christmas, as long as it's with both of you."

Ava reached over and squeezed Christian's hand. "That means a lot, Christian. Thank you."

Aussie's chest swelled with pride. This kid was incredible.

"Oh, I almost forgot. We'll need to let Judge Holten and my boss know what is going on," Ava said, turning to Aussie. "Christian's still technically the state's responsibility. It also might be best to have the FBI Agent there as well."

Aussie nodded. "I hadn't thought of that, but you're right. How soon can you talk to the judge?"

Ava pulled out her phone and typed a quick message. Moments later, she smiled. "Tomorrow morning."

Aussie raised his eyebrow in question. Did she have judges in her back pocket?

Ava grinned. "Judge Holten is also a good friend of mine. She said she'll make time for us."

Relieved, Aussie grabbed his phone and texted Derek. Within minutes, Derek replied, confirming he'd arrange for Agent Jefferson to meet them at Ava's office at ten.

"After we finish eating, both of you pack your bags," Aussie said, looking at both of them. "Once the meeting's over tomorrow morning and everything's squared away, we're leaving."

Christian finished the last bite of his sandwich and stood. "I'll start packing now."

Ava watched him go, then turned to Aussie.

"What about your bags? Don't you need to pack?"

"Snow is packing my bag for me. He said that he'll drop it off later this evening."

Ava walked over and wrapped her arms around his waist. "Thank you. For everything."

Aussie held her tightly, resting his chin on the top of her head. "I'd do anything for you and Christian. You're my priority now."

She looked up at him, her eyes glistening. "We're lucky to have you."

He leaned down and kissed her, pouring every ounce of his feelings into that single moment. They might have been caught in chaos, but as long as they were together, they'd find a way through it.

CHAPTER TWENTY-ONE

The atmosphere in the conference room at Ava's office was tense, with a mix of concern and determination reflected in everyone's expressions.

Around the long table sat Agent Jefferson, Derek, Judge Holten, Clint, Aussie, Ava, and Christian. Ava stayed quiet with her hands folded in front of her while Agent Jefferson took the lead and explained the situation to Judge Holten and Clint.

The room was silent except for Agent Jefferson's words. Ava could feel the weight of everyone's concern. Their eyes would occasionally glance toward Christian, who sat next to her. Even Clint, who was normally composed, looked unusually uneasy as his fingers tapped lightly on the table.

As Jefferson laid out the details, Judge Holten leaned forward, her sharp gaze directed at the agent. "And what exactly do you suggest for their protection while they're away?"

Jefferson nodded. He glanced at Aussie and then went back to the judge. "Aussie will ensure their safety. He has experience with situations like this and is more than capable of handling any threats that may arise. They will also have the backing of the FBI should it be needed."

The Judge absorbed that, nodding slowly. She then looked at Aussie. "So, you'll be staying with your family?"

"Yes, Ma'am," Aussie replied.

"And where do they live?"

Before Aussie could respond, Derek spoke up. "With all due respect, Your Honor, for security reasons, we don't disclose personal information involving the families of SEALs. What I can assure you is that the location is remote, private, and known only to Agent Jefferson and me."

The Judge's eyes flicked to Derek, studying him for a moment. Then, she gave a small nod of approval. "Good. The less who know, the better. If only a select few know where they are, that minimizes the risk. No one else needs to be aware of their whereabouts." She then turned her attention to Ava. Her expression softened. "I know this is a big upheaval for you and Christian, but I trust you'll do what's best for both of you."

Ava nodded, grateful for the judge's support. She could see in her eyes that she was fully on board with the plan.

Ava glanced at Clint again. He was still just sitting there, not really participating in the discussion. Normally, he was vocal in meetings, offering solutions or asking tough questions. Today, though, he seemed distracted. It was unlike him, and it gnawed at the back of Ava's mind.

Once everyone was on board with the plan, the meeting concluded, and everyone wished Ava, Aussie, and Christian a Merry Christmas. Ava was touched by the warmth and care they all showed, even in such a tense situation.

As people filed out of the conference room, Clint stopped her. "Ava, could I please speak with you in my office?"

"Of course."

After she told Aussie and Christian that she would meet them in her office, she followed Clint down the hall, her steps slow as an uneasy feeling settled in her chest. Once inside, the door clicked shut behind her.

Clint walked over to his desk and leaned against it. His arms were crossed, and his expression was tight.

"Why didn't you come to me first?" he asked, his tone sharper than she expected.

Ava blinked as she was completely caught off guard by his tone. "This all just happened the other day. Plus, I was following Agent Jefferson's instructions."

Clint's eyes narrowed. "I get that, but a little bit of a heads-up would've been nice. Plus, you're leaving, and we have three kids coming in. With everyone's scheduled vacations, do you know how stretched we're going to be without you here?"

"I understand," Ava said, trying to stay calm. "But I'll still be working remotely, and Sarah can help handle things here in person."

Clint's jaw clenched. "You don't get it. You're the one who has the most experience here. I personally don't think you should go." He muttered, but Ava heard him.

The lack of concern in his voice stung more than Ava wanted to admit.

"I'm sorry, Clint," she said quietly. "But right now, my priority is Christian and keeping him safe. You, of all people, should understand that."

He didn't respond. He just stared at her for a moment. His expression was unreadable. Finally, he signed.

"We can't do anything about it now. Just don't forget your responsibilities."

Ava frowned. She was unsettled by his lack of concern for her and Christian's safety. It was as if his focus was entirely on the agency's work and not her well-being. *But wasn't Christian's safety part of the agency's work?*

Before she could respond, his phone rang, and he answered it without another word to her, effectively dismissing her.

Fuming, Ava left his office and returned to hers, where Aussie and Christian were waiting. The moment Aussie saw her face, he stood.

"What's wrong?" he asked, his voice low and steady.

Ava shook her head. "Something's off with Clint. He was upset that I didn't come to him first and didn't seem to care about why I was leaving. He's never acted like this before."

"Maybe he's just stressed," Aussie offered, though his brow furrowed with concern.

"Maybe," Ava said, though her gut told her otherwise. There was something deeper at play, but she couldn't put her finger on it.

"Come on," Aussie said gently, resting a hand on her shoulder. "Let's get out of here."

As they walked out to Aussie's truck, Derek was waiting for them by the driver's side door.

"Just wanted to say goodbye," Derek said with a smile. "The team has your back. If anything comes up, you call me. Understood?"

"Understood," Aussie replied, shaking Derek's hand.

Ava couldn't help but feel a sense of awe at the way Derek and the others looked out for each other. The bond they shared was unshakable, and it made her feel safer knowing Aussie was part of it.

"Thank you, Derek," she said.

Derek smiled, "No thanks needed, honey. We always have each other's back. You guys drive safe," he said, stepping back. "And Merry Christmas."

"Merry Christmas," they echoed as they climbed into the truck.

As they pulled out of the parking lot and onto the highway, heading toward Indiana, Ava glanced at Aussie and Christian. Despite the tension and uncertainty, she felt a glimmer of hope. They were together, and that was what mattered most.

CHAPTER TWENTY-TWO

Ezekiel adjusted his tie as he sat at the long mahogany table in the City Hall meeting room, nodding along to the monotonous droning of the city manager. The room was packed with local business owners and community leaders, their polite smiles masking their impatience. Ezekiel's carefully cultivated public image as the owner of the largest furniture shop in town required him to attend these meetings, but his mind was elsewhere tonight.

For the third time, his phone buzzed in his pocket. He resisted the urge to pull it out, though his curiosity was piqued. Few people had his number, and even fewer would dare interrupt him during a city function.

When the meeting finally adjourned, Ezekiel was the first to stand, muttering a curt excuse to the mayor as he slipped past the crowd. He strode out of City Hall, ignoring the familiar faces who were trying to catch his attention for small talk. The chill of the night air hit him as he stepped onto the pavement, but he barely noticed.

By the time he reached his car, he had his phone out, looking through the missed calls. Jarod's name was at the top—three missed calls from him, all within the last hour.

He quickly called him back.

"Jarod," Ezekiel barked as soon as the line connected.

"Ezekiel," Jarod replied, his voice tight with unease. "We've got a problem."

Ezekiel leaned against his car, his knuckles whitening as he gripped the roof. "What kind of problem?"

Jarod sighed. The hesitation in his voice was making Ezekiel's blood boil. "It's about Christian and Ava."

Ezekiel's eyes narrowed. "Go on."

"Apparently, your little talk with Barrett and Chase about backing off of Christian went unheard."

"What do you mean? What happened?"

"It appears the two dumbasses royally fucked up and confronted Christian the other day and threatened him that if he didn't cooperate, they would take things further and go after Ava."

Ezekiel felt his blood pressure rising with each passing second.

"But that isn't all. Apparently, Christian told some people what happened, and now the FBI is looking for Barrett and Chase. As for Christian and Ava, they left town earlier today."

"Left town? Where did they go?"

"No clue. They left with the guy that she was dating. According to my source, he's a Navy SEAL, and his personal information is sealed tight."

Ezekiel's eyebrows shot up upon hearing that detail. But he didn't have time to waste worrying about who the woman was dating. Suddenly, the anger surging through his body returned in full force. He needed to cut off the lead that the police had.

Ezekiel sneered, pacing beside his car. He had noticed that Barrett and Chase had been getting a little too comfortable in their roles. Now, their stupidity has put everything that Ezekiel has worked for at risk.

"Barrett and Chase are going to pay for this."

"The FBI is tracking them," Jarod reminded him.

Ezekiel's lip curled. "Doesn't matter. I'll handle it. They won't be an issue for long."

Jardo hesitated before asking, "What about Ava and Christian? We don't know for sure if Barrett or Chase mentioned anything else to Christian that could potentially lead the authorities to us."

Ezekiel's mind churned. He would deal with Ava and the boy, too. Christian was a liability. He was nothing more than a loose end to be tied up. And Ava. She was an annoyance. Beautiful, but still an annoyance. Perhaps she could serve a temporary purpose before her usefulness ran out.

"Do you know where they went?" Ezekiel asked.

"No," Jarod admitted.

Ezekiel gritted his teeth. "Fine. But you'll let me know the second you hear anything. If they come back, I want to know before anyone else."

"Of course," Jarod assured him.

Ezekiel ended the call and slid into the driver's seat, his mind already shifting gears. He dialed another number. His tone was icy when the person on the other end picked up.

Find Barrett and Chase," Ezekiel ordered. "And make them disappear."

The person on the line grunted an acknowledgment before hanging up. Ezekiel's fingers tightened around the steering wheel as he started the car.

As he drove toward his warehouse on the outskirts of town, his mind raced with plans. He would need to lay low for a while, but when the time came, he'd make sure that nobody would interfere with his business again.

The thought of eliminating the threats coming at him brought a cold smile to his lips. He'd get what he wanted. He always did.

CHAPTER TWENTY-THREE

Ava yawned as she checked the time. It was just a little after six in the evening. The drive to Aussie's parent's house took a lot longer than they expected it to. When they left yesterday, they had driven for about two hours when they found out that the major highway on their route was completely shut down due to a major multi-car accident, and it wasn't expected to open back up for several hours. So, instead of sitting in standstill traffic, they decided to find a hotel and just hunker down for the night.

They got an early start in the morning, and after they had breakfast at the hotel, they were on the road by eight.

Ava sat quietly in the truck, her gaze drifting out the window as they neared Aussie's parents' house. The farmland that stretched for miles was dotted with weathered barns and grazing cattle. The golden light of the fading sun bathed the fields, giving the scene an almost ethereal glow. It was so peaceful, so untouched, that for a moment, Ava allowed herself to forget the chaos back in Virginia Beach. Here, it felt like time itself had slowed down, offering a rare glimpse of serenity.

"Here we are," Aussie announced as he turned the truck on the main road and onto a driveway.

As the truck rumbled down the long gravel driveway, Ava stared out the window, her breath catching at the sight ahead. The farmhouse that stood there was massive, with pristine white siding, dark green shutters, and a wraparound porch decorated with twinkling Christmas lights. Garlands hung from the railings, and a towering Christmas tree glimmered through one of the large front windows. Beyond the house stretched acres of rolling land with barns and a large paddock where a few horses grazed peacefully.

Christian let out a low whistle from the back seat. "This place is huge."

Ava couldn't help but smile. "It's beautiful," she agreed, her eyes lingering on the snow-covered fields. The entire scene looked like something out of a holiday movie.

"You have horses?" Christian asked eagerly.

"Yup," Aussie replied, pulling the truck to a stop in front of the porch. "Plenty of them. And yes, you can ride one."

Christian grinned as if Aussie had just handed him the best Christmas present ever.

Ava's gaze shifted to the couple waiting on the porch. Aussie's parents stood side by side, bundled in warm coats. Their faces were lit with welcoming smiles. His mom was petite, with short-cropped gray hair. His dad was tall and broad-shouldered. His weathered features were softened by the warmth in his eyes.

As soon as Aussie killed the engine, they walked down the steps to meet them.

"Aussie!" his mom called, her voice brimming with joy. "It's about time you got here!"

"Hey, Mom, Dad," Aussie said, stepping out of the truck. He came around to open Ava's door and help her down. He then gestured toward her and Christian. "This is Ava and Christian."

Ava barely had time to extend her hand before Aussie's mom pulled her into a hug. "It's so good to meet you, Ava," she said warmly. "Welcome to our home."

"Thank you," Ava replied, slightly startled but smiling.

Meanwhile, Aussie's dad bent slightly to meet Christian's eye level. "You must be Christian. I see you eyeing the horses. Do you like to ride?"

"I never rode before, but Aussie said I could ride one here," Christian said, his voice laced with excitement.

"You sure can. We have plenty to pick from," Aussie's dad said. "How about tomorrow you and I go out for a ride?"

Christian's eyes lit up. "Seriously?"

"Absolutely!"

Christian looked at Ava. "Is it okay if I go riding tomorrow?"

Ava smiled. "I don't see why not." She glanced at Aussie to see if he had any objections. But Aussie just grinned.

"I think it's a great idea. My dad knows all the trails back in the woods. You'll have a good time," Aussie told Christian.

"Come on inside," Aussie's mom said, wrapping an arm around Ava as they walked toward the house. "You've had a long trip, and I've got some dinner on the stove."

As Ava stepped inside, she was left speechless. The inside of the house was just as stunning as the outside. The living room boasted high ceilings with exposed wooden beams, a crackling stone fireplace, and cozy furniture adorned with plaid throws. A staircase wound its way up to the second floor, where Ava spotted several doors leading to what she assumed were the bedrooms. Not to mention, the whole house was decorated for Christmas with traditional décor of pine garlands and red bows that matched the red poinsettias placed all around the house.

"Why don't you three go upstairs and get settled? Dinner should be ready in about twenty minutes."

"Speaking of dinner. What are you making?" Aussie asked, his nose lifting into the air.

His mom smiled. "Your favorite."

"Baked pork chops with that garlic rub?" He asked.

"Yep. And roasted potatoes and steamed cabbage."

Aussie kissed his mom's cheek. "You're the best," he told her, and she laughed.

Watching Aussie and his mom melted Ava's heart. They looked so happy together.

"Alright, you three get going. Remember dinner in twenty."

Aussie looked at Ava. "I'll show you where you'll be staying," he said, picking up the bags and leading the way upstairs. Ava and Christian followed, their footsteps muffled by the plush runner on the stairs.

When they got to the second floor, they went left down the hallway. Aussie stopped in front of two doors. "Ava, this is your room," he said, opening the door to reveal a cozy space with a queen-sized bed, a dresser, and a window overlooking the fields. He turned to Christian. "And you're right across the hall. You each have your own bathrooms."

Christian darted inside to explore his room, which was just as inviting, complete with a twin bed and a small desk by the window. Both rooms even had a fully decorated Christmas tree.

Ava looked at Aussie. "Where is your room?"

He grinned and pointed two doors down from hers. "I'm right there. Don't worry, I'm close by." He winked, and she felt herself blush. "Go and get settled. I'll grab you guys in a few minutes."

As Aussie headed to his room and went inside, Christian came out of his room and followed Ava into hers.

"This place is amazing," Christian said.

Ava nodded in agreement. "It is."

"I like Aussie's parents already," he told her, and Ava smiled.

"They do seem like wonderful people."

Christian then turned toward Ava. "Are you really okay with spending Christmas here?" he asked her.

Ava cupped his face, her heart swelling at the concern in his eyes. "It doesn't matter where we spend Christmas, Christian. What matters is that we spend it together."

Christian nodded, his expression softening. "I really like Aussie," he said after a moment.

Ava smiled. "I do, too."

"I wish I could have a dad like him," Christian said quietly. "And a mom like you."

Ava's chest tightened, her emotions tangling between heartbreak and hope. "Christian," she began, but he was already pulling away and going back to his room.

His words lingered with her, though, sparking a thought. Could she adopt Christian on her own? Would Judge Holten think she had a chance? Maybe in a few days, she'd call and ask. For now, she wanted to focus on making sure Christian felt safe and loved.

A knock at the door pulled her from her thoughts. Aussie poked his head in. "You ready to head down?" he asked.

Christian shot out of his room and past Ava, already racing down the stairs. Ava smiled and walked to Aussie, who lingered in the doorway.

"Thank you," she said softly.

"For what?"

"For everything. For bringing us here, for caring. For being you."

Aussie stepped closer and wrapped his arms around her waist. Her hands went to his chest. "Ava, you don't ever have to thank me for doing something for you or Christian. You both may not realize it yet, but in the short time that we've known each other, you two have come to mean a great deal to me."

The sincerity in his voice made her chest ache in the best way. She nodded, not trusting herself to speak right at that moment. Instead, she lifted up on her tiptoes and kissed him softly.

"You mean the world to Christian and I, too," she whispered against his lips.

He grinned, took her hand in his, and led her toward the stairs.

As they descended the staircase, the aroma of baked pork chops and freshly baked bread grew stronger with each step.

Ava trailed slightly behind Aussie, feeling an odd mix of nervousness and warmth. She wasn't used to such cozy family dinners.

As they entered the kitchen, the sound of laughter greeted them. Christian was already seated at the table, leaning forward, talking with Aussie's dad about their plans for the horseback riding trip they had scheduled for the next day.

Ava smiled as she and Aussie pulled out chairs at the table. She sat beside Christian, who gave her a quick grin before diving back into his conversation. The table was adorned with a hearty spread. There were seasoned pork chops, roasted potatoes, steamed cabbage, and a basket of freshly baked rolls.

"This looks amazing," Ava said sincerely.

"Thank you, dear," Aussie's mom replied, beaming as everyone echoed Ava's compliment.

As the meal began, Aussie turned to his mom. "When are Angie, Rachel, and Wren getting here?"

Aussie's mom's smile dimmed slightly. "They're not coming this year, sweetheart. They're spending the holiday with their spouses' families."

Aussie's brow furrowed. "What? Why didn't anyone tell me?"

"I thought I did. That's why I was so thrilled when you said you'd be here. Your sisters and I agreed to pick a weekend after the holiday for us all to get together. It'll be like a second Christmas."

Aussie leaned back in his chair, still processing, but nodded. "Alright, fair enough."

Dinner moved on with lively conversation. The warmth in the room was palpable, and Ava found herself enjoying the easy dynamic of Aussie's family. When Aussie's mom brought the dessert to the table, Ava couldn't help but marvel at it. It was a double fudge chocolate cake, and on the side, she had vanilla bean ice cream to go with it.

"This is incredible," Ava said, savoring a bite."

"Thank you, Ava. I'm so glad you like it."

As the table settled into a post-dessert lull, Aussie's mom turned her attention to Ava. "Ava, dear, tell me about your family. Do they live nearby?"

Ava barely had time to process the question before Aussie interjected, his voice firm but gentle. "Mom, that's not really—"

"It's okay," Ava interrupted softly, placing her hand on Aussie's arm. She gave him a small, reassuring smile. "I don't mind."

Aussie hesitated but nodded, his concern evident. Ava turned back to his parents. "I grew up in foster care. My childhood wasn't the easiest. Most of my foster homes weren't great, and I wasn't treated well. But when I was seventeen, I met Evelyn. She's the one who finally saw me for who I was. She took me in, gave me a home, and believed in me when no one else did."

Aussie's mom's eyes glistened with emotion. "She sounds like an incredible woman."

"She was," Ava agreed, her voice filled with gratitude. "She's the reason I got into social work. I wanted to help kids the way she helped me."

"That's admirable, Ava," Aussie's dad said. "Taking Christian in, too, shows just how much heart you have."

Ava felt her cheeks warm under their praise. "Thank you."

As the evening wound down, Ava found herself stealing glances at Aussie and his parents. Their easy banter, the genuine care they showed one another was a dynamic she'd never experienced firsthand but always longed for.

As they left the table, Ava couldn't help but think how nice it would be to have a family like Aussie's. A place where warmth and laughter were constants, and love wasn't something you had to earn.

CHAPTER TWENTY-FOUR

The following afternoon, Ava found herself in what she could only describe as cookie boot camp.

The kitchen smelled heavenly. It was a mix of cinnamon, vanilla, and melted chocolate that wafted through the air. The soft croon of Bing Crosby singing *White Christmas* played from a small speaker on the counter.

Ava stood at the island, her hands dusted with flour as she rolled out sugar cookie dough, stealing glances at Aussie's mom, who was spooning cupcake batter into a cupcake pan.

"You've got a good hand for this," Aussie's mom said with a warm smile as she poured the remaining batter into the pan before glancing up at Ava. "Are you sure that you haven't done this professionally?"

Ava laughed, brushing a stray strand of hair from her face with the back of her wrist. "Not even close. This is my first time baking in, well, forever. I usually just buy cookies when I need them."

"Not anymore," she said with mock seriousness. "Around here, everything's made from scratch. You're officially in training."

Ava smiled as she cut another batch of star-shaped cookies. The light, cheerful atmosphere put her at ease, a welcome distraction from the chaos they had left behind.

"So," Aussie's mom began, her tone casual but her eyes sparkling with curiosity. "Tell me about you and my son."

Ava paused mid-roll, a blush creeping into her cheeks. "Um...what do you want to know?"

"Aussie's mom shrugged, though her expression betrayed her eagerness. "I've just never seen Aussie this smitten before. He's never brought a woman home to meet the family, let alone around Christmas. That's a big deal for him."

Ava felt her cheeks grow warmer as she focused on the dough. "He's amazing. Honestly, I don't know how I got so lucky to have him in my life."

Aussie's mom nodded knowingly. "And he'd say the same about you, I'm sure." She slid a tray into the oven and turned back to Ava, her tone softening. "You're good for him. It's obvious. And Christian? That boy is a treasure. He's so polite, so curious about everything. You've done a wonderful job with him."

Ava swallowed, touched by Aussie's mom's words. "Thank you. He's been through a lot, but he's such a good kid. If it were up to me, I'd adopt him tomorrow and make him mine forever."

Aussie's mom raised an eyebrow as she leaned against the counter. "So, why not do it?"

Ava sighed, cutting out another star. "Because the state doesn't exactly look favorably on single parents adopting kids. It's frustrating, but I'm not giving up on him."

Aussie's mom reached over and patted Ava's flour-dusted hand. "I can see how much you love him. And I can also see that you're not going to be single for much longer."

Ava blinked, caught off guard. "What?"

Aussie's mom chuckled, her eyes twinkling with mischief. "Oh, come on, sweetheart. You and Aussie are practically written in the stars. And let's just say I wouldn't be surprised if my son is already thinking about putting a ring on your finger."

Ava laughed, though her heart skipped a beat. "We haven't even been on a real date," she admitted.

Aussie's mom gasped, placing a floury hand on her chest in mock outrage. "You mean to tell me that man hasn't taken you out properly? That's a crime!"

"Well, in his defense, it's been a little crazy lately," Ava said with a grin. "I guess we just haven't had the chance."

"Well, that needs to change," Diane said firmly, wagging her finger. "Mark my words. I'll make sure it happens."

Ava shook her head, laughing softly as she finished the last of the cookies. "You're a force to be reckoned with, aren't you?"

"Always," she said with a wink.

They moved the last tray of cookies into the oven and began packing up the cooled batches into festive tins. The red and green containers that were adorned with ribbons were destined for the Christmas fair in two days, which was also Christmas Eve.

As they loaded a tray with an assortment of cookies, Aussie's mom placed a hand on Ava's shoulder. "Everything will work out, Ava. I have a good feeling about this."

Ava smiled, her heart feeling a little lighter. "Thanks. I hope so."

Together, they carried the trays of cookies into the study, where Aussie and his dad were seated, deep in conversation.

Aussie leaned back in the worn leather armchair in his dad's study. He had a steaming mug of coffee in his hands. The room smelled of pine from the crackling fireplace. Across from him, his dad sat in a matching chair, his hands resting on the arms, his gray eyebrows slightly furrowed.

Aussie had just finished giving his dad the cliff notes version of the situation back in Virginia Beach.

"You're sure this situation isn't going to follow you here?" his dad asked, his tone low and serious.

Aussie sighed, shaking his head. "As sure as I can be. Derek and the FBI agent are the only ones who know we're here." He hesitated, running a hand through his hair. "But it's serious, Dad. These people who have threatened Ava and Christian are believed to be behind the three murders in our town over the last few months."

His dad nodded, his expression thoughtful. "You're doing the right thing. Protecting them is what matters. But it's a hell of a responsibility, son."

"I know," Aussie admitted, his gaze falling to the flickering flames. "But they mean a lot to me. Ava is incredible, Dad. She's strong, kind, and smart. And Christian? That kid's been through so much, but he's still got this huge heart. I'd do anything for them."

The older man studied him for a moment before his lips curled into a small smile. "Sounds like you've got it bad for her."

Aussie chuckled softly. "Yeah, I guess I do." He paused, his expression turning serious. "It's only been a little over a month, but it feels like I've known her a lifetime. She's just different. She makes me think about things I've never really thought about before. About a future."

His dad leaned forward, resting his elbows on his knees. "I've never seen you like this. And that's saying something, considering I raised you."

Aussie laughed. "It's different with Ava. She's not just some passing thing. I want this to last."

"I'm happy for you," his dad said sincerely. "And for what it's worth, I like her. She's got a good head on her shoulders, and the way she looks at you, well, you'd be an idiot to let her go."

Aussie felt a rare warmth spread through his chest at his dad's words. "Thanks, Dad. That means a lot."

"And that boy," his dad added, nodding toward the TV room where Christian was sitting, talking on the phone to Katy. "He's a good kid. And I can tell you, after spending time with him earlier while we were horseback riding, that kid looks up to you. He respects you."

Aussie's chest tightened, his thoughts turning to Christian. "He's special. I don't know what his future holds, but if there's a way to keep at least him and Ava together, I'll do whatever it takes to make that happen."

Before his dad could respond, the door to the study opened, and Ava and his mom stepped in, balancing a tray of cookies.

"Cookie delivery!" Ava announced as she set a tray of sugar cookies on the table between him and his dad.

Aussie grinned up at Ava. "I see that you survived Mom's baking boot camp, huh?"

"Just barely," Ava teased, making everyone laugh.

Christian walked into the room carrying a tray of mugs. "I made us hot chocolate," he said as he carefully placed the tray down on another table.

"Thank you, Christian. That was very sweet of you," Aussie's mom told him, and Aussie smiled.

Christian turned toward Aussie's dad. "Thank you again for taking me horseback riding today. I had fun."

"You're more than welcome, son." his dad replied warmly, patting Christian on the back as he sat on the edge of the couch.

"Okay, the moment of truth," Ava said as she picked up a star-shaped sugar cookie and handed it to Aussie. "These are the first cookies that I ever made from scratch."

"So, you want me to be your guinea pig?" Aussie asked with a grin.

Ava rolled her eyes playfully. "Just eat it!"

Aussie bit into the cookie, and he had to suppress the moan that wanted to escape his mouth. The buttery sweetness of the cookie melted in his mouth. It was, without question, the best fucking sugar cookie he'd ever tasted. Though he would never tell his mom that.

But as Ava watched him expectantly. He knew that the anticipation was killing her. So, he couldn't resist teasing her.

He kept his facial expression neutral as he chewed it. "Well?" she asked as she leaned closer.

Aussie swallowed the cookie and then chased it down with a sip of hot chocolate.

"It's alright, I guess," he said, his tone deliberately nonchalant. He was fighting to keep a straight face.

Ava's eyes narrowed, and she swatted at his arm. "*Alright*? Seriously? I slaved over those cookies."

Before she could pull away, he caught her wrist and gently tugged her down onto his lap, laughing at her surprised yelp. He wrapped an arm around her waist, holding her close as he leaned in, his voice dropping to a soft murmur. "Okay, you win. It's one of the best cookies I've ever had. Happy?"

Her mock glare melted into a smile, and Aussie grinned, popping the last bite of the cookie into his mouth. "But I might need another one, just to be sure."

She rolled her eyes playfully, but the soft smile she gave him lingered, and Aussie felt the warmth in his chest grow.

As everyone settled in with cookies and hot chocolate, the room filled with chatter and laughter. For a moment, Aussie let himself believe that this was what life could always be like—safe, happy, and filled with the people who mattered most.

CHAPTER TWENTY-FIVE

Aussie lay on his back in bed, staring at the ceiling as the clock ticked past one in the morning. Sleep was a distant hope as his mind was a relentless jumble of thoughts.

He couldn't stop wondering about what was happening back home and whether the FBI had made any progress on tracking down Barrett or Chase. The uncertainty of that whole situation gnawed at him.

His thoughts then shifted to Ava and Christian, which was a welcome distraction. He smiled faintly, recalling how the three of them, along with his parents, had crowded around the living room, munching on Ava's sugar cookies and sipping hot chocolate while sharing stories. They had ended the night watching *How the Grinch Stole Christmas*. For the first time in what felt like forever, he'd felt at peace.

But now, the silence of the night was deafening. He sighed as he tossed the covers back. If sleep wasn't coming, he might as well get up. Padding softly down the hallway, he decided a cold glass of milk and a few of Ava's cookies might help clear his restless mind.

He made his way downstairs, careful not to wake anyone. As he approached the kitchen, he noticed a strange soft glow coming from the back porch. Curious, he walked over to the sliding glass door and peered out.

He was shocked to see Ava sitting out there with her laptop open on the small table in front of her. The light from the screen illuminated her face. She seemed lost in thought as her eyes focused on the screen. He could see she had tension in her body, and his heart ached for her. He knew she was carrying so much weight on her shoulders. Bracing himself for the cold, he slid open the door and stepped outside. But instead of the chill he expected, he was greeted by a blast of heat coming from the outdoor heater.

Ava looked up, and when she saw him, a soft smile spread across her face. "Hey," she said quietly, her voice breaking the silence of the night.

"Hey," Aussie replied, his own smile mirroring hers. She looked comfortable in her flannel pajamas, thick socks, and her hair pulled back into a high ponytail. She looked perfect, and a fleeting image of them snuggled up on the outdoor couch flashed through his mind.

"Mind if I join you?" he asked, gesturing toward the empty chair beside her.

"Not at all," Ava said, her smile widening as she closed her laptop. "Couldn't sleep?"

He grinned, shaking his head. "Nope. My mind won't shut off. You?"

She shrugged, her eyes darting back to the laptop for a moment. "Same. I figured catching up on some work might tire me out, but..." She trailed off, her expression softening as she looked at him. "It's not really working."

Aussie could see the exhaustion in her eyes, but he could also tell that something was bothering her. After a moment of silence, he decided to ask. "Everything okay?" he asked gently, his tone filled with concern.

Ava sighed. "My boss, Clint, is still being an ass."

Aussie leaned back in the chair. "What did he do now?"

"He is blowing up my email and phone with text messages, asking about things. I mean, Jesus, it's not like I'm the only person who works there."

Aussie reached over and took her hand in his. "I'm sorry. I can beat him up for you when we get back," he teased.

Ava chuckled. "I wish it was that easy. I just don't understand the man. One day, he acts like he hates his job and doesn't want to be there. But then the next day, he's up everyone's asses micromanaging them."

Aussie wasn't sure what to say. "Well, don't let him get you down. I'm not familiar with how the foster system works, but are there other agencies you could look into to work for?"

She shook her head. "No. Not unless I go out of the area."

Well, he didn't want her to do that.

"Well, I just hate seeing your beautiful smile disappear."

She blushed, and Aussie couldn't help but smile at how adorable she looked.

Ava turned her gaze to the snow-covered fields and woods beyond the porch. "It's beautiful out here," she said softly.

He followed her gaze, taking in the serene winter landscape. "Yeah, it is," he agreed, then added, "My sisters and I used to play out in those woods when we were younger. We'd spend hours out there, especially after a fresh snowfall like this."

Ava smiled, her eyes still on the woods. "That must've been nice, growing up in a big family."

Aussie knew she didn't have the best childhood, having been an orphan since birth. She had nobody, and he understood why she went on to be a social worker, helping others who were in the same position she was in back then. He admired her for that more than she probably realized.

She seemed lost in thought for a moment before she spoke again, her voice quiet. "When I was younger, during Christmas, I used to sneak out of my foster family's home late at night to walk into town and see all the Christmas lights. There was something magical about it, you know? No traffic, no people, just me and the lights." She smiled wistfully. "I'd walk up and down Main Street, then sit on the bench in the town square, taking it all in and wishing I had a family to share it with. After a few hours, I'd sneak back home and crawl into bed, hoping no one noticed I was gone."

Aussie listened intently, feeling a pang of sadness for the little girl she had been walking alone through the town, yearning for something as simple as a family. But as she spoke, an idea began to form in his mind. Without saying a word, he stood up and extended his hand to her.

"Come with me," he said, a mischievous glint in his eyes.

Ava looked surprised, but after a moment's hesitation, she took his hand, leaving her laptop behind. He led her inside, through the house, and into the garage. She followed silently, but he could tell by the look on her face that she was confused and maybe a little intrigued. He grabbed his truck keys off the key hook in the kitchen. Once they were in the garage, he handed her her winter coat and duck boots.

Now she was really giving him a strange look, and Aussie couldn't help but chuckle. "Trust me," he said with a grin.

She nodded, slipping on her coat and boots, though the curiosity in her eyes didn't fade. He grabbed a sweatshirt he saw on the washing machine and threw it on before slipping into his coat and boots. Once they were both bundled up, he led her outside to his truck.

He helped her up into the truck before hurrying around the driver's side. Once inside, he started up the truck and turned the heat on to a full blast.

"Where are we going?" She asked, giving him an amused look.

"It's a surprise," he replied as he looked for something he could use to blindfold her.

He smiled when he spotted a pack of bandanas that he had bought the other day. He reached into the back and got one.

Aussie held up a black bandana with a mischievous grin. "Alright, put this on. And no peeking."

Ava raised an eyebrow, crossing her arms. "Blindfolds, huh? This feels very *Fifty Shades*, Aussie."

He chuckled, shaking his head. "Trust me, if I were going for *that* vibe, we wouldn't be leaving the house. I'd be taking you to the basement."

Her cheeks flushed, and she swatted his arm. "You're impossible."

He winked, leaning closer. "Relax, it's just a surprise. I promise it isn't anything bad."

She sighed softly. "Alright," she grumbled. But Aussie could see the faint smile on her lips.

Once she was blindfolded, Aussie put the truck in gear and drove towards town.

The short drive was done in a comfortable silence. When he reached the downtown area of their town, he pulled into a parking spot.

"Don't take it off yet," he told her as he got out of the truck and walked around to her side.

He opened the door and then carefully helped her down. He took her hand and started guiding her down the sidewalk.

"Aussie, where are we?" she asked.

"We're almost there," he told her. God, he hoped she liked this.

Once he had her in the spot he wanted her in, he untied the blindfold and let it fall.

When he heard her gasp, he knew she loved it.

Aussie glanced over at her and saw tears welling up in her eyes as she stared at the town's little Main Street, all decorated and lit up, with not a soul in sight. It was exactly how she had described it. It was magical, quiet, and beautiful.

He chuckled softly, leading her down to the town square, where a few benches were scattered around. They sat down, and Ava took it all in, her eyes wide with wonder. "It's amazing," she whispered. "It feels just like it did all those years ago, except this time, I'm not alone. I have someone to share it with."

She looked at him, her eyes shining with gratitude, and Aussie felt his heart swell. "Thank you," she said, her voice thick with emotion. She leaned in and pecked his lips.

When she pulled back, she was smiling, and he couldn't help but smile back.

"Can I tell you my whole story, especially about the woman who saved me?"

Aussie felt his chest tightened. He knew that Ava kept her personal life very close to herself. She shared a few things from her past, but she never went into detail. And he never tried to pry. He knew that when she was ready to tell him, then she would.

He smiled as he brushed a strand of hair from her face. "I love to hear it."

For the next two hours, they sat on the bench, snuggled together, watching the lights twinkle in the night as Ava told him her story. It was a moment that he would cherish and never forget.

CHAPTER TWENTY-SIX

The morning after, Aussie found himself in the kitchen with his mom. He leaned against the kitchen counter, watching her knead dough for what he guessed was going to be another batch of cookies. The usual scent of cinnamon and nutmeg filled the room, and Christmas music hummed softly in the background.

"So," his mom began, not looking up from her task but clearly sensing his presence. "You've been hovering around me for ten minutes. Out with it, son. What's on your mind?"

Aussie chuckled, scratching the back of his neck. "That obvious, huh?"

She smirked. "You forget, I raised you. Spill."

He shifted his weight, suddenly feeling like a teenager asking for advice. "I want to plan something special for Ava. Like a date. But I need your help."

That got his mom's full attention. She paused her work and wiped her hands on a dish towel, turning to face him. Her smile was knowing, her eyes sparkling. "A date, huh? Alright, let's hear it. What does Ava like?"

Aussie shrugged, leaning his elbows on the counter. "She's not into anything flashy, that's for sure. She's more subtle. She's down-to-earth. I don't think she'd enjoy some big, fancy dinner out."

His mom nodded thoughtfully, tapping her chin. "I got that vibe from her too. She's sweet but not one for showy things. What about something romantic but simple? You know, something meaningful?"

"That's exactly what I was thinking," Aussie agreed. "I just don't know where to start."

His mom's face lit up. "Well, as it happens, your dad just finished renovating the barn. You know, the one by the big paddock?

He turned it into a little one-bedroom apartment. It's all decked out for Christmas since that's where Rachael and her husband will be staying when they visit."

Aussie's brow furrowed, intrigued. "Go on..."

"What if you took Ava on a sleigh ride?" she suggested, her voice tinged with excitement. "Then afterward, you could have a quiet, romantic dinner in the barn. The place is cozy and perfect for something like this. Lights, decorations, the works."

Aussie grinned, the idea settling in his mind like the final piece of a puzzle. "Mom, that's perfect. Ava would love that. She'd probably prefer it to any restaurant in town."

She clapped her hands together. "I thought so, too. And don't worry about Christian. I'll keep him busy for the evening. We'll bake some more cookies or do something fun."

"You're the best," Aussie said, his grin widening.

She waved him off, though she was clearly pleased. "I'll also make sure dinner's in the oven for when you two get back from the sleigh ride. Something hearty and warm. I'll handle all the little details. You just focus on Ava."

Aussie nodded, his chest tightening with gratitude. "Thanks, Mom. This is going to be great."

"It will be," she said with a knowing smile. "She's a special one, Aussie. I can see why you're so taken with her."

He nodded, his thoughts drifting to Ava. "She is. And she deserves something special."

She returned to her dough, humming along to the Christmas carol playing in the background.

Aussie lingered a moment longer, already picturing the evening ahead. Tomorrow night couldn't come fast enough.

"Thanks again, Mom," he said, heading toward the door.

"Anytime, sweetheart," she called after him.

Aussie laughed, shaking his head as he left the kitchen. His mom always had a way of making everything feel just right.

As Aussie was passing by his dad's study, he noticed the light was on, and he peeked in.

He saw Ava sitting in one of the oversized leather chairs with her legs crossed in Indian style. Her laptop was balanced on her lap. There was a steaming mug of coffee next to her on the table, along with a half-eaten cookie.

He leaned against the doorway and watched her work. Her brows were furrowed slightly as she concentrated on whatever was on the screen. She reached for the cookie and nibbled on it as she typed something on the keyboard.

She was beautiful. Her long black hair fell loosely around her shoulders. But it wasn't just her looks that had him captivated. It was the way she threw herself into everything she did. Whether it was protecting Christian, baking cookies with his mom, or sitting here now as she worked, she was all in.

Aussie couldn't help the smile that spread across his face as he straightened up. "Hey, beautiful," he said, stepping into the kitchen.

Ava's head lifted, and her lips curved into a smile. "Hey yourself," she said. "What are you up to?"

He walked over and leaned down, pressing a soft kiss to her cheek. She smelled like vanilla and coffee. "Just watching you," he said, grinning as he sat in the chair next to her.

She chuckled, closing her laptop halfway. "Well, that sounds productive."

"Very," he teased. Then, more seriously, he added, "You still have some Christmas shopping you wanted to do, right?"

"Yeah," Ava replied, taking a sip of her coffee. "There were a couple of things I still needed to pick up for Christian. Plus, I would like to get your parents something."

"How about we go tomorrow morning? I still need to grab a few things myself," Aussie said. "We could knock it out together."

Her smile softened. "That would be perfect."

Aussie leaned forward a little and rested his elbows on his knees. "I was also thinking…"

"Uh-oh," Ava teased, narrowing her eyes playfully. You already introduced me to blindfolds. Are handcuffs next?"

Aussie burst out laughing. "That was a good one. Though since you did bring it up…"

Her eyes widened, and she slapped his arm playfully. "Stop it!"

He laughed again. But then he reached over and took her hand into his. "Seriously. I was thinking this morning that we haven't exactly had an official first date yet, have we?"

Her head tilted slightly, curiosity dancing in her eyes. "No, I guess we haven't."

"Well," Aussie said, his voice warm, "I want to change that. Tomorrow night. Just you and me. I've got something special planned."

Her face lit up, a blush spreading across her cheeks. "Really? What are we doing?"

He grinned, loving the way her excitement bubbled to the surface. "It's a surprise," he said, tapping her nose lightly. "But I promise no blindfolds," he joked. "However, dress comfortably and warmly."

"You're not giving me any hints?" she pressed, but there was no frustration in her tone, just delight.

"Nope," he said, popping the "p" with a mischievous smirk.

"Fine," she said, laughing softly. "But now I'm really curious."

"Good," he said, leaning in closer. "That's the idea."

He didn't give her a chance to press for more details. Instead, he closed the distance, capturing her lips in a soft, lingering kiss. Ava sighed into it, her fingers brushing lightly against his jaw as she kissed him back. Just as the kiss deepened, a sharp buzz from Aussie's phone shattered the moment.

He groaned in frustration, reluctantly pulling away to glance at the screen.

His body tensed as he read the name flashing across it: *Derek*.

A call from Derek could only mean two things: either his team was being called up, or something had happened related to Ava and Christian.

"I need to take this," he said apologetically, stepping away. Ava nodded, her expression curious but understanding.

As Aussie answered, his gaze flickered to Ava again. She was still watching him, her brow furrowing slightly.

"Derek," Aussie said, his voice low as he stepped farther away. "What's up?"

"How's everything going up there?" Derek's tone was casual but carried an undertone of genuine concern.

Aussie allowed himself a small smirk. Derek had a funny way of always checking in on the women in his team's lives. He was such a big teddy bear, not that he would ever tell Derek that to his face.

"Things are good here," Aussie replied.

"That's good. I do have some news for you," Derek said.

"What's that?"

"Authorities located Chase and Barrett earlier this morning."

"That's good news," Aussie replied, his relief evident for a split second.

"Not exactly," Derek said, his tone heavy. "They were found dead."

Aussie froze. His blood ran cold, and his gaze instinctively snapped to Ava. She was watching him, her body tensing as if she could feel the change in his demeanor.

"What?" Aussie managed, his voice barely above a whisper.

"Their bodies were dumped in one of the parks up in Hampton Roads. Both of them were shot execution-style."

Aussie pinched the bridge of his nose, his mind reeling. "Do they know who did it?"

"No leads yet," Derek said. "But the evidence recovered at the scene ties them to the crimes in the area, including the three murders."

"What about any leads regarding who they were working for?"

"It's a dead end. However, I do believe that whoever is behind these deaths knew those boys were compromised and did one hell of a clean-up job. Although Agent Jefferson said they did recover a cell phone in the vicinity of one of the bodies. Hopefully, it belonged to one of them and contained viable information."

"So, what does this mean for Ava and Christian's situation?"

"I honestly don't know."

"Alright. Well, thanks for the heads-up," Aussie said, his voice firm despite the weight settling on his shoulders. "If you hear anything else, you'll call me, right?"

"Of course," Derek assured him.

They wished each other a Merry Christmas before ending the call.

As Aussie slipped his phone back into his pocket, he looked up and saw Ava was now standing a few feet away. She had her arms wrapped around herself as if bracing for bad news.

He walked over to her, his expression softening.

"What's wrong?" she asked, her voice low and laced with concern.

"Let's sit down, and I'll explain everything," he told her.

Ava nodded, and he took her hand and led her over to the couch.

Ava took a seat on the couch, and Aussie sat down beside her. He was close enough that their knees almost touched. For a moment, he didn't say anything. He stared at a spot on the floor as if gathering his thoughts.

"That was Derek," he finally said, his voice low.

Ava's chest tightened. Derek's calls were rarely casual. "What did he say?"

Aussie exhaled sharply, leaning forward with his elbows on his knees. "Barrett and Chase. They were found dead up near Hampton Roads this morning."

Ava's breath caught. Barrett and Chase, the two boys who had made Christian's life hell, were dead? She wasn't sure how to feel about that. Relief? Fear? Something else entirely?

"How?" she asked quietly, her voice barely audible.

"Gunshot wounds." Aussie's tone was grim. "But that's not all. Evidence was left at the scene—evidence that links them to all the recent crimes in the area, including the three murders."

Ava frowned, confusion mixing with unease. "What do you mean? They were behind it?"

"That's what it's supposed to look like." Aussie shifted to face her fully. "But Derek doesn't think it's that simple. He believes the evidence was planted. It was meant to frame Barrett and Chase and throw the authorities off the trail of whoever's really in charge."

The room felt colder somehow despite the warmth of the house. Ava's mind raced, trying to piece together what this meant. "So the real culprits are still out there?"

Aussie nodded. "That's what we think. We also think that whoever's pulling the strings knew about the FBI tracking Barrett and Chase."

Ava's hands curled into fists on her lap. "What does this mean for Christian? For us?"

He leaned back, his expression softening as he looked at her. "I don't know yet. Derek's still piecing things together. But at least for now, those two won't be bothering Christian anymore."

She wanted to feel reassured, but she couldn't shake the gnawing doubt in her gut. "You think this is over?" she asked, her voice barely above a whisper.

Aussie's silence was answer enough. He reached out, placing a hand over hers. "I don't know. All I do know is that whoever's behind this, they're still out there. But we'll figure it out. I'll make sure you and Christian are safe."

Ava nodded, but her unease didn't fade. She had learned long ago that trouble rarely ended when it seemed to. And this felt far from over.

CHAPTER TWENTY-SEVEN

Ava stood by the window in the living room, nervously twisting the hem of her red sweater as she glanced at the clock, waiting for Aussie to arrive.

Her thoughts drifted to the news he'd shared the day before and the shocking update about Chase and Barrett. It was a grim reminder of the chaos that had invaded her life.

But tonight wasn't about that, she thought to herself. Like Aussie had told her last night, there's nothing they can do about it right now.

So, she was determined that she wasn't going to let the darkness of yesterday cast a shadow over her first date with Aussie. For once, she was allowing herself to embrace something good, something worth smiling about.

Pushing all the negative thoughts aside, she let her mind wander back to earlier in the day. Her lips curved into a soft smile. She and Aussie had spent the morning in town shopping for Christmas gifts.

She could still feel his hand wrapped around hers as they walked through the bustling streets, snow falling gently around them. Every time he introduced her to someone he knew, he'd say, *"This is Ava, my girlfriend,"* with so much pride it made her heart flutter. And he didn't just say it. He showed it. The way he would lean closer, brush a strand of hair out of her face, or hold her tighter when the crowd pressed too close made her feel cherished.

Her phone buzzed, breaking her reverie. It was a text from Aussie.

Aussie: *Grab your coat and meet me on the front porch.*

Her heart leaped with excitement. She grabbed her coat, slipped it on, and checked her reflection quickly in the hallway mirror. She'd kept her outfit simple but warm. She wore black jeans and a soft red sweater that she had picked out while they were shopping. She opened the door and stepped out onto the porch. The air was crisp, and the snow glistened under the soft glow of the porch lights and Christmas lights.

A minute passed, and then she heard the faint jingle of bells. Her breath caught as a horse-drawn sleigh came into view, gliding up the driveway. A beautiful white horse pulled it. The sleigh was adorned with garlands and red bows. Ava's eyes widened in awe as her gaze drifted to the sleigh's seat, where Aussie was sitting, grinning at her.

He hopped off gracefully, his boots crunching against the snow as he approached. He was dressed in jeans and a cream-colored sweater that hugged his frame just right. *God, he was freaking gorgeous, and he is all mine,* she thought to herself.

"You look beautiful," he said softly when he reached her. He leaned in and brushed a quick kiss against her lips, making her heart skip a beat.

"Aussie," she started, still stunned by the sleigh, "this is amazing."

"Just wait," he said, his grin widening as he took her hand.

Ava let him lead her down the porch steps, her excitement bubbling over as they approached the sleigh. She recognized the driver immediately. It was a gentleman who Aussie had introduced her to earlier in town. "Hi again," Ava said, smiling, and the driver tipped his hat with a chuckle.

Aussie helped her into the sleigh, his hands firm but gentle as he guided her up. Once they were seated, he pulled her close, draping a thick blanket over both of them. From beneath the seat, he pulled out a thermos.

"Hot chocolate?" he offered, winking at her.

She laughed, her cheeks warming despite the cold. "You thought of everything."

The sleigh began to move, and the bells jingled softly as they glided over the snow. The world around them was quiet, the woods blanketed in white.

Ava leaned into Aussie, her head resting on his shoulder. Every now and then, she'd steal a kiss, and he'd laugh softly before kissing her back.

It was peaceful and magical, and for the first time in a long time, Ava felt completely at ease.

After about an hour, the sleigh slowed to a stop. Ava lifted her head, her eyes widening as she took in the sight before her. One of the barns on Aussie's parents' property was glowing with warm Christmas lights strung up along the roofline and windows. The scene was straight out of a Christmas movie. It looked romantic and breathtaking.

"It's beautiful," she whispered.

Aussie jumped down first, then turned to help her. His hands were warm as they steadied her on the snowy ground.

"Thank you," she said softly to the driver, who nodded with a kind smile before steering the horse away.

Aussie retook her hand and led her to the barn's front door. "My parents had this barn renovated a few months ago," he explained. "It's basically a second home now. I thought it'd be the perfect spot for the second part of our date."

When he pushed open the door, the smell of spices and roasted meat wafted out, making Ava's mouth water. Inside, the barn was transformed into a cozy haven. A Christmas tree stood in the corner, decorated with twinkling lights and ornaments, and the dining table was set for two, illuminated by candlelight.

Ava's throat tightened as emotion welled up. "Aussie, this is incredible. You didn't have to do all this."

"I wanted to," he said simply, watching her reaction. "I know you're not a fan of big, flashy dates, and I wanted this to be special. Something you'd enjoy and remember."

Tears prickled her eyes, but she blinked them back, laughing softly instead. "You're going to make me cry." She reached up, pulling his face to hers for a kiss.

The kiss started soft and tender but quickly deepened, heat sparking between them. Ava's hands slid into his hair as he wrapped his arms around her, pulling her closer. With a low growl, Aussie lifted her effortlessly, her legs wrapping around his waist as he pressed her against the wall.

Her heart raced the warmth of his body against hers, chasing away any lingering chill from the sleigh ride. She could feel the strength in his arms, the controlled intensity in his kiss, and it left her breathless.

When he finally pulled back, both of them were breathing heavily. His grin was lopsided and teasing. "We better eat before the food gets cold," he said, his voice husky.

Ava laughed, her head resting against his shoulder for a moment before he set her back on her feet. "Fine," she said, brushing her lips against his one last time. "But only because you worked so hard to put this together."

As he led her to the table, she couldn't stop smiling. This wasn't just a date. It was a memory she'd treasure forever.

A while later, the plates were empty, and Ava leaned back in her chair with a content smile on her face. "That was amazing, Aussie," she said, her voice warm with appreciation. "I had no idea you were such a great cook."

Aussie's cheeks flushed slightly as he ducked his head. "Well, I had a little help." He scratched the back of his neck sheepishly. "An elf may or may not have given me some tips."

Ava laughed, the sound light and carefree. "An elf, huh? Does your mom know that you call her an elf?"

"She'd probably take it as a compliment," he said with a chuckle. "But don't tell her. She'll start wearing one of those pointy hats and claim she's Santa's favorite."

Their laughter filled the room, and Ava couldn't remember the last time she'd felt this light, this genuinely happy, yet even as she savored the playful banter, a warmth stirred inside her that had little to do with the food or the ambiance. Her mind wandered back to earlier and the way Aussie had kissed her against the wall, how his hands had felt on her, strong yet gentle, possessive yet tender.

She caught herself staring at him. He was standing now, holding out his hand to her with a boyish smile that sent her heart fluttering.

"Dance with me," he said.

She didn't hesitate, slipping her hand into his. He led her to the living room, where soft Christmas music played from a speaker. The lights from the Christmas tree twinkled, casting a warm glow around them. Aussie turned to face her, pulling her close as they began to sway to the music.

Ava melted into his embrace, her hands resting lightly on his chest as his arms wrapped securely around her waist. The moment felt timeless, as though the world beyond the barn didn't exist. The gentle notes of the music blended with the quiet hum of their breathing, and for a while, they simply moved together, wrapped in one another's presence.

Breaking the silence, Ava tilted her head back to look at him. "Thank you," she said softly.

"For what?"

"For everything." Her voice wavered slightly, but she held his gaze. "For tonight, for making Christian and me feel safe, for just being you."

His expression softened, and she could see the emotion swirling in his eyes. She took a deep breath, her heart pounding as she continued. "I care about you so much, Aussie."

Before he could respond, she rose onto her tiptoes and kissed him, surprising them both.

At first, the kiss was gentle, but it quickly turned wild, the pent-up emotion and desire between them igniting like a spark to dry kindling. His arms tightened around her, pulling her impossibly closer while her fingers threaded through his hair.

Ava broke away just enough to whisper against his lips, her voice breathless. "I want you, Aussie."

His eyes darkened, a mixture of hunger and restraint flickering across his face. "Ava," he began, but she silenced him with another kiss, making her conviction clear.

This wasn't just about desire. It was about trust, connection, and the overwhelming need to be close to him in every possible way. Ava knew what she wanted, and for the first time in a long time, she wasn't afraid to reach for it.

Aussie couldn't look away from Ava. She stood in front of him, the glow of the Christmas lights casting a soft halo around her as if she were something out of a dream. Her lips curved in a way that made his chest tighten, and the words she'd just spoken echoed in his mind.

"I want you," she said. Her eyes had locked with his. They were unflinching and sure.

Her kiss lingered on his lips, searing and soft all at once. It was a promise and a plea, and Aussie felt something inside him give way. She had him completely.

He cupped her face, his thumb brushing over her cheek as he searched her eyes for any hint of hesitation. "Ava," he said, his voice low, rough with restraint. "If you want to stop, you better tell me now. Because once we start, I'm not going to be able to stop. You're too damn tempting."

She smiled, "I don't want to stop, Aussie. I want this. I want you."

The last thread of his restraint snapped. He claimed her lips in a kiss that was deep and consuming. It was one that left no question about how much he wanted her. Without breaking their kiss, he slid an arm under her legs and the other around her back, lifting her as if she weighed nothing.

Ava gasped softly, her arms looping around his neck as he carried her toward the bedroom. When he nudged the door open with his foot, the warm, inviting space welcomed them. A king-size bed sat against one wall, dressed in soft, neutral linens, while a small Christmas tree in the corner twinkled with tiny white lights. The festive charm of the room was intimate and magical, a perfect reflection of the moment.

Aussie set her down on her feet. His heart was racing.

She looked up at him. Her dark blue eyes shimmered with a blend of anticipation and vulnerability that hit him straight in the chest.

He reached out, tucking a strand of hair behind her ear, his fingers lingering against her cheek.

"You're so beautiful," he murmured, his voice husky, filled with awe.

Ava's lips curved into a shy smile, her gaze never leaving his. "You're not so bad yourself."

"Not so bad?" he teased, leaning in closer. "I was going for devastatingly handsome, but I'll take it."

She rolled her eyes, but the grin tugging at her lips gave her away. "Devastatingly handsome is a little much," she said, her voice light and teasing.

"Well, let me work on convincing you," Aussie murmured, slipping his hands beneath the hem of her sweater. Her breath hitched as his knuckles grazed the smooth skin of her back.

"Your hands are cold," she said, laughing softly.

"Sorry," he said, grinning as he leaned in to kiss her shoulder. "Don't worry, things will heat up soon."

Ava giggled, swatting at him playfully, but she didn't pull away. As he lifted her sweater over her head, her hair tumbled free, and she looked at him with a vulnerability that tugged at his heart.

"Your turn," she said as she reached for his sweater and started lifting it up. But she could only lift it so far because of her height. Laughing, Aussie bent down, and she pulled off the rest of the way.

She stared at his chest. "You've been hiding this all day," she said, her voice soft but teasing as her hands brushed over his chest.

"You should've said something sooner," he replied, his grin widening. "I'd have walked around shirtless just for you."

She laughed, her cheeks flushing deeper, and he leaned in, his lips brushing hers. "I love that sound," he murmured against her mouth.

"What sound?" she asked, her breath warm against his lips.

"Your laugh. It's one of my favorite sounds," he said, his tone soft but sincere.

Her gaze softened, and she cupped his face, pulling him into a deeper kiss. The rest of the world faded as their laughter quieted, replaced by the growing intensity between them.

Piece by piece, they undressed each other, their movements unhurried, as though savoring every second. Her laugh was soft and breathless when his hand brushed her side, and he couldn't help but grin, leaning in to kiss the corner of her mouth.

When they finally stood bare before each other, the air around them felt electric. Every glance and touch was charged with anticipation. Aussie guided her to the bed, lowering her gently onto the soft covers.

"I've never been this nervous," Ava admitted, her voice barely above a whisper.

"Me either," Aussie confessed, brushing a strand of hair from her face. "But it's the good kind of nervous."

She smiled, her hand slipping to rest on his chest. "Yeah. It is."

Aussie covered her body with his. He leaned down and cradled her face with his hands as he kissed her deeply. He poured all the unspoken words and emotions into the moment. Every movement felt like a declaration, every touch a vow to cherish and protect her.

Pulling from her mouth, he moved his lips slowly down her body. He made sure to worship each and every inch of her delectable body. Hearing her soft moans and gasps of pleasure fueled his drive.

"Aussie, please…" she pleaded as he started to make another pass down her body.

He could hear the need in her voice, which made his cock even harder.

But he ignored her pleas as he continued southward until his lips met the prize he was seeking.

As soon as his lips made contact with her pussy, he couldn't hold back. As his tongue lapped at her folds, it wasn't long before he felt her legs start to tremble, and he knew that she was just seconds from detonating. He applied pressure to her clit with his thumb and began rubbing it.

"Oh, fuck! I'm so close!" she panted.

Knowing that he wouldn't last long either, Aussie quickly moved back up her body and settled his body between her thighs.

"Fuck, you are so beautiful," he told her, leaning down and kissing her. He made love to her mouth, giving her a preview of what was to come.

Ava gripped his shoulders and pulled her mouth from his.

"Please, Aussie. I need you inside of me."

He grinned. "Your wish is my command."

Lining up his cock, he slowly entered her. Her walls felt like a vise was gripping him. She was so fucking tight. He pulled out, then pushed in a little further. He repeated that again, but then Ava shocked him when she bucked her hips, causing him to slide all the way in her.

The way she stilled and the small hiss she elicited, Aussie thought that he had hurt her.

"Fuck, Ava. Are you okay? Did I hurt you?" he asked. The panic was evident in his tone.

But then she cupped his cheek and stared into his eyes. She smiled.

"I'm fine, Aussie. Make love to me."

Those were the only words that he needed to hear. He kissed her again as he started to move again.

Ava's hands moved over him, her touch igniting a warmth that spread through him like fire.

Their movements became a rhythm, a dance that was equal parts passion and tenderness. Every sensation was heightened, every whispered word and soft moan a testament to how deeply they felt for one another. The only thing that existed was this moment, this connection, and the love that flowed between them in waves.

As the room filled with sounds of their lovemaking, the sensation soon became too overwhelming, and Aussie started to feel the familiar tension building inside of him. He was close.

As his thrusts became quicker and more urgent, he felt Ava's vaginal walls clench down on his cock, signaling that she was close too.

Two more hard thrusts and Ava cried out. Aussie quickly followed with his own release.

Aussie held her close, his forehead resting against hers as they caught their breath.

He pressed a gentle kiss to her lips, his voice a hushed confession. "I'm falling in love with you, Ava."

Her eyes glistened as she smiled, her hands framing his face. "I already fell in love with you," she admitted, her voice trembling with emotion. "The moment you stood up for Christian and me, you had my heart."

Their lips met again, a kiss full of promises for the future, and as they held each other in the quiet glow of the Christmas lights, Aussie knew that he would do whatever it took to protect her and the life they were beginning to build together.

Ava lay in Aussie's arms, her head resting on his chest as his steady heartbeat filled her ears. His arm wrapped securely around her waist, anchoring her to him, and she couldn't remember a time when she had felt so safe, so loved.

She traced light patterns on his skin, her mind swirling with emotions she couldn't quite put into words. Gratefulness swelled in her chest as she thought about how much her life had changed since

Aussie walked into it. Everything with him felt right, as if he had been meant to find her and be a part of Christian's and her life.

Her thoughts were interrupted by his voice, soft but full of concern. "You okay?"

Ava tilted her head to look at him. His soft, hazel eyes searched hers, and his brow furrowed slightly.

She smiled, running her fingers through his hair. "Everything is perfect," she assured him. "I was just thinking about how grateful I am for you. For us. For all of this."

His hand shifted to cradle her cheek, his thumb grazing her skin. "I'm grateful for you, too," he murmured.

She hesitated, then began to share her thoughts. "I've been thinking about how things will be when we get back home. I don't want this to change."

"It won't," he said firmly. "In fact, I was going to talk to you about that. I want to stay with you and Christian when we get back home. Not to rush anything between us but with the threat still out there…" He trailed off, his expression serious. "I don't want to take any chances."

Ava's heart warmed at his protectiveness. "I was going to ask you the same thing," she admitted, her voice soft. "I want you to move in with us, Aussie. Not just because of the threat, but because it feels right."

He kissed her forehead, his lips lingering there. "Then it's settled."

She sighed, her smile fading slightly. "I still don't know what will happen with Christian's case after the holidays. I don't want to lose him, Aussie. He's already been through so much."

Her voice cracked, and he tightened his hold on her, pressing a reassuring kiss to her temple. "You won't lose him," he said with conviction. "If there's anything I can do, anything at all, to help convince the court and the state that he belongs with you, I will. I promise."

Tears welled in her eyes, and she tilted her head to kiss him, her lips soft and full of gratitude. "Thank you," she whispered against his lips. "You have no idea how much that means to me."

They shared a few tender kisses, their connection growing deeper with every touch. When Ava pulled back slightly, a mischievous smile played on her lips.

"Can I ask you something?"

"Of course."

She tilted her head, curiosity lighting her expression. "What's your real name? And how did you get the nickname Aussie?"

A faint blush crept up his cheeks, and Ava raised an eyebrow, intrigued. "What's so embarrassing about that?" she teased.

He chuckled, the sound deep and rich. "My real name is Ty Mitchell."

"Ty," she repeated, testing the name on her tongue. "I like it. But I like Aussie too."

He smirked. "Aussie has a bit of a backstory."

"Do tell," she urged, snuggling closer.

He sighed, running a hand through his hair. "Before I joined the Navy, I had a pretty bad stutter. To the point where I wasn't sure the SEALs would even accept me. But I was determined to make it."

Her heart ached for him as he spoke. She could hear the vulnerability in his voice, and it only made her love him more.

"I tried everything," he continued. "Techniques, exercises, the whole nine yards, but nothing really worked. It was frustrating, to say the least. But then I discovered something. When I spoke in a slight accent, I didn't stutter. It was like flipping a switch."

Her eyes widened. "Really? And that's where Aussie came from?"

He nodded, a sheepish grin tugging at his lips. "Yep. It stuck during training because I used it so often. At first, it was just to avoid blocks, but then it became part of who I am."

Ava placed a hand on his cheek. "Thank you for sharing that with me," she said sincerely. "I can't imagine how hard that must have been. But I think it's amazing that you found a way to overcome it. It's just another reason to admire you."

His smile softened, and he leaned in to kiss her, his lips brushing hers in a gesture of gratitude and affection.

They talked a little longer, discussing his work in the Navy as much as he was allowed to share. Ava assured him that she was okay with his job and that she would be proud to stand by him no matter what.

When he kissed her again, it was searing and full of promise. Without a word, he rolled her onto her back, his hands framing her face as he deepened the kiss.

"Round two?" he teased, his voice low and full of warmth.

She laughed softly, her eyes sparkling as she pulled him closer. "Absolutely."

And as the night unfolded, their love grew stronger, solidifying the bond they had both been searching for.

CHAPTER TWENTY-EIGHT

The soft morning light filtered through the curtains as Aussie carefully slipped out of bed. Ava was still sound asleep, her dark hair fanned out across his pillow. Her breathing was steady and peaceful. He paused for a moment, taking in the sight of her. There was no way she was ever sleeping alone again. She belonged in his bed and in his arms.

Quietly, he grabbed a pair of sweatpants and a hoodie and made his way downstairs. The house was silent, save for the faint ticking of the grandfather clock in the hallway. The warmth of the kitchen greeted him, and he moved on autopilot toward the coffee maker, his mind replaying the events of the night before.

Their date had been nothing short of perfect. Dinner, dancing, and laughter had led to a night that had changed everything. After spending hours wrapped up in each other, they'd reluctantly pulled themselves from bed to clean up the barn house. Ava hadn't even put up a fight when he asked her to stay in his room, and the memory of her shy smile was seared into his mind.

They'd also decided to talk to Christian about Aussie moving in with them when they got back home. It wasn't just about keeping them safe. It was about starting something real. Something permanent.

Pouring himself a cup of coffee, Aussie leaned against the counter. He'd never felt like this about anyone. Ava wasn't just someone he cared for. She was it. She was his everything. She was smart, strong, and fiercely compassionate, and he knew deep down that he'd never find another woman like her.

"Merry Christmas Eve, sweetheart," came a cheerful voice behind him.

Aussie turned to see his mom entering the kitchen, her robe tied loosely around her waist and her slippers shuffling softly against the tile. She leaned up to kiss his cheek before reaching for a mug.

"Merry Christmas Eve," he replied, smiling as he sipped his coffee.

His mom gave him a knowing look, the corners of her mouth twitching upward. "How'd the date go?"

Aussie chuckled, recognizing the playful gleam in her eyes. She knew exactly how it had gone but was clearly enjoying making him squirm.

"It was amazing," he said, deciding to play along. "Thanks for helping with dinner and everything. It wouldn't have been the same without your touch."

She patted his arm. "It's what moms are for. But I can tell by the way you're glowing that it was more than just dinner."

He shook his head, grinning. "Okay, fine. It wasn't just dinner. It was perfect."

Her eyes softened as she leaned against the counter. "I know you like her, but how serious is it, Ty?"

He didn't hesitate. "I love her."

His mom's face lit up, and she clasped her hands together. "Oh, honey, I'm so happy to hear that. Ava is wonderful, and Christian? That boy has stolen my heart. I can already see them both as part of our family."

Aussie's heart swelled at her words, but he tempered his excitement with caution. "I feel the same, but we don't know how Christian's situation will play out. The courts and the state could still—"

She held up her hand, stopping him from continuing. "I believe everything will work out. Ava is exactly the person Christian needs.

Anyone with half a brain can see that. You just keep doing what you're doing, supporting them both. The rest will fall into place."

Before Aussie could respond, the sound of footsteps approached, and Christian appeared in the doorway. His shoulders were slumped, and his expression was clouded with uncertainty.

"Morning, buddy," Aussie greeted, setting his mug down. "What's wrong?"

Christian hesitated, rubbing the back of his neck. "It's nothing," he muttered.

Aussie turned to face him and met his gaze. "Hey, if something's bothering you, you can tell me."

Christian sighed, his cheeks turning pink. "It's just I wanted to get Ava something for Christmas. Something meaningful, you know? For everything she's done for me. But I don't have any money."

Aussie's heart broke a little, but he was also deeply impressed by the boy's thoughtfulness. He reached out, placing a hand on Christian's shoulder. "You know what? I was planning to run to the store this morning. How about you come with me, and we'll pick something out for Ava together?"

Christian's face lit up, his eyes wide with excitement. "Really?"

"Really," Aussie confirmed, ruffling his hair. "Go grab your shoes and coat."

Christian bolted out of the kitchen, leaving Aussie standing with his mom, who was watching him with tears glistening in her eyes.

"I'm proud of you, honey," she said softly. "You've got a big heart. Just keep following it, and everything will be okay."

Aussie smiled, her words sinking deep into his soul. "Thanks, Mom."

She reached up to squeeze his hand before turning to refill her coffee. As Christian reappeared, ready to go, Aussie grabbed his keys and gestured toward the door.

꿈

Ava slowly blinked her eyes open and looked around the room. At first, she was confused, but then she remembered that she was in Aussie's room.

Her thoughts drifted back to the night before, their date replaying in vivid detail. The sleigh ride, and then the way he held her close as they danced. The way his eyes locked onto hers was like she was the only woman in the world. And then the way he'd kissed her and made love to her, taking her breath away and unraveling her defenses completely.

She blushed, her smile deepening as she thought about their night together. Aussie had been everything—passionate yet gentle, assertive yet tender. He hadn't just made her feel wanted. He'd made her feel loved. Ava ran her fingers across the pillow next to her, already missing him.

But reality was beginning to settle in. She would have to talk to Christian about all of this. They had to be honest with him about how serious her and Aussie's relationship was becoming. Deep down, she knew he wouldn't mind. Christian adored Aussie, but it was still a conversation that couldn't wait.

With a sigh, she rolled out of bed, shivering slightly as her bare feet touched the cool floor. The room smelled of pine from the Christmas tree in the corner, and the festive decorations made her smile again. Grabbing her robe, she slipped out of Aussie's room and padded back to her own to shower and get ready for the day.

After freshening up and pulling on a long-sleeved t-shirt and jeans, Ava made her way downstairs. The enticing aroma of fresh coffee and baked goods greeted her as she entered the kitchen.

Aussie's mom was there, humming softly to herself as she worked at the counter.

"Good morning," Ava greeted, grabbing a mug and pouring herself some coffee.

Aussie's mom turned, her smile warm and inviting. "Good morning, sweetheart. Did you sleep well?"

Ava felt a flush creep up her neck, but she nodded. "I did. Thank you."

"Good." Aussie's mom wiped her hands on a towel and gestured to the empty room. "Aussie had to run into town for a few things. He took Christian with him."

Ava smiled, glad they were spending time together. Christian admired Aussie so much, and she knew it would mean a lot to him.

"Can I help you with anything?" Ava asked, setting her coffee down and moving toward the counter.

"Desserts," Aussie's mom said with a grin. "I've got all the ingredients ready for the cookies and pies. You just tell me what you want to start with."

Ava glanced over the array of ingredients and pulled her hair back into a ponytail. "Let's do cookies first. I feel like I'm becoming a pro at those."

As they worked together, Ava couldn't help but feel at ease. Aussie's mom was warm and kind, her laughter filling the kitchen as they chatted and shared stories. Ava felt a pang of longing for her own mother, but she also felt a sense of belonging here.

Aussie's mom glanced up from the dough she was rolling, a playful glint in her eyes. "So, how was the big date?"

Ava froze for a second, heat rushing to her cheeks. "It was really nice," she said, trying to keep her voice casual, though she could feel the blush creeping up her neck.

"Really nice?" Aussie's mom repeated with a chuckle. "That's all I'm getting? Come on, I've known Aussie his whole life. I can tell when something's different, and something is *definitely* different."

Ava laughed nervously, brushing her hands on her apron. "Okay, okay. It was amazing, from the sleigh ride to the dinner. It was all just perfect. It was like something out of a movie."

"That boy," Aussie's mom said, shaking her head with a proud smile. "He's always been a romantic at heart, even if he tries to act tough." She paused, her expression turning sly. "And how about after the date? Did he behave himself?"

Ava nearly dropped the cookie cutter she was holding. "Uh, well, he was a gentleman," she stammered, her face practically glowing now.

Aussie's mom let out a hearty laugh, waving a hand. "I'm just teasing you, dear. I'm glad the two of you were able to enjoy the night together."

Ava smiled. "Me too."

Aussie's mom reached out and gave Ava's hand a gentle squeeze. "I'm so glad that you came with Aussie. We've loved having you and Christian here. It's been such a joy sharing the holiday with you both."

Ava felt a lump form in her throat. "Thank you for letting us be a part of it. This whole experience has been more than I could have hoped for."

Aussie's mom smiled warmly, her eyes shining with emotion. "You've made my son happy, Ava. I haven't seen him this lighthearted in years. And that makes me happy, too."

Ava blinked back the sudden sting of tears. "He's made me happy, too," she admitted softly.

"Well," Aussie's mom said, her voice brightening as she gestured to the tray of cookies, "then it sounds like this is the start of something wonderful. Now, let's get these in the oven before the boys come home and eat all the dough!"

Ava laughed, her heart feeling full. She knew she'd found something special here—not just with Aussie but with his family.

CHAPTER TWENTY-NINE

The air was filled with the scent of roasted chestnuts and peppermint as Ava, Aussie, and Christian strolled through Santa Land. The town festival was a wonderland of twinkling lights, glittering garlands, and Christmas cheer. Snow had started to fall as they walked, coating the cobblestone streets in a light powder and adding a magical touch to an already enchanting evening.

Ava clutched Aussie's hand tightly, her cheeks flushed from the cold and the warmth of being so close to him. On her other side, Christian walked with wide-eyed wonder, occasionally darting ahead to check out the vendor booths.

"I still can't believe this place," Ava said, her voice soft and amazed.

Aussie glanced down at her, a smile tugging at the corner of his mouth. "It's pretty awesome. When we were kids, my mom made sure we never missed it, no matter how busy life got. Santa Land was her way of making Christmas unforgettable."

"The place does have a magical feel to it," Ava said.

They passed a vendor selling hot chocolate, and Aussie stopped to grab three cups. He handed one to Ava and another to Christian when he came bounding back.

"Thanks," Christian said, his smile bright. "This is so cool. There's, like, everything here. Did you see the guy carving ice sculptures over there?"

"Not yet," Ava said, laughing at his enthusiasm. "Lead the way."

Christian nodded and darted off, sticking close enough to keep them in sight. Ava watched him go, her heart swelling. He looked so happy and carefree, and it was moments like these that reminded her just how far they had come.

"I think he's having the time of his life," Ava said, her gaze following Christian.

Aussie chuckled, slipping his arm around her waist. "Good. That's what tonight is about—having fun and making memories."

As they walked, the soft notes of Christmas carolers floated through the air. A group dressed in old-fashioned Victorian costumes stood near the center of the festival, harmonizing to *Silent Night*. Ava paused, taking it all in. The little shops and vendor booths were decked out with wreaths and twinkling lights, their windows displaying handcrafted ornaments, cozy scarves, and homemade pies.

"Have you ever seen anything like this before?" Aussie asked, pulling her a little closer.

Ava shook her head, her eyes glistening. "Never. It's beautiful. I feel like I've stepped into the North Pole."

"Good," he said, his voice low and warm. "You deserve this kind of magic, Ava. You and Christian both."

Her heart swelled at his words, and she leaned into him, her head resting on his shoulder. "Thank you for sharing this with us," she whispered.

They continued strolling, eventually making their way to the center square where a grand Santa's workshop had been set up. A line of kids waited eagerly to meet Santa, their laughter and chatter filling the air. Christian had rejoined them by then, tugging Ava's sleeve.

"Do you think I'm too old for a picture with Santa?" he asked, a mix of hope and embarrassment in his tone.

Ava smiled, brushing a hand over his hair. "You're never too old for Santa. Go for it."

Christian grinned and turned to Aussie. "You coming with me?"

Aussie chuckled, nudging him forward. "Not this time, kid. This one's all you."

They watched as Christian joined the line, talking animatedly to a boy around his age. Ava's gaze softened as she turned back to Aussie. "He's really fitting in, isn't he?"

"He is," Aussie said, his voice full of pride. "He's got a good heart. You've done an amazing job with him, Ava."

She blinked, surprised by the sudden emotion welling up inside her. "It's not just me. He's come so far because of people like you and your mom and dad. He can see what a real family is like and that it really does exist."

Aussie stopped walking, turning to face her. Snow dusted her hair, and her cheeks were pink from the cold. He cupped her face gently, his thumb brushing along her jawline. "You're my family now," he said softly. "Both of you."

Ava's breath hitched, and she felt the sting of happy tears in her eyes. Before she could respond, Christian's voice called out.

"Hey! I'm next!"

They both turned, laughing as they watched Christian sit on Santa's chair, grinning for the camera. Ava felt a warmth settle over her, one she hadn't felt in years. This was more than a magical night. It was a new beginning.

Aussie reached for her hand again, interlacing their fingers. "Let's make this our tradition," he said.

Ava smiled up at him, her heart full. "I'd like that."

As they strolled past a booth filled with trinkets and holiday ornaments, Christian suddenly stopped, his gaze fixed on a silver charm bracelet displayed under twinkling fairy lights. The delicate bracelet featured a small snowflake charm that sparkled under the glow.

"What caught your eye?" Ava asked, stepping beside him.

Christian hesitated, his cheeks pink from the cold or maybe embarrassment. "Katy mentioned once that she wanted a charm bracelet," he admitted softly.

Ava's heart melted at his thoughtfulness. She liked Katy and thought it was sweet that Christian was thinking of her. "How about I get it for you to give to her when we're back home?" she offered with a warm smile.

Christian's face lit up. "Really? You'd do that?"

"Of course," Ava said, reaching out to squeeze his shoulder.

Without warning, Christian threw his arms around her, hugging her tightly. "Thank you, Ava. You're the best."

Ava's heart swelled, and she wrapped her arms around him, holding him close. Moments like these made her wish more than anything that she could keep Christian for good. She couldn't imagine her life without him anymore.

The night continued with everyone laughing, sipping cocoa, and enjoying the festival's magic. Ava was admiring an intricate ice sculpture of a reindeer when Aussie's phone buzzed. He glanced at the screen and sighed.

"It's Derek. I need to take this," he said, his tone apologetic.

"Go ahead," Ava assured him. "We'll walk around a bit more."

Aussie gave her hand a squeeze before stepping away, leaving her and Christian alone. They wandered toward the edge of the square, where the snow was falling more heavily. As they stood near a tree wrapped in golden lights, Christian's expression grew serious.

"Ava?" he began hesitantly, his voice barely above a whisper.

"What's on your mind, kiddo?" she asked, giving him her full attention.

He hesitated, shuffling his feet in the snow. "Would you ever think about trying to adopt me? I mean, I love living with you, and you actually care about me. You pay attention, you know? No one's ever really done that before."

Ava felt her throat tighten, emotion welling up inside her. His words were so raw, so honest, that they hit her like a wave. Tears pricked her eyes, but she smiled through them.

"Christian," she said, her voice thick with emotion, "you mean the world to me. I promise you that I'll do everything in my power to keep you with me. You're already my family in my heart."

Christian's eyes glistened as he hugged her again, and she held him close, her resolve to fight for him stronger than ever.

When Aussie returned, his expression was unreadable, but Ava could sense something wasn't right. She handed Christian some money. "Why don't you go find some of that white chocolate cocoa we saw earlier?" she suggested gently.

"Okay," Christian said, bounding off with a smile.

As soon as he was out of earshot, Ava turned to Aussie. "What's wrong?" she asked softly.

Aussie exhaled, running a hand through his hair. "It's what I've talked about before—my job. I'm always on call, and sometimes that means leaving at a moment's notice."

Her heart sank, but she nodded, understanding the weight of his words. "When do you need to leave?"

"Not until the day after Christmas," he said. "We're not deploying for sure, but we need to be ready just in case."

Reality hit her like a cold gust of wind. She would soon have to return to her real life in Virginia Beach, and Aussie would head off on a mission. The thought of being apart from him weighed heavily on her, but she forced herself to stay strong. The last thing she wanted was to add to his stress.

Aussie must have sensed her unease because he pulled her into a hug, his arms wrapping around her securely. The embrace was warm and comforting, grounding her in the moment.

"Listen," he said, his voice low and steady. "Until then, we're going to focus on Christmas. We're going to enjoy this time together and make it amazing for Christian. Deal?"

Ava nodded against his chest, his words soothing some of her anxiety. "Deal," she whispered.

He tilted her chin up and kissed her, slow and sweet. The moment felt like a promise, a reassurance that they would face whatever came their way together.

But as they stood there under the falling snow, Ava couldn't shake the nervous feeling creeping in. Going back home meant returning to uncertainties. She pushed the thoughts aside, determined to enjoy the time they had left. For now, that was all she could do. She would just live in the moment.

CHAPTER THIRTY

Aussie lay in his bed with Ava tucked against his side. Her head rested on his shoulder, and she had one arm draped possessively across his chest. Her body fit perfectly against his.

For a moment, he stayed perfectly still, his heart full as he watched her sleep. There was something profoundly peaceful about waking up beside her, a feeling he hadn't realized he'd been missing until now. With Ava, everything felt right, as if all the scattered pieces of his life had quietly fallen into place.

She stirred, her lips curving into a sleepy smile before her eyes fluttered open. "Morning," she murmured, her voice husky with sleep.

"Morning, beautiful," he replied, brushing a strand of hair from her face.

Ava stretched lazily, her hand coming to rest on his chest. "What time is it?"

Aussie glanced at the clock on the bedside table. "A little after seven. Looks like we're up before Christian."

She chuckled softly, her laughter warming him from the inside out. "A Christmas miracle."

"Guess that means we've got some time to ourselves," Aussie said, his tone playful as he leaned down to press a kiss to her forehead.

Her eyes sparkled as she looked up at him. "What did you have in mind?"

"Well," he began, his fingers trailing lightly over her arm, "I was thinking we could start by staying right here a little longer. Maybe talk about how lucky I am to wake up next to you."

Ava rolled her eyes, but her smile betrayed her. "You're laying it on thick this morning."

"Because it's true," Aussie said earnestly, his voice softening. "I can't believe I get to wake up with you."

Her expression softened, and she reached up to trace the line of his jaw. "You're pretty amazing yourself, you know."

"Not amazing enough to deserve you," he teased, though his heart felt full just hearing her say it.

"You're ridiculous," Ava said, laughing as she playfully pushed his chest.

"And yet, you're still here," he shot back, his grin widening.

They stayed like that for a while, trading soft words and laughter as the morning light grew brighter.

Eventually, Ava propped herself up on her elbow, her expression thoughtful. "We should probably get up before Christian comes looking for us."

Aussie groaned dramatically, pulling her back down against him. "Just five more minutes."

Ava laughed, but she didn't resist, settling into his arms once more. "Fine, but if he bursts in here, I'm blaming you."

"I'll take my chances," he said, his voice full of warmth.

As they lay there, the scent of pine and the faint sound of Christmas music from downstairs filled the air. Aussie couldn't imagine a better way to start the day than having Ava in his arms and the promise of a future with her in his heart.

About an hour later, and after two cups of coffee, Ava sat cross-legged next to the Christmas tree, watching as everyone opened presents.

Christian sat beside her as he tore into a brightly wrapped box with his name on it. Across the room, Aussie lounged in an armchair, his signature easygoing grin in place as he watched the scene unfold.

His parents were seated nearby, exchanging knowing smiles as they handed out the last few gifts.

"Whoa, check this out!" Christian exclaimed, holding up a sleek skateboard emblazoned with bold, vibrant designs. His eyes were wide with disbelief as he turned to Ava. "This is awesome!"

Ava laughed softly, "I'm glad you like it. Just promise me you'll wear the pads and helmet that go with it."

"Of course!" he said with a grin that didn't quite convince her.

Aussie chuckled from his spot, raising a mug of cocoa in a mock toast. "If he's anything like me at that age, good luck getting him to keep the helmet on."

"Not helping," Ava shot back playfully, her lips curving up into a smile.

Aussie winked at her before leaning forward to grab a gift from beneath the tree. "Speaking of rebels, this one's for you, Ava." He handed her a small box wrapped in silver paper, tied neatly with a red bow.

"For me?" Ava asked, glancing at him suspiciously as she took the box.

"Just open it," he said, his grin widening.

Ava carefully untied the ribbon, her fingers trembling slightly, though she wasn't sure why. She peeled back the paper to reveal a black velvet box. When she opened it, her breath caught. Inside was a delicate silver bracelet and a charm in the shape of an anchor.

Her throat tightened as she looked up at Aussie. "It's beautiful," she said softly.

"It reminded me of you," he said, his voice quiet but steady. "Strong, grounded, always holding steady no matter what storms come your way."

Ava felt her eyes sting, and she blinked quickly to keep the tears at bay. "Thank you," she whispered, fastening the bracelet around her wrist.

"You're welcome," Aussie replied, his voice warm. "Merry Christmas, Ava."

"Merry Christmas," she said, her smile trembling but genuine.

Before she could dwell on the emotions bubbling in her chest, Christian nudged her arm. "Ava, this one's for you, too," he said, holding up a brightly wrapped gift.

Ava took it, laughing as she tore into the paper. Inside was a framed photo of her, Christian, and Aussie, taken just a few days earlier when they had been outside and engaged in a snowball fight. The three of them were laughing. She had forgotten that Aussie's mom had been out there taking pictures.

She traced the edge of the frame with her fingers, "This is perfect," she said, her voice thick.

"You're stuck with us now," Aussie teased, his grin softening the words.

"I wouldn't have it any other way," Ava replied, glancing at Christian, then back at Aussie.

CHAPTER THIRTY-ONE

Ava stood next to Aussie's truck. Her heart was heavy as she watched Aussie's mom hug Christian tightly. His shy smile widened when she kissed the top of his head and whispered something in his ear that made him giggle.

The past six days had been a whirlwind of warmth and laughter, filled with stories shared over hearty meals, games played in the backyard, and late-night conversations that felt like peeling back layers of a life she never knew she could have. She felt a pang of sadness as she thought about leaving this newfound family.

"You better bring him back soon," Aussie's mom said, turning to Ava and pulling her into a firm embrace. "And you too, sweetheart. You're family now."

Ava swallowed the lump in her throat and managed a smile. "Thank you for everything. I had so much fun."

"It was our pleasure," Aussie's dad added, his gruff voice softening as he clapped Aussie on the shoulder. "You've got a good one here, son. Don't mess it up."

Aussie chuckled, wrapping an arm around Ava's waist. "Don't worry, Dad. I know."

As they piled into Aussie's truck, Ava glanced back one last time, waving at the couple standing on the porch. Christian's hand shot up enthusiastically, his face glowing with the happiness he'd found here. She felt a bittersweet ache. She couldn't wait to come back.

The truck rumbled to life, and moments later, they pulled out onto the road. The familiar hum of the tires on the pavement and the faint strains of a country song on the radio filled the cab as they settled in for the twelve-hour drive back to Virginia Beach.

Christian's excitement had finally worn him out, and Ava glanced back to see him slumped in his seat, sound asleep.

Just as they merged onto the highway, her phone buzzed. She glanced at the screen and saw a text from Judge Holten.

"Can you be at the courthouse tomorrow at 3:00 pm?"

Ava's brows furrowed as she quickly typed back, *"We should make it as long as we don't hit any delays. What's going on?"*

The response came almost immediately.

"Christian's case. There's been a development that needs to be addressed ASAP."

Her stomach twisted. The last time she'd spoken to Judge Holten before their trip, the judge had mentioned taking the rest of the year off. Why the sudden urgency now? She typed back quickly, *"What kind of development?"*

But this time, the reply was frustratingly vague.

"Just be there at 3. I'll explain everything then."

Ava's chest tightened, and her mind raced with possibilities. She stared out the window, her thoughts spiraling. Had something happened with his foster parents? Was the placement falling through? The unknowns gnawed at her, making it hard to breathe.

"Everything okay?" Aussie asked, glancing at her briefly before returning his focus to the road.

She hesitated, glancing back at Christian. He was still sound asleep, his face peaceful. Not wanting to wake him, she lowered her voice. "Judge Holten just texted. She needs me at the courthouse tomorrow at three. She said it's about Christian's case and that there's a development, but she won't tell me anything else."

Aussie's jaw tightened, but his tone was steady as he said, "Well, that doesn't mean it's bad news. Maybe it's just procedural or something minor."

Ava shook her head. "She wouldn't call me in like this unless it was important. I don't know what to think. I'm scared."

He reached over and squeezed her hand. "Hey, whatever it is, we'll deal with it. You don't have to do this alone. I'm here for you and for Christian."

His words were a balm to her fraying nerves, but the knot in her stomach remained. She nodded, taking a deep breath and trying to steady herself.

"Thanks."

"No matter what happens tomorrow," he added, his voice firm but warm, "I'm not going anywhere. You and Christian have me for the long haul. Got it?"

Ava looked at him, her eyes glistening with gratitude. "Got it."

As the miles stretched ahead of them, Ava leaned back in her seat, trying to calm the storm of emotions swirling inside her. Tomorrow felt like an ominous shadow, but for now, she focused on the positive of having Christian with her now. Whatever awaited them at the courthouse tomorrow, she knew she wasn't facing it alone.

CHAPTER THIRTY-TWO

Ezekiel sat in the dimly lit corner of his office, the blinds drawn to shield him from prying eyes. A cigarette burned between his fingers, its ash collecting in a glass tray overflowing with discarded butts. He had been laying low for weeks, ever since the heat had turned up on the gang's operations. The kid, Christian, had been a thorn in his side, meddling in business that was none of his concern. And Ava? She was a problem Ezekiel intended to eliminate, one way or another.

The buzzing of his burner phone broke the silence. Ezekiel exhaled slowly before answering, his voice sharp and impatient. "What?"

"It's Jarod," came the gruff reply. "I just found out something you're gonna want to hear."

Ezekiel leaned forward, his eyes narrowing. "What is it?"

"Ava and the kid," Jarod said, lowering his voice as if someone might overhear. "They're back in Virginia Beach."

Ezekiel's grip on the phone tightened, his pulse quickening. The corner of his mouth curled into a sneer. "You're sure?"

"Positive," Jarod confirmed. "They got back late last night. Been laying low at her place."

Ezekiel's thoughts churned as anger bubbled beneath the surface. He had been waiting for the right moment to clean up this mess, and now it seemed the opportunity was presenting itself. "Good," he growled. "Send someone to track them. Watch their movements. When the time is right, take them out—both of them."

Jarod hesitated. "Actually," he began, his tone shifting, "I already know where they're gonna be later today."

Ezekiel's brow furrowed. "What are you talking about?"

Jarod cleared his throat. "They're going to court. Something about the kid's case. They'll be there this afternoon."

The sneer returned to Ezekiel's face. This time, it was sharper and more sinister. "Perfect. That makes things easier. I don't care how you do it. Just make it happen. Take them out."

"You got it," Jarod said. "I'll handle it."

Ezekiel hung up, a sense of satisfaction washing over him. He leaned back in his chair, propping his feet up on the desk. Things were finally falling into place. With Ava and Christian out of the picture, his business could get back on track, and the gang's operations would flourish once more. He allowed himself a rare moment of relaxation, his lips curling into a smirk.

That moment was short-lived.

The door to his office burst open with a thunderous crack, the sound of splintering wood echoing through the room. Ezekiel jolted upright, his feet slamming to the floor as armed officers and FBI agents flooded the space, their weapons drawn.

"Ezekiel Torres," one of the agents barked, "you're under arrest!"

"What the—" Ezekiel started, but the words died in his throat as two agents grabbed him, forcing him to the ground. The cigarette fell from his fingers, its ember snuffed out as it hit the floor.

His heart raced as cuffs snapped around his wrists. "You don't know who you're messing with!" he spat, struggling against their grip.

"Oh, we know exactly who you are," Agent Jefferson replied coldly. "You've got a long list of charges to answer for, including murder."

As another agent walked Ezekiel out of his office while reading his rights to him, Ezekiel's mind reeled. How had this happened? He had been so careful, staying out of sight, making sure nothing could trace back to him. And now, his plan to eliminate Ava and Christian was crumbling before it even began.

As he was hauled to his feet, he saw that his office was now swarming with law enforcement. The smirk on his face was long gone and replaced by a mask of fury and disbelief. His carefully constructed empire was crumbling around him, and there wasn't a damn thing he could do to stop it.

FBI Agent Jefferson stood in the chaos of Ezekiel Moore's office. The adrenaline was pumping through his veins. This was the moment he'd been working toward for months. Finally, they had the mastermind behind the wave of violent crimes and gang-related operations that had swept through the region.

Jefferson's chest swelled with pride as he watched the infamous criminal hauled off in handcuffs as his rights were being read to him.

This was justice in action.

Jefferson couldn't suppress the smirk tugging at the corners of his mouth. *Got you, you slimy son of a—*

"Agent Jefferson!" a voice called sharply, breaking his triumphant reverie.

Jefferson turned to see Agent Reed standing near a desk in the corner of the room. He had a look of unease on his face. "You need to see this," Reed said, gesturing to a computer screen.

Jefferson frowned and made his way over, weaving through the swarm of agents cataloging evidence. "What is it?" he asked, leaning down to look at the screen.

What he saw made his blood run cold.

The monitor displayed an email from Judge Jarod Brown that was timestamped less than an hour ago, stating that Ava Morgan and the boy, Christian, who she was caring for, were scheduled to be at the courthouse at three o'clock for a hearing with Judge Holten.

Jefferson froze, his brain scrambling to process what he was reading. His pulse thundered in his ears as the gravity of the situation sank in. *Fuck! Ava and Chrisitan were walking into a death trap.*

"Somebody get VBPD on the line and have them get to the courthouse," Jefferson barked, his usual calm demeanor slipping into urgency.

He pulled out his phone and immediately dialed Derek Connors, the SEAL team commander who was working closely with their task force.

Derek answered on the second ring, his voice steady. "Agent Jefferson, what's up?"

Jefferson didn't waste time with any pleasantries. "We've got a problem. Do you know where Ava and Christian are?"

"From my understanding, they're at the courthouse," Derek replied. "Why? What's going on?"

Jefferson pinched the bridge of his nose, fighting to keep his voice steady. "Get to the courthouse now. Ava is in danger. I've already called for backup."

"What kind of danger?" Derek's tone sharpened.

Agent Jefferson quickly went over the situation with the arrests of Ezekiel and Judge Brown before explaining the email that they just found on Ezekiel's computer.

"Fuck!" Derek swore. "My team and I are on our way. We'll also try to reach Ava."

"I'll meet you there."

Jefferson disconnected the call and turned to the room full of agents.

"Everyone, listen up!" he barked. "We've got an active threat at the courthouse. I need all available agents there immediately. Let's move!"

As the agents sprang into action, Jefferson grabbed his gear as his mind raced. His earlier elation was gone, replaced by a gnawing sense of dread. If they didn't get there in time, the consequences could be catastrophic.

He pushed through the crowd, his jaw clenched as he headed for the door.

CHAPTER THIRTY-THREE

Aussie sat at the back of the classroom, staring blankly at the PowerPoint slides projected on the wall. The annual Navy-mandated substance abuse training was the same every year. It was long, boring, and delivered in the most monotone voice possible.

The instructor, a gray-haired civilian contracted by the Navy, droned on about the dangers of alcohol abuse, sounding like she'd rather be anywhere else. Aussie was right there with her.

He stifled a yawn, propping his chin on his hand. His leg bounced under the table as his mind began to wander. *Ava.* He hadn't been able to stop thinking about her since they'd left her house that morning. The court hearing weighed on him. They still didn't know the full details, but the fact that it involved Christian's case was enough to keep a knot of worry in his gut.

He checked the clock on the wall, willing it to move faster. *Come on, let's wrap this up already.* He hated being stuck here when all he wanted was to be by Ava's side, supporting her and Christian through whatever the judge had to say.

Originally, they were just supposed to be briefed in the morning on a potential situation that was flaring up in the Middle East. As soon as the briefing ended, Aussie was planning to head to the courthouse to attend the hearing with Ava. But that plan was shot to hell when they were informed that they had to attend the stupid required class.

Just as his patience was about to snap, the classroom door burst open with a bang, startling everyone inside. Derek strode in, his face set in a grim mask. "Class is over, gentlemen," he announced, his voice cutting through the monotony like a knife.

Aussie's head snapped up, his stomach twisting. Obviously, something had gone down.

"What's going on?" Bear asked as he was already halfway out of his seat.

Derek scanned the room, locking eyes with Aussie. "I just got a call from Agent Jefferson. That cell phone they found near Barrett and Chase's bodies had some incriminating texts on it. The FBI just raided both Ezekiel Moore and Judge Jarod Brown's offices. Both are in police custody. One of the agents found some evidence in Mr. Moore's office that shows that Ava and Christian could be in immediate danger."

The words hit Aussie like a punch to the gut. His body was already moving on instinct. His chair scraped against the floor as he stood. "What kind of danger?" he demanded.

"Not sure about all the details yet," Derek said, motioning for the team to move. "But we're not waiting around to find out. Let's go. I'll explain more on the way. Agent Jefferson is already en route, and the police have been notified."

The team began rushing out of the room, grabbing their gear as they went. The instructor, clearly flustered by the sudden interruption, huffed and puffed, clutching her clipboard to her chest. "Excuse me, Commander, but this is an important—"

Derek cut her off with a sharp, sarcastic smile. "Oh, I'm sure your lecture on the dangers of wine coolers has been riveting, ma'am. But we've got lives to save. You'll survive without us."

A few snickers filtered through the room as the team filed out, leaving the instructor sputtering behind them. Aussie followed Derek into the hallway. His heart was pounding as he ran through worst-case scenarios in his head. He didn't say a word as he climbed into Derek's SUV.

Derek slid into the driver's seat, slamming the door shut before starting the engine. He glanced at Aussie, his expression hard but laced with a hint of disbelief. "You're not gonna believe who's tied up in all of this."

Aussie's jaw clenched, his grip tightening on the dashboard as they sped out of the parking lot. "Try me."

Derek let out a sharp exhale, his knuckles white on the steering wheel. "Clint Meyers, Ava's boss."

Aussie's eyes widened in shock. "Are you fucking kidding me? That guy is involved?"

"Apparently so. And if what Agent Jefferson said is true, the guy is planning on being at Ava's hearing." Derek muttered as he sped down the road.

Aussie's stomach sank further as Derek's words hung heavy in the air. This was bigger than any of them had imagined. And Ava and Christian were right in the crosshairs.

"I need to warn Ava."

"Call her."

Aussie pulled his phone from his pocket and dialed Ava's number. As the phone rang, Aussie prayed to God that she wasn't in danger.

Ava sat on the wooden bench outside Judge Holten's chambers. Her foot tapped nervously against the polished floor. The courthouse was busy with the usual sounds of shuffling papers, murmured conversations, and the occasional clatter of footsteps echoing down the marble halls. But Ava barely noticed. Her focus was entirely on Christian, who sat beside her, scrolling through something on his phone. He looked calm, but Ava could tell he was as uneasy as she was.

She wrung her hands in her lap, her thoughts swirling. *What's going to happen in there?* The possibility of losing Christian clawed at her chest, making it hard to breathe.

Ava's mind drifted back over the past few weeks. She thought about Christian's laughter echoing through the house, their late-night conversations, and how he always helped her in the kitchen, even when he complained about chopping onions. He wasn't just a kid in her care anymore. He was like a son to her in every way that mattered. The thought of that being ripped away was unbearable.

And then there was Aussie. She bit her lip, glancing at her phone. *Where is he?* She hadn't heard from him since early that morning, but she knew he'd had a meeting with his Commander about a potential deployment. After that, he mentioned some mandatory class he and the team had to sit through. She hoped he'd make it in time. She needed him here. She needed his calm presence to ground her.

The sudden blare of fire alarms jolted Ava out of her thoughts. Christian looked up, his brows furrowed in concern. "What's going on?" he asked, pocketing his phone.

"I don't know," Ava said, standing and scanning the hallway. People were already moving toward the exits.

"Do we need to go outside?" Christian asked.

"I think we should," Ava said, grabbing his arm gently. "Let's follow everyone else."

They joined the flow of people heading toward the exits, the sound of the alarms grating against her ears. "I don't smell smoke," Christian said, his voice tinged with suspicion.

"Neither do I," Ava admitted, glancing around. She didn't see any signs of fire, but the courthouse staff were ushering people toward the doors, so she decided it was better to be safe.

Once outside, the chilly air hit her face, and she breathed deeply, trying to calm her nerves. People milled around the courthouse steps and the nearby sidewalks, talking in hushed tones. Ava and Christian moved toward the parking lot, thinking it would be quieter there.

As they descended the wide stone steps, a familiar voice called out, stopping Ava in her tracks. "Ava!"

She turned, startled to see Clint, her boss, hurrying toward them. "Clint?" she asked, frowning. "What are you doing here? I thought you were off until after the New Year."

Clint gave her a tight smile, his hands shoved deep into the pockets of his coat. "I was," he said, glancing around nervously. "But I heard Judge Holten wanted to meet about Christian, so I decided to come by."

"Oh," Ava said slowly, her unease growing. She didn't like how jumpy Clint seemed. His eyes darted around, and his posture was stiff, almost defensive.

"That's thoughtful of you," she added, trying to sound neutral.

Clint nodded quickly. "Yeah, well, I wanted to make sure everything's in order." He gestured toward the parking lot. "Where are you headed?"

"We were just going to wait in my car until the fire department clears the building," Ava said. She kept a close eye on Clint, who seemed to fidget more with each passing second.

"I'll walk with you," Clint offered.

Ava hesitated, her instincts screaming that something was off. She glanced at Christian, who looked up at her questioningly. Forcing a small smile, she nodded. "Alright," she said, her voice even. "Let's go."

As they walked toward the parking lot, Ava's grip on her car keys tightened. Something about Clint's behavior didn't sit right with her. She made a mental note to stay alert and keep Christian close. Something told her this wasn't just a coincidence.

The cold air stung Ava's cheeks as she walked briskly toward her car, Christian beside her and Clint trailing just a step behind. Her keys jingled in her hand, the sound barely registering over the growing sense of unease in her chest.

Her phone buzzed in her pocket, startling her. She fished it out and saw Aussie's name on the screen. Relief washed over her—maybe he was on his way after all.

"Hey," she answered, trying to keep her voice steady.

"Ava," Aussie barked, his tone sharp and urgent, unlike anything she'd ever heard from him. "Where are you?"

She froze mid-step, her heart lurching. "I'm walking to my car with Christian and Clint. The fire alarm went off in the courthouse, so we decided to wait in the car until they clear the building."

There was a beat of silence on the other end, and then Aussie asked again, his voice colder this time, "Clint is with you?"

"Yes," Ava replied slowly, her stomach twisting. "Why?"

"Get away from him," Aussie snapped. "Right now. He's part of the criminal network that the FBI is bringing down. He's dangerous, Ava. I'm on my way, and so are the police."

Ava's breath caught, her grip tightening on Christian's hand. She glanced over her shoulder at Clint, who seemed oblivious to her sudden tension.

"They're already here," she whispered, spotting flashing red and blue lights heading toward the parking lot.

"Good," Aussie said, his voice barely audible over the blood rushing in her ears. "Stay calm, but don't let Clint suspect anything. I'm pulling into the lot now."

Before Ava could respond, the situation erupted into chaos. Police cars screeched to a halt, officers spilling out with their guns drawn. Men and women in FBI jackets appeared in front of them with their weapons aimed squarely at Clint.

"Clint Meyers!" an agent shouted. "Get on the ground! Now!"

Ava froze, her mind struggling to process that this was really happening. Christian tugged on her arm, his voice trembling. "Ava, what's going on?"

"I don't know," she whispered, her eyes darting between Clint and the advancing officers.

Clint's demeanor shifted in an instant. His nervousness evaporated, replaced by raw panic. "Stay back!" he screamed, his hand darting into his jacket.

"No!" Ava gasped, realizing too late what he was doing.

Clint pulled out a gun, aiming it first at the officers, then swinging it toward her and Christian. The world seemed to slow as he barked, "If anyone shoots me, they die! Back off!"

The officers froze, their weapons still trained on him. Ava's heart pounded in her ears, her vision narrowing as the barrel of Clint's gun wavered between her and Christian.

"This is all your fault!" Clint snarled, his eyes wild as he focused on Christian. "You ruined everything! Do you have any idea what you've done?"

Christian clung to Ava as he trembled against her side. "I didn't—" he stammered, tears welling in his eyes.

"Stop it!" Ava snapped, her voice shaky but fierce. "Whatever this is, it's not his fault. Leave him alone!"

Clint's eyes burned with rage, his grip on the gun tightening. "You don't get it! He's the reason everything fell apart!"

Ava's mind raced. *Think, Ava. Do something.* But before she could move, Clint turned the gun fully toward Christian.

"No!" Ava screamed. Without a second thought, she threw herself in front of Christian just as Clint pulled the trigger.

The crack of the gunshot echoed in her ears, and a searing pain tore through her chest, stealing the breath from her lungs. She collapsed to the ground, the cold pavement biting into her skin.

Somewhere in the distance, more gunfire erupted, but all she could focus on was the unbearable agony radiating from her upper chest.

Blood pooled beneath her, sticky and warm.

"Ava!" Christian's voice broke through the haze, panicked and choked with tears. He knelt beside her, his hands pressing against the wound, though he couldn't stop the flow of blood.

Suddenly, two large figures appeared next to her. One seemed very familiar, though her vision was blurry.

"Ava, love. Stay with me," one of the individuals said.

"Aussie…" she whispered. Her eyes felt heavy.

"Yes, it's me. No, don't close your eyes. Keep looking at me," he told her.

Suddenly, another face popped into her line of vision.

"Christian," she said. Her voice sounded weak.

"Why, Ava?" he cried, his face streaked with tears. "Why did you do that?"

Ava forced herself to meet his eyes, her lips trembling as she managed a weak smile. "Because," she whispered, her voice barely audible over the chaos around them, "I'll always protect my son."

Her vision dimmed as the world around her began to fade into darkness. She couldn't hold on anymore. The last thing she saw and heard was Christian's tear-streaked face and Aussie yelling at her not to close her eyes before everything went black.

"No!" Aussie yelled as he gently shook Ava. "Ava, don't you dare! Stay with me!"

The paramedics arrived, pushing him aside as they worked to stabilize her. Aussie stumbled backward, his legs barely holding him up. Time seemed to freeze for a moment. Then suddenly, the entire scene replayed in his mind but in slow motion.

Tears streamed down his face as he watched Ava throw herself in front of Christian, shielding him from the bullet meant to end his life. Her body jerked backward from the force of the bullet before slamming into the ground.

Christian broke free from Snow's grasp and ran into Aussie's arms. Aussie held him tightly, shielding him from the sight of the medics working on Ava.

"Is she going to die?" Christian sobbed, his hands clutching Aussie's shirt.

Aussie's voice cracked as he answered, "No. She's not going anywhere. She's a fighter, Christian. She's going to make it."

The team closed in around them, forming a protective barrier as the paramedics worked on Ava before loading her into the ambulance.

"I can't lose her," Christian whispered, his voice trembling.

Aussie tightened his hold on the boy, his throat constricting as tears blurred his vision. "Neither can I," he said softly.

As the ambulance doors closed and the siren wailed, Aussie stood there, clutching Christian tightly, praying with everything he had that he wouldn't have to face a world without Ava.

CHAPTER THIRTY-FOUR

The roar of the C-130 engines faded into the distance as Aussie and his team stepped onto the tarmac. It had been a grueling two weeks of training, but they were finally home. Despite the ache in his muscles and the exhaustion tugging at his every step, Aussie's thoughts were on his next mission. But this wasn't just any mission. Ava's court hearing was scheduled for the following day, a day that could change her life, Christian's life, and his own.

One month. That's how long it had been since the chaos unfolded, since the day that Ava had thrown herself in front of Christian to shield him from a bullet that was meant to end his life. The memory still haunted Aussie. The sight of her crumpled on the ground, pale face, and the blood staining his hands as he tried to keep her conscious. She had nearly died, and that moment had shattered him in a way no battlefield ever could.

It had been a stark reminder of how much she meant to him. He couldn't lose her. She wasn't just the woman he loved. She was the woman he wanted to spend the rest of his life with. And Christian? That boy wasn't just Ava's world. He was Aussie's world as well. He couldn't stop imagining what life could be like with her and Christian as a family.

Tomorrow, the court would decide. He had been counting down to it for weeks, planning every detail of his support for her and Christian.

As the team approached the hangar, Aussie immediately noticed something was off. Derek stood just outside the building, his arms crossed, his expression tense. He wasn't the type to linger without good reason, and the way his eyes locked onto them sent a jolt of unease through Aussie.

"Shit, it is never a good sign when he picks us up," Bear muttered as they picked up their pace.

The team slowed as they reached Derek, who wasted no time. He looked at Aussie.

"Ava's court date got moved up. It's happening right now."

"What?" Aussie's voice shot up, his stomach dropping. "Right now?"

Derek nodded, his tone brisk. "It started about fifteen minutes ago. Get in," he said, motioning toward the van.

Aussie froze, the weight of Derek's words crashing into him. His pulse thundered in his ears. If the hearing had already started, there was a good chance he'd miss it entirely.

"Move your ass, Aussie!" Derek barked, snapping him out of his daze.

Aussie shook himself from his thoughts and practically threw himself into the van, his teammates following with a mix of confusion and urgency.

"Why would they move the day?" Playboy asked, his tone laced with disbelief.

"I have no idea," Aussie shot back as Jay Bird slammed the door closed, and the van lurched forward, tires squealing as they sped toward the courthouse.

The van ride was a blur. Every stoplight, every turn, felt like an eternity. Everyone was silent, and the tension was thick in the cramped van. Aussie tapped his foot anxiously against the floor, silently praying that he would get there in time. He had promised Ava that he'd be there.

He had planned to speak on her behalf, to tell the court how fiercely she loved Christian and how much she deserved to be his mother. But he had something else planned as well. It was something he hadn't shared with anyone, something that might surprise them all.

The courthouse finally came into view, and Aussie was out the door before the van had fully stopped, his team following close behind.

Once they made it through security, the echoes of their boots filled the marble hallways as they searched for the right courtroom.

When he found it, he burst through the doors, his heart pounding. But then he froze at the sight before him.

Inside, near the front of the room, Ava sat at one of the tables, surrounded by Jocelyn, Clover, Hannah, and Gabby. Tears streamed down her face, and her shoulders shook as she hugged Christian tightly.

Aussie's heart sank. He was too late.

"Ava," he whispered as he crossed the room in three long strides. She looked up, and the moment their eyes met, she launched herself into his arms. Her sobs wracked her body as he held her close, his own eyes burning with unshed tears.

"I'm so sorry," he murmured, his voice thick with emotion. "I should've been here."

Her sobs softened, and she pulled back just enough to look at him. Her beautiful face was streaked with tears. But there was something else in her expression. It was a spark that he didn't understand. "Aussie," she started, but he shook his head, cutting her off.

"No, let me finish." His voice was thick with emotion. "I love you, Ava. And I love Christian like he's my own son.

He took a deep breath, reached into his pocket, and pulled out a small velvet box. Ava's eyes widened as Aussie dropped to one knee and opened the box, revealing a sparking diamond ring. Gasps rippled through the courtroom as some clasped their hands to their mouths in shock and delight.

"Ava," he said, his voice trembling, "you are the strongest, most incredible woman I've ever known. You've shown me what it means to love without fear, to fight without hesitation. I want to be the man who stands by you every day for the rest of my life. Will you marry me?" He then looked up at Christian, who was wide-eyed, looking between him and Ava. "And Christian. I want to be your dad if you'll let me."

For a moment, Ava stared at him, her tears falling faster. Then, to his surprise, her sobs turned into laughter, a sound so unexpected that Aussie blinked in confusion.

What the fuck? He thought to himself.

"Aussie," she said through her laughter as she reached out and cupped his cheek, "I love you, too. And I'd love nothing more than to marry you. But," her laughter grew as she wiped her cheeks. "I'm not crying because the court didn't approve me. I'm crying because they did. Christian is staying with me. He's my son, officially."

Aussie's jaw dropped. "Wait…what?"

Christian grinned, tears glistening in his own eyes. "She's not lying, Aussie. She's my mom."

Laughter echoed through the room as Aussie stood up and rubbed the back of his neck, clearly embarrassed. But relief flooded through him. The vise that was squeezing his heart loosened, letting his heart swell with joy. "Well," he said, grinning at her, "that still doesn't change the fact that I want to marry you. And Christian, I still want to be your dad."

Ava wiped her tears, smiling up at him. "Then yes, Aussie, a thousand times yes. I will marry you!"

Aussie smiled as he slipped the ring onto her finger before pulling her into his arms and kissing her. When they broke apart, he saw Christian standing there, but when Aussie held out an arm, the boy rushed into the hug, burying his face against Aussie's chest.

"What do you say, Christian?" Aussie whispered. "Can I be your dad?"

Christian nodded, his shoulders shaking as he started to cry. "I want that," he said, his voice muffled against Aussie's body.

The moment was broken by a soft cough. When they looked in the direction of the front of the room, Judge Holten was sitting at the bench with an amused smile.

"Well, this was certainly unexpected. But for the record, as soon as you two tie the knot, I'd be honored to approve the paperwork for Mr. Mitchell to adopt Christian officially."

The courtroom erupted in applause and cheers. Ava laughed, wiping her tears as she looked up at Aussie. "I love you."

He smiled back at her, "I love you, too," he said, leaning down and kissing her warm lips.

Before the moment could settle, Clover clapped her hands for attention. "Alright! Enough crying and kissing for now. We've got a party planned at Bayside tonight to celebrate!"

Ava looked at Clover like she had two heads. "You already planned a party?"

Clover grinned and nodded. "Yep."

"But how did you know what the outcome would be?" Ava asked her.

Her grin grew by the second, and she glanced at Judge Holten. "I might have had a heads up," she said sheepishly.

Aussie chuckled as Ava's jaw dropped, and she looked at her friend and colleague, Judge Holten, who had just winked before leaving the room.

Aussie pulled Ava close. "I guess tonight we have a lot to celebrate," he said.

She smiled. "Yeah, I guess we do."

Aussie pulled her and Christian into another hug, his heart fuller than it had ever been. For the first time in his life, everything felt exactly as it should. They were a family. And nothing would ever change that.

EPILOGUE

Bayside buzzed with laughter and cheer as everyone gathered to celebrate Ava, Aussie, and Christian.

Nails leaned back in his chair, sipping his beer and watching Aussie pull Ava close, her ring catching the light as they laughed at something Christian said. It was a good fit, the three of them. They looked like a family straight out of a picture frame, and that made Nails genuinely happy for his teammate. Aussie deserved this. He deserved a partner who loved him, a son who admired him, and a future filled with promise.

"Never thought I'd see the day," Nails muttered, shaking his head with a grin.

"What's that?" Snow asked from the chair beside him, raising an eyebrow.

"Aussie settling down," Nails replied, gesturing toward the trio.

Snow chuckled. "He's earned it. You thinking about following in his footsteps?"

Nails scoffed, but his grin softened. "Nah, not my style. Though, seeing them like that, I get it. Maybe someday."

Snow smirked, clearly amused, but didn't push further.

Nails' thoughts drifted as the party continued. The camaraderie was great, but for some reason, his mind kept circling back to his mom. It had been a while since he'd called her. The Outer Banks weren't far, but life had a way of getting in the way. Pulling out his phone, he stepped away from the group and headed outside to the back patio, where it was quieter.

He dialed his mom's number, and it rang a few times before she answered. "Well, this is a surprise! My boy remembers his mother."

Nails chuckled. "Hey, Ma. Thought I'd check in. How's everything going?"

"Oh, you know, the usual. Staying busy with my garden club and keeping the neighbors in line," she said with a laugh.

Her voice eased something in him like it always did, but then he caught it. There was another voice he heard in the background. It was faint but distinct. It was a woman's voice.

"Who's there with you?" Nails asked, his tone casual but laced with curiosity.

There was a pause, just long enough to make his gut tighten. "Oh, it's nothing, just the TV," his mom said a little too quickly.

Nails frowned. "Doesn't sound like the TV, Ma. Who's there with you?"

Her hesitation spoke volumes. "It's just a friend," she said finally, her tone light but forced.

"Uh-huh," Nails said, not buying it. "What kind of friend?"

"Nails, don't start," she replied, her tone shifting to a mix of exasperation and defensiveness. "You don't need to worry about it."

But he did worry. The tightness in her voice wasn't like her, and it gnawed at him. "Alright, Ma," he said finally, keeping his tone even. "If you say so."

After a few more pleasantries, they ended the call, but Nails couldn't shake the feeling that something was off.

He returned to the group, but his mind was elsewhere. Snow noticed immediately. "What's up?"

Nails sat down beside him and took a swig of his beer. "I just talked to my mom. She's acting weird."

"Weird, how?" Snow asked, frowning.

"Like she's hiding something," Nails replied, running a hand through his short, spikey hair. "She had someone there with her. It sounded like a female. When I asked who was there, she wouldn't really say. She just said that it was a friend."

Snow leaned back, considering. "You think it's something serious?"

"I don't know," Nails said, his jaw tightening. "But I'm thinking I might take a trip down there, see for myself."

Snow nodded. "Want company?"

"Sure." Nails replied. "Maybe next weekend. Does that work for you?"

"Count me in."

As the party carried on around him, Nails stared out at the water, his mind racing. Whatever his mom was hiding, he was going to find out. And something told him it wasn't going to be as simple as she'd made it seem.

Nails and Riley's story is coming soon!
Pre-order Available

BOOK LIST

The Trident Series
ACE
POTTER
FROST
IRISH
STITCH
DINO
SKITTLES
DIEGO
A Trident Wedding
A Trident Christmas Baby
Protecting Charley *(2025)*

The Trident Series II – BRAVO Team
JOKER
BEAR
DUKE
PLAYBOY
AUSSIE
NAILS *(2025)*
SNOW *(2025)*
JAY BIRD *(2025)*

Other Books
Identity Risk (The Billionaire Experience)
Grateful Hearts (Home for the Holidays)

ABOUT THE AUTHOR

Jaime Lewis is a *USA TODAY* bestselling author who entered the indie author world in June 2020, with ACE, the first book in the Trident Series.

Coming from a military family she describes as very patriotic, it's no surprise that her books are known for their accurate portrayal of life in the service.

Passionate in her support of the military, veterans and first responders, Jaime volunteers with the Daytona Division of the US Naval Sea Cadet Corps, a non-profit youth leadership development program sponsored by the U.S. Navy. Together with her son, she also manages a charity organization that supports military personnel and their families, along with veterans and first responders.

Born and raised in Edgewater, Maryland, Jaime now resides in Ormond Beach, Florida with her husband and two very active boys.

Between her two boys and writing, she doesn't have a heap of spare time, but if she does, you'll find her somewhere in the outdoors. Jaime is also an avid sports fan.

Follow Jaime:
Facebook Author Page: https://www.facebook.com/jaime.lewis.58152
Jaime's Convoy: https://www.facebook.com/groups/349178512953776
Instagram: https://www.instagram.com/authorjaimelewis/
BookBub: https://www.bookbub.com/profile/jaime-lewis

Made in the USA
Columbia, SC
23 July 2025